The Falmouth Model

The Third Catrin Sayer Mystery

ALLAN JONES

ISBN: 978-1-9993813-0-1

Cover: Falmouth harbour (author photograph)

THE CATRIN SAYER MYSTERIES

*This book is a Kindle Direct Publishing paperback.
The series is also available as e-books from
Amazon Kindle eBooks and other suppliers*

Allan Jones

CONTENTS

'A period may be spent in swinging in the action,
proportions and construction of the figure
with long lines…'

THE HUMAN FIGURE, by John H. Vanderpoel, 1907.

PROLOGUE
SMITH SQUARE

Catrin Sayer and Melanie Farrell exchanged smiles as Melanie's partner complained about her nervousness yet again.

"I'm not sure about all this, Catrin," Jean Hughes intoned. "You said it was going to be just a conversation in front of a video camera. Look at it all!"

The three women were standing in the windbreak offered by the entrance to the Kings Building in a corner of Smith Square, Westminster, avoiding as much as possible the light gusts of wind laced with spray. In front of them was a flurry of activity. Two large umbrellas had been erected to provide a temporary haven from the intermittent showers. Beneath one of the umbrellas two videographers were getting their cameras and lights ready and under the other Simon Cleary was busy setting up his boss's easel and other painting equipment.

Around all of them bureaucrats and business people entering or leaving the building were glancing their way interested, amused or irritated by the sudden carnival in an otherwise quiet square in London.

Catrin and Jean were waiting for the conversation on camera with a watercolour painter in the less than ideal weather. The crew were racing against time; it was late afternoon and dusk was not too far away. Despite Jean's nervousness, for Catrin Sayer this was light relief after her recent activities.

The artist at the centre of it all, Mason Carrington, was across the road staring at the features and weatherworn stone of the former church which dominated the centre island in the square. St. John's was a magnificent example of English baroque architecture dating from 1714, now a concert hall in this upscale neighbourhood only a few minutes' walk from the Houses of Parliament.

Mason was in his early forties, trim, tanned from long hours outdoors and with a head of curly, wildly-unmanageable hair. He seemed oblivious to the occasional splatter of drizzle and unperturbed that in a minute or two he was expected to produce on camera a superb painting of the church and square while simultaneously holding a conversation with his guests. This was a part of a series he was recording for entertainment and training purposes; a digital media set of watercolour paintings completed outdoors in London while talking with other artists.

In this case the victims were Catrin and Jean, two ceramic artists. Jean was a formally trained and gifted potter; Catrin was developing a reputation as a ceramic decorator of note. For all Jean's nervousness, Mason was relaxed and happy; a globally-acclaimed 'expressive' watercolourist, he was in his element painting outdoors.

Catrin looked across at him and smiled. Cornishmen don't mind rain and spray; they can't afford to with that windswept coastline, she thought. And he is lost in concentration; his paintings may be impressionistic and loose, developed rapidly in a series of watercolour washes, but the angles of the church and shapes of its ornamentation had to be just right.

Melanie was making reassuring noises about the recording session to come.

"Think of the exposure, the sales potential," she said to Jean, encouragingly. Carrington's videos sold well internationally in the visual arts community. Jean and Catrin had been promised a good slot to talk about their work together at the Cwmbran Kiln, the boutique pottery in Spitalfields Arts Market that Jean and Melanie co-owned and where, as time permitted in her other professional life, Catrin decorated works that she and Jean created.

Her partner replied, "Melanie, at present I am thinking of how not to throw up, the way my stomach feels."

Catrin smiled. "It will be fine, you will see, Jean, once we get started. He is a great conversationalist."

Catrin's 'other professional life' was a police officer; a detective sergeant in the Art Crime Unit, part of the Serious Crime Command in the Metropolitan Police Service. A number of far more disturbing events in the past month had led up to this meeting with Carrington. A video session wasn't troubling her that much at all.

Life had got really busy, she thought, with the sudden and unwelcome subpoena to appear as a witness at a trial in Glasgow. It had been non-stop since then, principally in Cornwall. As Simon called over to his boss that everything was ready and the video director asked for Carrington, Jean and Catrin to take their places, Catrin suddenly wondered when the Falmouth case really began, given its impact on her life and the strange developments that were now headline news.

1 BRUSSELS MIDI

Arno Hintzen sat quite relaxed on the bench at the station, his sketchbook open, drawing in black ink a view of the entrance area. His technique was not rhythmical or continuous. As his eyes took in each element of the composition he decided on the strokes, applied them, then stopped and looked again, his head bobbing up and down like a bird. Nothing was imprecise about his art. Nothing was imprecise about anything he did.

He had opened the sketchbook to a fresh page after he sat down. As he did so, he had flipped through a number of other drawings made at different locations and other times. For a moment he held one open, showing a park in Frankfurt. He smiled to himself, recalling the event.

The image he was looking at linked to his work on the Ingersoll project. Eighteen months ago, Peter Ingersoll had found some of his banking transactions listed in an exposé article in a leading Dutch current affairs magazine, carefully positioned against a quote he had made on the latest Greek financial crisis. In a press conference tied to a meeting at The Hague, he had called for debt-laden countries to establish systems where all citizens shoulder their responsibilities to pay taxes according to fair and transparent rules.

Unfortunately the bank transactions shown in the article suggested that Ingersoll was exempt, somewhat, from his own advice. In fact, it was clear that he hadn't been following too many rules at all, particularly his own state's tax laws. As a result the Eurocrat was placed under investigation and he had resigned from his post at the European Commission within a week. No-one knew how the bank statements had been obtained and the magazine with the scoop was not revealing its sources.

The sketch of the park brought back to Arno the memory of a discussion with an intense young Greek man there. Ingersoll had not been a major player in the European bureaucracy. Hintzen was careful not to overplay his hand in such projects; he didn't want the heavyweights in cybercrime on his tail. But as the Greek said, Ingersoll was on his way up the ladder and, unless stopped now, he would be a much bigger problem in the years to come. Arno had been glad to assist, for his usual fee.

Marilyn Greaves arrived in Brussels on the Eurostar train from St. Pancras Station, in London. She was middle-aged, casually but well-dressed and carrying only a small backpack as she joined others exiting the train. As she cleared the barrier and moved out of the throng a little way, she pulled out his 'treasure hunt' notes. She had thought of the humorous name for his email with its explicit instructions about what to do on arrival. When she first read them she had almost added at the end 'then walk ten paces north and dig'.

It is a large train station, she realised, as she entered

Brussels Midi and made her way into the main concourse area; I am glad he gave me directions. This was part of the first real step of an important journey she had put off for far too long. In the bustle and noise of the busy terminal she paid close attention to the guidance now, following the pedestrian signs and noticing the shops he had pointed out. Near the end she saw the bench, one of three unprepossessing benches in a waiting area. Now she wasn't excited; she was apprehensive.

Why did I expect this hacker person to be young and wearing a hoodie, or to be scruffily dressed? She had read too many novels, she realised. He was sitting on the seat he had mentioned, the sketchbook in his hand. The hacker was working away, drawing something in the busy station concourse, apparently oblivious to other people. The man looked tall and about her age and was wearing a nice sports jacket and slacks with creases, she noted, fresh from the cleaners. A professional man, it appeared, taking time out of the office to enjoy his hobby.

Within a few feet of him she simply said, "Hello?"

He was a complete stranger, but hopefully the right complete stranger and not by coincidence someone else who liked to draw.

The man stood, waving his sketchbook to encourage the ink to dry. He had been using a fountain pen, Marilyn realised. Then he shook her hand formally. "It's my pleasure to meet you," he said, "Shall we have lunch?"

He had a German accent but he spoke English very well. She wondered fleetingly why he bothered with this other world she was about to enter.

He led her to the Brasserie restaurant in the station and they were taken straight to a table for two. He had 'presence', the sort that caught the attention of waiters and maître d's; a decisive man who expected good service and got it. She was nervous and not that hungry but they needed a place to meet and talk.

"Let's order first," he said.

Before the meal arrived she passed over the memory card.

He took it and said, "So, did you do it as I told you, only look at the images from the camera on your computer screen, not download the files?"

She replied, "Yes, I did it that way."

The hacker had given her complete instructions, down to the electronics store in Plymouth and the camera model to use. In fact he knew the answer already; he had already accessed her computer and searched the hard drive; nothing was resident. He was still assessing her.

He said, "Good, I will review this now. One moment, please."

The memory card was quickly inserted into a slot into a small black tablet computer that came out of his battered leather briefcase. It was a computer brand she did not recognize, but she was no expert to judge anyway, she thought. As he waited for it to boot up Hintzen said, "Chinese", reading her stare. "It's not connected to the internet either; never has been outside China."

He quickly looked at the images she had supplied, the tablet at an angle that prevented her and others from observing. His fingers moved over the screen, expanding the images, checking magnification clarity. Then he said, "This will be fine. I can do this. And the payment, please, may I ask?"

Marilyn passed over a fat envelope. It contained ten thousand euros in hundred euro notes and she said before he asked, "I did this part as you suggested also;

withdrew it in different size batches over several weeks."

It was a lot for her; part of her inheritance from her mother's estate held in the only bank account to which she had sole access.

Hintzen nodded, but didn't comment or open it. He just added the envelope to his briefcase. A trusting soul, she thought, for a person who was an illegal surveillance expert, an image manipulator and a hacker, yet also a man who avoided the internet as much as possible, it appeared.

The waiter brought their food over. As he approached the table the computer, memory card and envelope were safely stored in the briefcase out of sight.

When they were alone again Hintzen said, "Now, it isn't at all necessary but I like to understand why clients want my services. It can help, I say, but in truth it doesn't do a lot other than give me a rationale. Perhaps in this case it will guide me a little more clearly."

His voice was light but she sensed it was more important to him than he was claiming.

"I am happy to tell you," she said. She wasn't; but it seemed the right thing to say. She wanted this to succeed; it had been on her mind for a long time.

When they had finished the meal, during which she found out nothing about him at all, he reached into his briefcase again and pulled out a large Ziploc bag. In it was a smaller sealed Ziploc bag and, within that, an unsealed sturdy envelope on which the delivery and sender addresses had already been completed neatly, she saw.

As Arno opened the outer bag allowing her to take its contents, he said, "Hopefully you won't need this but if you do, put the five thousand euros inside the map that is already in the envelope. It has enough paper and printed images to get the money past any cursory scan. But I suggest you wear disposable gloves to do so."

"No traces," she said.

"No traces, right." He wasn't smiling, making pleasantries. He returned the larger Ziploc bag to his briefcase.

"And the address?" she said, looking through the plastic at the envelope.

"It's a post box for a small company that distributes bulk stocks of toothbrushes to dental practices; the ones they give away to patients with each checkup. But I will be notified."

"Hopefully I won't need to use it," she said. Then she added, "But you go to extreme lengths to avoid using the internet for someone who… breaks into web sites. I thought you were able to do that undetected, or without being traced, whatever it is."

"I can," Arno replied, "but my clients can't, in communicating with me. And it is prudent to keep any traceable elements to the minimum."

He looked down at his wrist. "What time is your train back to London?"

She looked at her own watch. "In about forty-five minutes, I should have been watching a little more carefully."

"The Eurostar; there is plenty of time, I will show you the way." Hintzen had chosen his own train connections home with a departure ten minutes after her train left.

He put the payment for the lunch in euros on the table with the bill and signalled to the waiter who had served them.

~~

Some days after the meeting, alone in his apartment in Stuttgart, Arno closed the lid of his Toshiba Kirabook leaving it in standby mode. The laptop was his main computer platform for this work; a powerful, high-end computer with excellent screen definition. He worked mainly with it disconnected from the internet, apart from any routine software updates and some time spent regularly connecting it to specific websites. When he was connected, either on this laptop or his more aged desktop, he carefully presented a very different online profile.

There he was a knowledgeable and careful stamp collector. One could see that philately was clearly a passion, if they chose to look into his email history. In other areas he was much slower to deal with online correspondence.

They would see also that he had a satisfying but undemanding academic job, it seemed. Anyone checking him out would get the impression that for him the internet and email were reluctant struggles with a changing world. He was happier with physical rather than electronic documentation, with hand-produced text and images, with history rather than technology. He had no Facebook account and he bought virtually nothing on-line other than rare stamps.

The scans of his quite-impressive sketchbook pages he sometimes sent to friends were of variable quality; the scanned images usually were fine but occasionally could be awful. The emails would then contain an apology for the bloody awful scanner function on his all-in-one printer. If the response pointed out the age of the equipment he used, it generated a pithy reply or a joke about a time when one's belongings used to be made to last.

It was all carefully orchestrated, just in case the authorities ever checked him out. Arno tried to be an ultra-careful man.

The client's request had been strange, no more warped than some others, but uniquely weird. He had worked hard to add the sense of savagery that her explanation over lunch had warranted.

He transferred later the prints of the altered images to a sealed envelope in his 'clean' room. It looked to anyone else like an unused spare bedroom in which he happened to store some items. The sealed courier envelope would contain nothing to tie back to him and its exterior would be carefully wiped before dispatch. He would then wait for the phone call confirming its suitability before placing the image on the website.

But he was quite sure it would meet the contract requirements, at least the first phase. The pre-payment for two altered images had been made, after all, so he still had more work to do on her instruction.

All that the courier pack contained was the sealed envelope, unaddressed. In it were three photographs. Two were duplicates of the same image showing a young woman being sexually assaulted by a man; him naked, the woman dressed. That had been part of the challenge. The other specific item the client had required in the image was there also.

The third photograph was an enhanced view of a dark portion of the first image with that item now more visible. It was a vase.

2 GLASGOW

"Catrin Sayer."

The Macer, the Scottish courtroom official spoke her name quietly in the doorway of the small room. His tone was as authoritative as if she was being called to Courtroom 1 from the larger witness waiting room. Catrin had been subpoenaed to appear at the High Court of the Judiciary in the Saltmarket in Glasgow.

She was sitting on one of the chairs surrounding the table with her hands on her lap, waiting. One of her assigned security officers, Constable Jim Halliwell from the Diplomatic Protection Branch, had been standing outside the door but she now saw that he was checking the corridor on each side. Sayer was no diplomat; she was a serving police officer. Protection on this trip from the DPB was unusual but, as they say, it had 'history' to it.

She was back in Glasgow, the city where a drug kingpin, Dominic Connolly, had allegedly called for her execution nearly two years ago in retribution for her arrest of Colin Cheney, one of his gang members. Hence the protection today. While the threat had never been fully substantiated, Superintendent Jack Taylor at Scotland Yard had insisted on the same security arrangements as used for her trip south from Glasgow two years ago. At that time she had just been released from Glasgow Royal Infirmary. This was her first trip back to the city.

Cheney's defense counsel had called her as a witness to testify at his trial for an unrelated crime. He was now accused of the second degree murder of Roland McGuire, another prisoner in Barlinnie prison. She had no direct knowledge of that incident nor had she any indication from the defense team why she had been subpoenaed.

Police officers are normally summonsed as witnesses for the prosecution, with considerable pre-trial discussion with prosecuting barristers, or advocates, as they are referred to in Scotland. In this case all Catrin had received was a secondhand set of messages from the prosecutor's office to Inspector Keith Marshall, her colleague. They were 'observations'; general comments that were as close to the wire as the legal counsel for the opposition was allowed to make prior to the trial itself. It was no wonder she was nervous.

Catrin had been trying to deal with her anxiety about her role as a witness by thinking about taking time off when she returned to London. The Macer's call had brought Catrin out of her reflections. She gave Jim a quick glance as she walked out of the door past him.

He put his thumb up, wishing her luck as he spoke briefly into the sleeve microphone letting his partner, Constable Henry Walsh, know the status update. Walsh was outside the building at present in the secure parking, checking their vehicle for the return to London. Until Sergeant Sayer returned from the courtroom the two officers knew she was in the hands of others, the security officers in the courtroom.

"Good luck, Catrin," Halliwell said softly, as she followed the Macer across the corridor into Courtroom 1.

Catrin was led through the wood-paneled room into the witness box. As she was sworn in she took her first look at the defendant, the man who had damaged her left cheek. Colin Cheney kept a neutral expression on his face but there was enjoyment in his eyes, she saw. She wasn't sure if that was to do with seeing her face, the scar quite visible as his handiwork, or her discomfort at being called as witness for his defense.

The memory of her sessions with the police psychologist Dr. Herrington after the incident came to mind. 'When you wake up at night and see him, I want you to think immediately about how damaged he is', he had told her. 'It will diminish him; hopefully stop the nightmares, the broken sleep'.

He had been right; it had. But looking at Cheney again in the flesh she thought he may be sick, but he is still a dangerous man.

Michael Lyon, the prosecutor, had told Keith Marshall that Sayer's appearance was nothing to do with the McGuire case but with her direct interactions with the accused. That could only really relate to the few minutes at Kinnington Church, right? Have her think about that, he said, have her refresh her mind on the details.

After the swearing-in, Robert McKenzie stood up and bowed formally to the judge. He was the defense advocate, a white-haired veteran of the Scottish Bar.

He said to Catrin, "Please state your name and occupation for the record."

His voice was even, reasonable. It would not stay that

way, she had been warned, he could be aggressive and she would have to weather it through until cross-examination.

"My name is Catrin Sayer. I am a police officer, a detective sergeant with the Metropolitan Police Service based at New Scotland Yard, London."

"What are your duties, Sergeant Sayer?"

"I am part of a team called the Art Crime Unit. The mandate of the team is to assist in the investigation of art-related crimes anywhere in the UK."

"You were still a constable, I believe, in this same Art Crime Unit when you participated in a case two years ago in Glasgow which involved an incident at Kinnington Church. Is that correct?"

"Yes."

"You, in fact, arrested Mr. Cheney there, did you not?"

"I did, although he was formally cautioned and taken into custody by Sergeant McPherson of Police Scotland."

Peter McPherson had left his job during the subsequent enquiry into the conduct of the police by PIRC, the office of the Police Investigations & Review Commissioner. He and his wife had opened a Day Care.

"My Lord," said McKenzie, addressing the judge, "Having called Sergeant Sayer for the defense of the Accused and establishing her role, I ask that if required I may treat this witness as hostile?"

It was patently evident to the jury now that Sayer was unlikely to be supportive of Cheney's case.

"You may, Mr. McKenzie."

He looked in turn at Catrin and at the jury. "Members of the jury, this is nothing to do with the demeanor of this witness. It is simply allowing a style of questioning for Mr. McKenzie to use."

He looked at the defense advocate. "Judiciously, that is. Please proceed."

It's not about the demeanor of the witness, Catrin thought; it is about the demeanor of the lawyer. He was going to grill her over hot coals; she could see it in his eyes.

"My Lord, thank you. Miss Sayer, at that time you had been a detective constable for less than a year; is that correct?"

"Yes."

"So not a lot of experience, I take it?"

Catrin replied, "I have now been a police officer for over six years."

Remind her to keep to the facts, Lyon had said to Marshall. The prosecutor was a little further along from McKenzie on the Advocates bench. He was watching her impassively but he nodded slightly at the response.

McKenzie continued, "Indeed, but you had only about four years' service in total at the time of the incident, according to my calculation.

"So on the day in question, you were dressed in plain clothes and positioned initially in a van being used as an observation post, a stakeout as it is sometimes called, near the church; correct?"

"Yes."

"What police service equipment were you carrying at the time of the incident other than your mobile phone?"

Catrin responded. "I wore a service belt beneath my jacket. It had an ASP telescopic baton, a small torch and a set of regulation handcuffs; Speedcuffs they are called. I also picked up the large service torch, a Maglite, as I left the vehicle and ran towards the church."

She had seen the battered and scuffed Maglite that had been used at the incident in an evidence bag on the table in the courtroom. It was next to a tagged ASP baton similar to the one issued to her. She thought she knew exactly where this was heading now.

McKenzie asked, "Would you say you that you were appropriately experienced to handle the incident that occurred there?"

His voice had developed an edge.

Catrin answered, "I was appropriately trained to arrest a suspect. No-one can predict entirely how each incident will unfold."

She was addressing the jury, not the advocate, precisely as she had been coached to do during her training course for courtroom examination.

"As a police officer I have made a number of arrests in my prior duties. It is part of my training, part of my job."

Some members of the jury were starting to look bored.

McKenzie addressed the court officer. "Please show the witness Exhibit 11."

The officer brought the long, black-metal Maglite torch in its evidence bag towards Catrin. The torch was over 30 centimetres long and about three-quarters of a kilogram with its batteries, she knew. Catrin recognized this specific one, scratch marks and all. She tried to control the slight shudder as the memory of the incident came back to her.

McKenzie asked, "Without being asked to validate the chain-of-custody tag, does this look like the Maglite you used?"

"It does."

He repeated the same question with Exhibit 12, the ASP baton. Catrin told him it was not hers, but appeared identical to her own baton.

McKenzie asked, "Detective Sayer, can you please demonstrate the use of the ASP baton?"

Michael Lyon rose. "Objection, My Lord. The officer is here as a witness. She did not use a baton at the incident and she is not here to demonstrate service equipment used by Police Scotland."

The judge looked sourly at the defense advocate. "Sustained, Mr. Lyon. Mr. McKenzie, I am not clear where you are going on this issue of the baton, but I will let you proceed; for now."

"Thank you, My Lord. Exhibit 12 to me, please."

He took the baton from the court officer and expertly flicked it open with a crack into its 3-segment length.

He then said, "Please pass Exhibit 11 to the jury."

The court officer took the bagged torch over to the jury.

McKenzie said, "Members of the jury, would you please compare these two instruments. The police baton I am holding is a weapon with a precise purpose, tensile strength and tip. Used by an expert, such as a trained police officer, it can immobilise an aggressor without causing major damage. The Maglite, well look at it, feel the weight, it is more a club, a cosh, is it not?"

He turned his head to face the witness box "Sergeant Sayer, did you hit the defendant with the Maglite?"

"On his ankle, yes."

"While he was prostrate on the ground, correct?"

"Yes."

"You did not use your baton, did you?"

"No."

Lyon continued, "Did you during that arrest also kick him violently between his legs, a kick to the testicles, in fact, as he lay face down on the floor; a blow with sufficient force to make him scream and vomit?"

"Yes."

Catrin hated saying it and not explaining further.

Several jury members looked upset, one woman shaking her head silently.

McKenzie said again, forcefully, "Did you, at the time, give any thought to the damage you were inflicting on the defendant?"

"No."

"You gave no thought to the possible longer-term damage to the defendant?"

He was pounding at her, she felt. She knew she had to keep steady; she had been warned he would do something like this.

She kept her voice even. "No, I was making an arrest; that was what I was thinking about."

Catrin tried to keep her face impassive and consciously resisted the desire to grimace or bite her lower lip. McKenzie was building his case that her kick had led to diminished sexual capability in Cheney and the resulting condition had ultimately lead to the confrontation in Barlinnie and the death of Roland McGuire.

She had been instructed by Keith Marshall, 'Don't explain or elaborate when you answer. If you do the defense counsel will burrow away at your reasons, try to show them to be a vengeful retaliation to Cheney's attack on you. The more you talk, the more you give him opportunity to pick at you'.

She controlled the urge to explain, looking at the lawyer. He said nothing, letting the last set of questions soak in. In the silence Catrin looked away, first at the jury, then at the judge. She didn't want to look down, look defeated.

After a few seconds, the judge said, "Mr. McKenzie, will that be all?"

"No, my Lord, thank you. Sergeant Sayer, please

confirm, yes or no, did you undergo training to become an armed officer with the Metropolitan Police?"

"Yes, I did only the initial training course in firearms familiarization and use at the Milton Training Centre."

"But you are not authorised to carry a police firearm?"

"No."

Catrin recalled a similar comment from one of the investigating officers from PIRC during the enquiry. McKenzie must have read the transcript of the interview. It was designed to bait her then - and now. She stayed silent.

She saw that Michael Lyon was poised for the next question or comment from McKenzie. But the defense advocate didn't make a snide remark, as the investigator in the enquiry had. Again, he just stayed silent, letting the jury members draw their own conclusions. Some may interpret, he hoped, that Sayer did not have the temperament to be granted firearms status.

Lyon rose anyway. "Objection, My Lord; this is irrelevant."

But Robert McKenzie had already sat down. He had finished.

3 RESPONSE

The Crown Advocate waited a second or so, looking at the judge for permission to proceed. The judge was looking at McKenzie, his exasperation clear. He addressed Catrin directly.

"Sergeant Sayer, why did you not complete the firearms course, may I ask?"

Catrin saw he was giving her an opportunity to address the slur.

"My Lord, I decided during firearms training that I preferred a career direction in criminal investigation rather than in an armed tactical response unit, which is where continuation of the firearms training to the next level would have taken me. The position at the Art Crime Unit then came up and I applied. I joined a unit that does not need me to complete a firearms qualification at present."

'Thank you, Judge' she thought to herself.

The judge looked at the defense advocate.

"The jury will disregard this last line of questioning of Sergeant Sayer regarding firearms. It is not relevant to the matter in hand. Please continue, Mr. Lyon."

Michael Lyon put his first question. "Detective Sergeant Sayer, where did you obtain the injury that gave you the scar on your cheek?"

Through Marshall he had asked her to avoid using any make-up to hide the scar at all.

She said, "During the same incident, at Kinnington Church. The defendant hit me with a steel baton while committing the robbery. It broke open my cheek."

McKenzie rose. "My Lord, I object. The defendant's actions at that incident are not for this jury to consider. He was tried and convicted for those offences and is serving his sentence now."

The judge said evenly, "Overruled, Mr. McKenzie. Sergeant Sayer is called as your defense witness and you opened the issue of the Kinnington Church robbery with her. Mr. Lyon, please continue."

Lyon said, "The blow was from a baton that Mr. Cheney had purposefully modified, truly a club as my learned friend referred to Exhibit 11. The force was sufficient to damage your cheek badly and knock you down the steps outside the church. Is that correct?"

"Yes."

"Why did you hit Cheney with the torch on the ankle rather than use your own baton?"

"It was dusk. I had taken the torch to look inside the church doorway, as I had seen a man fall there while I was in the van. He was a parishioner at the church that I had met previously during my investigation. He had also been injured by the defendant; more severely than myself, I would add.

"After I was knocked down, Mr. Cheney tried to escape but fell himself. He had stepped on the Maglite torch I had dropped and he lost his footing. The torch skidded towards me; that's why it is so scuffed. As he tried to get up I picked it up as it was then close to hand. I hit him on the ankle to stop his escape as he had ignored my warning that he was under arrest."

"Did you then instruct the defendant to lie prone? I believe it is standard procedure in a violent situation of this nature? You instructed him not to move?"

"Yes I did."

"And did he do so?"

"Yes; initially he did. Then he tried to get up."

Lyon said, referring to a document he picked up from his desk, "Sergeant Sayer, the enquiry into your action at this incident by PIRC, as the office of the Police Investigation and Review Commissioner is known, contains a report of an interview with you. You stated then that the defendant was about to jump up and attack you as you approached to handcuff him. He had become aware how badly you were injured and thought he could overpower you. That is why you kicked him, is it not? That was your perception."

"Yes," said Catrin, "It was a moment's decision, to prevent him from jumping up."

"Why?"

She looked at Cheney.

"I had told him he was under arrest after he attacked me. He had demonstrated that he was a dangerous man. If he got up to attack me further I would have no alternative other than to hit him with the torch again, to use as much force as necessary to enable me to constrain him and prevent him inflicting further injury to myself or others. That is consistent with the law."

Lyon looked at the defendant for a moment and then at the jury. "So in fact your quick-thinking saved this man further significant injury, did it not? It's alright, Sergeant Sayer, you don't need to answer that."

McKenzie was rising to object to this speculation as Colin Cheney said loudly from the dock, "I would have killed the bitch, torch or no torch."

McKenzie's eyes closed briefly as the judge brought down his gavel.

"There will be no outbursts of this nature in court. Mr. McKenzie, if your client speaks again I will remove him and we will proceed without him present. Is that clear?"

"Yes, My Lord," said the defense advocate. His voice showed his annoyance with both the way Cheney had made an outburst and the way in which Michael Lyon had baited him into doing so.

Lyon waited for a moment then said, "For the record, the investigation by the Police Investigation and Review Commissioner into the incident concluded with what finding?"

Catrin said, "It was dropped. PIRC concluded there was no case against Police Scotland, the Metropolitan Police or myself, I was told."

"Quite so," said Lyon. He looked at the defendant. "You were found to be the innocent party."

He smiled briefly at Catrin. "Detective Sergeant Sayer, thank you. My Lord, this concludes my questions of this witness."

As she was dismissed and left the courtroom Catrin glanced at the jury box checking their expressions, noting particularly the three jurors who had shown signs of concern about her kick to Cheney's groin. The two male jurors were now looking at her sympathetically. The female juror was still regarding her with thinly-disguised distaste.

You weren't there, lady, she thought, so who are you to judge me?

4 TRURO

Marilyn Greaves had nearly finished her drawing of the older nude male. He was an experienced model and was holding a pose that required very careful observation of the different hip and shoulder lines and their relative perspectives. Get those wrong, she knew, and the rest would be out of balance, no doubt leading to a comment from Lyman, the teacher. She was particularly pleased with the drawing and with being back in this particular studio; happy also to be through the first phase of her plan.

She had been so tense about the whole thing the last time she was here. Now she consciously avoided looking at the spot where the camera had been placed. The hacker had been very specific on the camera model when they had talked beforehand.

"Some of the cheaper 'pen' type recorders do not produce a suitable quality image for me to work with," he had said on the phone, "and you only need a recording during the session, not a surveillance camera to cover longer periods."

Placement and retrieval had been her great fears; what would happen if she was discovered during either stage? It was her imagination running wild; no-one was interested in a student going into an empty studio early or returning sometime after the class emptied out of the room, fussing about leaving something under her seat.

She was glad that the class today didn't have the Mitchell woman posing. She had nothing against her really; but cared nothing for her, either. She had just been a useful windfall; a piece which made the puzzle fit together neatly.

Marilyn looked at the young people around her. There were only two mature students in the group, her and a retired doctor. All were busily drawing, other than Graham, of course. He was now listening to his music on his earbuds with his eyes closed, something that irritated Lyman no end, she knew. The student would have finished already; his drawing would be excellent and Lyman may again suggest to him that he should use the time more productively, perhaps draw the model from a different position. If given, it would be advice which the young man would ignore; his drawing skills were streets ahead of the rest of the class.

At one time in her life the combination of talent, arrogance and bloody-mindedness had impressed her. No longer. Now she would dearly like to slap the young man; knock the earbuds off his head and shock him.

As she looked back at her drawing she found that Lyman was looking over her shoulder.

"Nicely done, Marilyn. You caught the abdomen very well, particularly, I think."

She smiled but said nothing. It's the advantage of an older woman married to an older man, she thought; I am used to belly folds on older people more than most of the students in the room.

~~

She had tracked the delivery of the photograph to its intended target on-line, a padded envelope sent 'no signature required' from a real 'senders' address, but not her own. The hacker's message in Brussels had come over clearly; leave no traces. On the day of delivery she made a small excuse about a change of plans; a visit with someone that quickly had her husband, Callum, telling her to enjoy herself, as he ran around doing the hundred and one things a school principal does. He would have forgotten about it in minutes, she knew, and would be busy until well after school closed, as usual.

Later that morning, sitting in her car she waited patiently, but getting quite excited when she saw the postman appear, walking along the other side of the road. She timed it nicely to exit the vehicle and walk past the house as he pushed through the letter slot in the front door several envelopes and a thin package, a padded envelope she recognized.

It was a complete morning spent on something that would happen anyway, but it gave her special satisfaction to see the envelope delivered. As she drove back she called her friend who, delighted with an opportunity for an impromptu natter, agreed to meet her at a café they often used. Later, after supper, she would impart some details of her friend's life to Callum who would, at best, half-listen.

5 JAGUAR

They were in the car heading south, Henry driving, Jim in the front passenger seat; a reprise of the trip after collecting her two years ago following her surgery at the Glasgow Royal Infirmary. Catrin had the back seat to herself. It was a Jaguar XF they were using this time and Henry wasn't sparing the horses at all.

As soon as Catrin was out of the courtroom she had said to Jim, "I need the loo before we go anywhere."

He smiled. "I am not surprised. You could hear Cheney's voice from out here. There is a private washroom near the waiting room we were in; I think it is for court staff."

He waited outside with a Police Scotland female PC; she was refusing entry to other women until Catrin reappeared. Then Jim and the uniformed officer were escorting her to the side door and their vehicle.

They set off south led by a Police Scotland car flashing all its lights until they got to Junction 5 on the M74 motorway where it said goodbye.

"A long way for little time in the box, Catrin," said Henry, as they cleared Abington. They were in the fast lane with little traffic around them now.

Catrin replied, "The defense advocate, McKenzie, just wanted another person to blame McGuire's death on, so he chose me. I was wondering how long I would stand there after he established that I had kicked Cheney, letting it soak in. The judge had to force him to proceed.

"Mr. Lyon's approach was right. I had thought it was weak, letting McKenzie put all those questions without allowing me to respond properly. When Lyon led me to say that I would have taken Cheney out with the Maglite, the man just lost it, said how he would have killed me. I'm sure that went down well with the jury.

"But seeing him there, how dangerous he is, he was probably right; he would have finished me. Thank God he is locked away, the evil sod."

She took a sip from her water bottle.

"Anyway, we did as we were told. I turned up and fulfilled my obligation to the Scottish court. Now we just hope that there isn't media coverage this time."

She sat back and closed her eyes, recalling the first journey south with these two men, straight from the hospital, her face swollen and wrapped in dressings. She had been with her boss DCI Jane Worsley and her friend Jian Li Yeung, a friend she met on her first ACU case in North Wales. I was in a mess in more ways than one at the time, she thought. I need to snap out of it; it's done now.

Superintendent Taylor had explained the reason for the security arrangements.

"Sayer, you are called as a witness so you will have to appear. But Police Scotland has never formally told us that the death threat to you by Connolly was unfounded, we only have the unofficial word from Superintendent Strachan after the incident. In fact, after PIRC dropped the enquiry, Police Scotland said nothing about you, not even acknowledging your significant contribution to their investigation. So we are reminding them. In our eyes nothing has changed, and it should have."

"It's politics then, sir?"

"Politics and peace of mind, Sayer. Glasgow is still Connolly territory even if he is in Shotts."

HM Prison Shotts; a high security facility for male prisoners, he meant.

He smiled. "And Sayer, it is the same two security officers assigned, Halliwell and Walsh. They pushed for it once it was on the work schedule, I hear."

He looked enigmatic, expecting a question from her, but was forestalled by a chuckle and a comment from the other person present at the briefing, Jane Worsley.

She said, "Jim told the others that he and Henry wanted to see what you really looked like; your head was wrapped up like the Invisible Woman last time, he said."

~~

Catrin was hoping that Worsley would give her an assignment that was office-based or in the London area when she got back. It was Norfolk last week and Glasgow now, she thought.

Last week she had been on a case involving a theft of a painting by the artist Canaletto from Halsting Hall, near Norwich, a country estate belonging now to the National Trust. There she had interviewed two elderly visitors to the Hall who had been injured during the incident. She needed a break, she thought.

But until then she had other police work to consider, too. She pulled out her mobile and called John Obi to get an update.

Henry and Jim heard Catrin's comments and responses in her conversation with her colleague. She's a long way from the wreck we drove home last time, Henry thought. He heard her finish the call, raising her voice to ensure that he and Jimmy heard it clearly.

"Henry, what time about will we be at the M6/M42 interchange?"

He gave her an estimate. She passed it on to Obi.

"My staff and I will collect you in my Jaguar," she said, as haughtily as her Welsh lilt would allow.

Jim laughed. "Listen to her, Henry; 'my staff.'"

She closed the call, chuckling at Jim's comment.

"West Midlands will have DC Obi there waiting for us."

DC John Obi, the newest member of the ACU, had been assisting the West Midlands Police in enquiries near Birmingham.

The text from DCI Worsley she had received while talking to Obi simply said 'Call me when you get the chance'.

Her first question was, "How did it go?"

Catrin gave her the thirty-second version. Her boss listened then said, "So it turned out OK; we will keep an eye on the outcome and the sentencing provisions for Cheney. I don't think he likes you very much.

"Where are you now?"

Catrin told her.

"So you haven't picked up Obi yet?"

"No, ma'am, I just called him; it will work, though, we will collect him."

"Well before you do, I would like you to make a note to add in something next Monday, covering for me. I was going to a meeting near Bristol with DCI Coltrane but have had to cancel; I would like you to do it. It relates to the Halsting Hall case, possibly, so you have more background anyway."

"Yes, ma'am."

"I will give you details when you get back. Also, tomorrow, you are lined up to see a DI Charles Steadman in PCeU here. A case they want help with, Keith tells me; sounds weird, but it involves a vase, I hear. It's a Devon & Cornwall Police matter, but find out whether it's a fit for us, OK?"

Catrin said, "PCeU; the cybercrime people? Computers?"

Worsley said, "Yes, computers, and its e-crime, Catrin, that's the official term; the Police Central e-Crime Unit."

Catrin had been making brief notes, a habit built up over the years working with Worsley; she could impart a lot of information and associate work assignments in a short time, Catrin knew.

"And Catrin, if it turns out to be something we should help with, it has not escaped me that Weston-Super-Mare is about half-way to Exeter. Let's talk after you see Steadman."

Catrin acknowledged the news, realizing that next week might not be a good time for her to ask for time off to start new ceramic projects, after all. And it was Weston-Super-Mare she was going to, not Bristol. The reference to Exeter, she knew, meant the headquarters location of the Devon & Cornwall Police.

Worsley's closing comment was, "Say hello to Jim and Henry and tell Henry he is driving too fast."

Worsley had previously been a DCI in the Diplomatic

Protection Branch and knew the two security officers.

She closed the call and passed on the message.

Jim said, "She always says that."

Henry responded, "I remember she didn't say that last time we brought Catrin south; she never mentioned it once then."

~~

"It's a Malaysian ceremonial knife, Sarge, a kris."

Jim, looking directly ahead, smiled to himself. The Midlands accent on the tall, black officer who had joined them and his ease of use of the slang for sergeant made him wonder how Catrin had adjusted to having responsibility for a junior officer.

Catrin had made the introductions and said, "John, we can talk openly in the car. Everything stays here, right, Jim?"

"That's right, Sergeant Sayer, you remember from the last time."

No more 'Catrin' now she had a subordinate with her, he thought.

Obi said, "I am glad DCI Worsley sent me up here. The Midlands people thought the painting and the knife were unusual and that the painting was the 'art'. The painting was nothing special, I think, but I spotted that the kris is valuable, very valuable. I arranged for Professor Suharto from Birmingham University to visit the Edgbaston 'nick' tomorrow and see it; they are holding it there for now. Suharto remembered me from my undergrad, would you believe?"

Catrin half-listened as Obi went through his notes, then yawned.

Obi asked, "Tired?"

She nodded. "Knackered. I didn't sleep well at all last night, given I had no idea which line they would take once I was on the stand."

He stopped talking.

Catrin put her head back. Her last thought was that she needed to know nothing about Malaysian ceremonial knives; she had enough work on her plate.

She woke to the quiet conversation of Obi with the DPB officers talking about football, Obi defending himself for being a Coventry City fan despite now working in London. She heard him say, "With Kaila and my daughter, I get little enough time to watch these days anyway, so it hardly matters."

John was married; his parents were from Kenya. He met his wife at college, also a second-generation immigrant; his wife's parents were from Pakistan. Catrin got the impression that the two families, one Muslim, one Christian, got on well. His wife was expecting their second child.

Henry saw in the mirror that Catrin had woken and said, "We know where you live, Sergeant Sayer, we take it we will drop you off there. But John, where do you need to go?"

Obi said, "The Tube near Catrin's flat will be fine, Henry; I live in Tower Hamlets."

"Aldgate East it is, then," the driver responded.

Catrin realised that they were approaching London; they were almost home.

6 PCeU

The following day, Friday, Catrin sat in DI Steadman's office in the PCeU section at New Scotland Yard. She had seen the police officer around the building but did not know him personally. Given the size of the Met Headquarters, that wasn't unusual.

Worsley had briefed her before the meeting on both the Weston-Super-Mare and the PCeU cases. The latter had come up in a discussion during a break in a squash game on Tuesday between Keith Marshall and Charles Steadman, it turned out. "Interdepartmental co-operation, Catrin," said Worsley.

Steadman began, "DS Sayer, the idea of involving ACU wasn't mine; it was the computer crime technician in Exeter who came up with the idea for a female police officer with artistic skills to help. They couldn't identify anyone locally, so Keith thought it might work for you.

"We have been on this case about a week now, so the suggestion seemed worth pursuing. We aren't looking for a police artist, don't get me wrong. It's an artist's eye on the problem and, in part, a ceramic art expertise, which I hear that you have."

He was about Keith's age, she thought, also fit and well-dressed. She could see how the two of them got along socially and probably connected on playing squash.

"Well sir, I decorate ceramics, but Sergeant Reynolds in Art & Antiques is an expert in that area if you are trying to track a specific piece. He also has a range of specialist experts he works with that he can call on."

Steadman nodded. "Let's go back to that later; we can review it at the end of the meeting. First, let's talk about the investigation underway."

"An image, an altered image, of a second-year student at Falmouth University was posted a little over a week ago on her Facebook wall by a hacker. It would be very disturbing for anyone and certainly has been traumatic for the young woman involved. Surprisingly enough, it is not a nude image of her from some 'selfie', that sort of thing. It is sexual and violent.

"It now turns out that it is probably based on a real image of her, but at first the woman couldn't pin down where the original was obtained - until Tuesday. We heard the update just before I had my squash game with Keith, hence the discussion. I will explain in a moment but I want you on the same page before I do, so I will show you the image, OK?"

He was checking her preparedness.

Catrin nodded. He probably thought that being in an art specialist unit, she would be a little insulated from the image he was about to show her. He had no idea of the sort of stuff she had seen earlier in her career while working in support of the Drug Squad in Brixton, the length people will go to support their addictions.

He swung the large display screen on his desk round so they both could view it. Catrin absorbed it, keeping her face as neutral as she could.

The woman was standing, leaning forward. She was in a tasteless-looking gaudy dress, hanging low enough at the loose neckline to reveal most of her breasts. The naked male was behind her, his arm extended forward holding a knife to the side of her neck. He was taller, stronger and appeared to be dominating the woman. His posture and expression gave the inference he was penetrating her. The dress was hiked up at the back, its crumpled folds trapped between the two bodies.

The girl's features were clear and her face seemed to be tense, open-mouthed, animated. The overall image conveyed violence far more than sex, though. The focal point, she saw, was clearly the knife at her throat with the light flashing from its blade. It pulled the eye of the viewer to the image then the line of the weapon led the viewer back to the point of their coupling.

One of her arms was reaching back; the other was pointing down, just touching a small, square coffee table made of a dark wood, the table increasingly unclear as the light level dropped away from the figures. It had nothing on its surface, it appeared. However, it had a lower shelf and on it a blurred indistinct shape could be seen. Part of a vase, was Catrin's thought, the one Worsley had mentioned to her.

Steadman looked at Catrin. "Last Tuesday, the woman in the photo, Janis Mitchell, phoned Inspector Stephen Hicks; he is the officer who is leading this case with the Devon & Cornwall Police. She told him she thought that she now realised where the base image could have come from, but wasn't completely sure. It was the body angle and her arm reaching back which gave her the idea. We had been working on the basis that it was a completely composite image.

"Ironically, it is quite possible she was naked, not dressed, when it was taken. She models for an art class. She thought it was consistent with a pose from one of a series of 30-second sketches she had undertaken for the class. You know about that sort of thing?"

"Yes," said Catrin, "I have been in figure drawing and painting classes over the years. But these classes would not allow cameras, or visitors; they are not photographic sessions."

Steadman said, "That's what I understand. Keith and I wondered if you went down to work with the team there, talk to her, could it help?"

Catrin asked, "Your earlier reference to the ceramic art element of it, sir; what was that about? This area, I take it, contains a vase?"

She pointed to the shape on the shelf.

He nodded. "The technician down there has done some good work pulling it out."

He switched the image.

"Colours may not be accurate, but... we thought it might mean more to you. It looks as if it has been placed there specifically; it is not just part of the background."

Catrin looked closely. This enhanced image of the vase was a lot easier image to take.

It was a conventional 'olpe' shape vase, she saw. Vase shapes have Greek descriptions, but she wasn't sure what level of detail DI Steadman was looking for. The colours weren't right, she knew instinctively, but she could see the edge of two patterns.

"Can we magnify - this bit, and then this?" she asked.

He did so. After a minute she spoke.

"It's nothing I recognize. My first impression is that this is not an antique or a commercial product line and not by any ceramic artist I have come across so far. Perhaps it's a one-off, but it looks to be very good quality, very symmetrical and it is nicely decorated. I think the decorative elements are too identical to be freehand work, unless the artist was very good. It could be what we call transferware; the pattern is made on a master sheet then copied to each section using a tissue and pigment process."

She looked at him, his face not showing any reaction.

She went on.

"The colours aren't right, I feel, but I can't really say why at present. But whoever made this was very competent and, if a one-off, it is probably a piece by a professional artist."

Steadman smiled. "I think you must know a lot about this subject, as Keith said."

He continued, "Fortunately Janis Mitchell had a Facebook friend on-line as the image came up and she called her. Mitchell took it down within a few minutes. She had been in a lecture at the time and only checked her message because her phone kept vibrating. Her friend had kept trying to call her and text her.

"She was clever enough to save a copy to her computer despite being upset but anyone could have seen it by then if they were on-line. The hacker overrode her privacy settings making all her site material totally public, not only available to her friends. She then called the police and made a complaint also to the Facebook people."

"Mitchell is devastated by it, as you can imagine. She has stopped going to classes, she stays off the computer and away from her phone. She is isolating herself in the hall of residence, we understand. The university offered counselling but she doesn't want it."

Catrin said, "I understand; people who need it generally don't want it at first."

She was thinking about herself and Dr. Herrington after the Glasgow incident. She hadn't needed a psychologist, , she thought. But she was wrong.

He continued, "Local police interest, of course, is to track the perpetrator. Our interest in PCeU is primarily in the person who prepared the image and hacked the web site. Her hacker identity is clear, if it is a 'her'. It is included in each hack she makes somewhere in the image at the pixel level. The name she puts there is 'Adrestia', after a Greek goddess."

Catrin looked blank and DI Steadman smiled. "I had to look it up, too. A Greek goddess of retribution, I gather. This person has a history of hacks into systems; placing information or stealing it. Some attacks are similar to what you have just seen; some are simply revealing secrets, providing embarrassing facts or damaging information about someone.

"We think that 'Adrestia' was contracted to do this attack. That is the thinking of police units in other countries dealing with similar security breaches under the same name. I won't go into details but leave it to Chris Treneer when you get to Falmouth. For a local computer tech he is very good; proactive despite the 'geek crap' he gets.

"Geek crap?" Catrin asked.

He nodded, grimacing.

"It's not unique to Devon & Cornwall. In the e-crime

world some of the officers we interact with can be 'old school'. 'Policing is for policemen', they think. Since Pankhurst chained herself to the railings they now have to admit that women can do some of the work as well. But civilian computer experts… let them give an opinion on a case, never."

Catrin laughed. "Thanks for the warning. If I am sent there I will wear pants, not a skirt. Mind you, there are some like that back in Brixton, where I served last."

He smiled. "Most people we deal with have been fine, but this sort of treatment can be hard on the technicians given the terms 'geek' and 'nerd' are already tied to computer work."

Catrin thought of the people she worked with generally. "That's not the case in my area, the art stuff. The civilian forensic people are really well-regarded, I think, and the SOCOs are just plain feared. If they take over the scene, run before they throw you out."

The site management authority and discipline of the Scene of Crime Officers was well known; he nodded in agreement.

He said, "Have you worked on cases in the West Country before?"

Steadman was smiling as he posed the question. She had the impression he knew the situation from Keith already.

"No," replied Catrin, "DCI Worsley always seems to cover cases that arise there herself. I think she likes that part of the world. DI Marshall did some work around Bournemouth, but that is as far west as I think he has been for the ACU."

He turned serious. "So will you do it, Catrin, go down and see?"

Catrin made the decision. She had hoped to be able to walk away but she thought of the young woman hiding from the world.

She said, "Yes, for a day or so; after I attend an interview near Bristol with DCI Coltrane next Monday. I can be down there the same evening, be in the Exeter HQ or the Falmouth station on Tuesday, if that works. I'll give it a go."

"Great," he said. "Who do I need to confirm it with?"

Catrin smiled. "DCI Worsley, I suggest. I will be entering her domain."

As she left to return to the ACU, she thought Inspector Steadman was a nice guy. He also had a wedding ring on his left hand. She noticed the status of men she met almost routinely these days.

Part of the issue currently was the departure of Helen Banks. She had been Catrin's flatmate until just under two months ago, but had moved to live with her fiancée. Helen had been the original tenant when Catrin was looking for a place after joining the ACU. The flat was located in Spitalfields, not far from the Art Market and the Cwmbran Kiln, so it was very convenient for Catrin. Now she had the flat to herself and her 'single' status seemed to play more on her mind.

Helen and Catrin had met with the owner and he had been happy to transfer the agreement to Catrin. "When you find another person, look for someone who is going to fit in, that's all I ask," he said. It was a quiet residential street; she knew exactly what he meant.

"I will look, but not for a month or two," she said to both of them at the time. "My art has been selling well and so I will splurge, have a couple of months being by myself. Since I left home for university I have always shared accommodation, so it will be a change for a while."

That window was now closing. She enjoyed having the place to herself but not the total cost. It was on her 'to do' list when she wasn't busy working.

7 ASSIGNMENTS

"So let me make sure I understand this, ma'am," said John Obi. "DI Marshall is heading to Nantes, France, to replace you interviewing a Brit there. DS Sayer is going to Weston-Super-Mare with Detective Chief Inspector Coltrane, probably in his fancy car, and then she gets to visit the English Riviera. And I am going to…"

He paused for emphasis.

"… 21, Waterson Avenue, Coventry. I am being sent to Coventry. Back to the case I was on last week, the kris thing."

Catrin snorted with laughter at John's act; he did pathos well. He had come out of his shell since his hesitant reserve and nervousness on his first day.

Jane Worsley nodded, playing along.

"Put like that, John, you are showing great potential for leadership, summarizing a situation so well. Keith will enjoy good French cuisine, Catrin will enjoy the pleasures of Cornwall and you will get some home cooking from your mum, providing you are still in her good books. Your parents don't live that far away, right?"

John came from Rugby, not far from his assignment for the next day or so.

The Art Crime Unit was conducting its regular briefing session on Monday morning, taking stock of existing cases and balancing assignments accordingly.

Catrin noticed that Worsley had not said anything about her own plans. Normally she did so, even if it was no more than 'I will be in meetings for two days with Jack Taylor in Guilford', or something similarly vague when it was confidential.

John said, laughing, "And you, ma'am, will you be somewhere equally exotic?"

Catrin saw Aina Jinnah's face change, suddenly serious and concerned. Aina, the civilian Administration and File Officer, was Worsley's right hand and closest confidant.

"And I - ," Worsley paused.

"And I will be near here, in the Royal Marsden, having a lump removed. Sorry, I don't know how else to drop it on you."

The Royal Marsden Hospital was a specialist cancer hospital in London.

She looked at Aina, who was now getting tears in her eyes. "At least it is out now; you can climb down off the broken glass you were walking on."

John Obi's face was in shock. "ma'am, I am sorry, I didn't mean to pry and -."

Worsley said, "Relax, John; I was looking for a way to mention it sometime but didn't know when. You gave me the perfect entry, in a sense. It's OK, alright?"

Catrin was hit hard and saw that DI Marshall had already been told; his face was wooden, impassive but his eyes gave it away. He was covering for Worsley in Nantes this week; she was covering for her in Weston-Super-

Mare, she had just realised.

"I will be away for the week and probably all of next week, they say. That's all I know. I will communicate through Aina. You can look after yourselves for a week, I think, and if something comes up you can go through Keith to Jack. He is aware, of course."

Taylor was Jane's direct boss and the founder of the Art Crime Unit.

Worsley looked back to normal after breaking the news even if her team were not.

"So we all have things to do and Catrin, I want to see you before you go off with Neville Coltrane. It's about the Falmouth thing, the case briefing you had with DI Steadman last Friday."

Clearly the ACU Monday morning meeting was over.

~~

Catrin sat across from DCI Worsley in her glass-walled office. She had been signalled to close the door as she walked in.

"Before you ask or look at me like you want to ask but can't, the tumor is in my left breast, deep. They will take it out - a lumpectomy they think - and decide what to do next. Hopefully I will be back when I said. If the surgery gets more serious... well, we will see.

"I want you to keep an eye on John, particularly if my absence is prolonged; I know you will be in different places for the next few days but he can phone and text you. It will be good for him and for you. He still needs a lot of direction; more than you did at this stage, I might add.

"Keith will have his work cut out when he gets back from Nantes both with his own caseload and covering some of mine, particularly the admin and bureaucracy here, which he hates. But he is the Inspector and it goes with the seniority."

Catrin said, "Yes, ma'am; I would be happy to help in any way I can. I am sorry to hear your news and I wish - ."

She stopped, knowing she needed to control her emotions.

Jane nodded, understanding, but she was focusing on the work, it was clear.

"This Falmouth thing this week; I am not sure how much it is in our bailiwick, or should I say ball court given its origin, but you decide. Despite what you heard on Friday, we need to walk away if it doesn't meet our mandate. Talk to the victim but don't get wrapped up in the investigation, OK? But you make the call when to leave, no-one else locally; you are not assigned to the D&C Serious Crime Team for the duration.

"That's it. Enjoy the drive down with Neville."

It was clear she needed to get on with other things so Catrin stood up to leave.

"And with the De Marr interview today with DCI Coltrane, ma'am; anything more there you want particularly from me?"

She was thinking about the first assignment in Weston-Super-Mare, before she went on to Cornwall.

Worsley said, "Play the 'bad cop', just as we discussed with Neville. You saw the Pickersgills in Norwich. It should help."

"Yes, ma'am; it certainly does."

Mr. and Mrs. Pickersgill were the old couple Catrin had interviewed in Norwich, the ones who found themselves in the middle of the robbery at Halsting Hall. She recalled the stitches in the old man's balding head and the bruise on the face of his wife, terminally ill. It had only been the week before last, but the trip to Glasgow had been dominating her thoughts since she returned from Norfolk.

8 FALMOUTH

Catrin climbed out of the comfort of the plush leather seat of DCI Coltrane's silver Bentley Supersport at Bristol Temple Meads train station. They had arrived in good time for her train to Falmouth. She had enjoyed the ride down from London, the smooth motion of the vehicle and the admiring glances at them from other drivers on the motorway. How the other half lives, she thought.

Neville Coltrane had spent most of his adult life in London, in Mayfair, and his knowledge of the side roads and shortcuts across London was on par with the best chauffeurs in town. She knew it was his personal vehicle. Coltrane was very wealthy; wealth derived from a line of Coltranes who had built a family fortune. They had also spawned the Coltrane Foundation, an art endowment and philanthropy group. The Coltrane name gave him a VIP reception across the art world, she had been told.

He was also Jane Worsley's counterpart, the director of the Art & Antiques Unit of the Metropolitan Police, part of the Specialist Crime Command. There the similarity ended. The A&A was a well-resourced, highly visible unit. Coltrane had four investigative teams led by inspectors and a number of civilian support staff, all with a range of art world and art crime specialist expertise. When insurance companies talked about the recovery of stolen art, A&A were in the 'first team list'.

Towards the end of the M4/M5 motorway section on the drive down from London they had dried up on work discussion. After a silence, Coltrane said, "I see that Liz Marshall is having an event for you and Sarah Chambers, the post-realist, next week. Sylvia and I plan to come."

Liz Marshall was Keith Marshall's sister. She owned a gallery shop off the Fulham Road specialising in works by contemporary British artists. She had been selling Catrin and Jean's work for three years now.

'Sylvia' thought Catrin; his partner, perhaps. She knew nothing of Coltrane's personal life.

"Yes sir, a week tomorrow; Tuesday. My potter Jean Hughes and I have made some new pieces and several collectors have loaned Liz some of our earlier works for the event. The same for Sarah's paintings, I believe. A brief chat from each of us about our art, then wine and cheese and a chance to talk with people."

"And sell more pieces, I hope," said Coltrane. "Which is mainly why Sylvia and I are attending. She may have a commission work, a platter-type centrepiece - or perhaps three? I am not sure. But I will leave her to talk about that, if she wishes, after she sees your work."

Catrin was intrigued. "Can I ask who Sylvia is, sir, if you don't mind my curiosity?"

He smiled. "Who is Sylvia? And not a Shakespearean question, Catrin. We are going to have to broaden your social circles, get you out of The Cwmbran Kiln and the Yard."

She was supposed to know perhaps, she realised.

"The Honorable Sylvia McNair is the director of The Fens Trust, the wetlands charity that hits the news every now and again. She is also the daughter of Baroness Cleary and the widow of Joshua McNair, the skier - remember his accident in the news? And she is my partner. We met at a charity event two years after Josh's death and, well, we have been together for the last three years. Does that help?" he said, dryly.

"Thank you, sir, I didn't know, honestly. I am glad you have someone in your life."

Coltrane heard the subtle tone in her response and said nothing. Sayer clearly wants someone in hers but platitudes wouldn't help, he knew. Perhaps expanding her social circle might, he thought.

"We are coming up on the Somerset Avenue turnoff; now I have to concentrate on following this thing."

He was looking at his satnav, muttering.

Catrin was thinking, I am close to home here, too; a pity. Pontypridd was about sixty miles away, she knew.

The interview with Peter De Marr in Weston-Super-Mare had gone well, at least from their perspective. He had been coy and had protested his innocence and ignorance of any useful information when they talked about the Halsting Hall case. Catrin had told him that the thieves, Kevin and Martin Sloan, two brothers, had been apprehended only thirty miles from Weston-Super-Mare.

She said, "We thought you might have a guess, a suggestion of who they delivered the Canaletto to; fellow travellers, so to speak."

Crooked art dealers know crooked art dealers, she meant. After all, she thought, you know the Sloan brothers, you just made that clear.

De Marr looked at her and at first said nothing. Then he looked at Coltrane. "I don't think I can help you further. It wasn't me, as I said."

Catrin had sounded as irritated as she could. "Then, Mr. De Marr, we may need to take you up on your earlier offer to search the place; or get a warrant if you retract it. We will call in the locals. There will be cars, flashing lights outside; we will keep them here for a while. And after the next art theft that we can link to anyone west and south of Watford Gap we will have them all come back, again and again. Until we get some help."

She had seen De Marr look across at his wife, who was upset, then angry. Nancy De Marr was thinking of the talk, the revelations, the gossip and perhaps the possibility of the need for yet another new start somewhere else. They had been trying to live quietly since De Marr was released from prison.

He had told them what they needed to know; an artist's shop in Cardiff was now on Coltrane's team radar. De Marr knew full well that the ACU were focused on catching criminals; they would have followed up on Catrin's threat, he was sure, they had that reputation. That is why Neville had suggested originally that Jane Worsley should join him.

~~

She had settled back in the First Class seat trying to clear her head of the De Marr discussion. Now that the perpetrators of the Norfolk robbery were in custody, the investigation of the fate of the Canaletto had been transferred to the Art & Antiques Unit; it was no longer an ACU matter despite her role today. Nor, she thought, was the next thing on her agenda in Falmouth really, but she had agreed, so…

Catrin was looking forward to visiting Devon and Cornwall. Although she didn't consciously copy art or designs from other artists, her experience was that images seen in new places, indoors or outdoors, stimulated her creativity and gave her ideas for new ceramic works. She rarely travelled without a small sketchbook and drawing pencils. An idea would come to her; she would spend a minute or two jotting it down. Much of the time she would come back to it a few days later, wrinkle her nose and say 'no', but sometimes she would find her mind had made progress with the image. She would then be keen to get to the Kiln and talk to Jean about preparing a clay 'bisque', the blank hardened ceramic from the first-firing that would effectively become Catrin's canvas.

The furthest she had travelled into the West Country previously was to Taunton in Somerset, to a volleyball competition held there one weekend while she was at university. She knew the area south of Bristol fairly well having been to Bournemouth and Weymouth on the coast for family holidays, but anywhere west of Taunton was new ground for her.

She was checking messages on her Blackberry when her mobile rang. It was John Obi.

"Sarge, I need some advice and DCI Worsley told me to come to you for everything now. Are you on the train to Cornwall yet?"

"Yes, John, I am just settling in for the ride. What do you need?"

He said, "The West Midlands people say the Malaysian items can be released now that they have a confession, and the items don't belong to the victim. I have more on the Malaysian knife from Suharto, and think I should contact the Malaysian Embassy formally. Should I just go ahead and do that?"

She thought for a moment. "No. Email your reason for the contact to our liaison at the Foreign & Commonwealth Office; Aina will give you the details. And it's a High Commission, not an embassy. Then set up a meeting, based on FCO advice on who to approach; we don't want to get cross-threaded on the politics. And have someone with you. If I am back I will go, but otherwise make sure there are two officers present. The FCO may also offer to send someone."

He got the picture. There was to be no misunderstanding of what was said.

He then went on, "My second question, then. The kris is valuable; the painting is not, I think. Should I mention the painting to the High Commission or will it make us look foolish doing that if it is trash?

Catrin recalled John's brief description of the painting and the image he had shared with the team at the briefing.

"We don't know the background and it is not simply a financial evaluation. It was obtained in the same manner as the kris, perhaps. We should raise it; let them make the call. Flag it but make it clear we are uncertain as to its significance as it does not appear to be a particularly high quality painting. Where are you now?

"I am about four miles from my parent's home; going for dinner, as DCI Worsley said." He paused. "It was a shocker this morning, though."

Catrin replied, "Yes it was. But all we can do is hope for the best for her and do a good job. I have just talked with Aina while I was waiting for the train. She is in the office by herself now, so perhaps tomorrow, when you get back...."

"Right, Sarge, I will check her out, have lunch in the

cafeteria with her, or we can go out. You could see how worried she was this morning."

She closed the call. Worsley was right in her remark about John needing a lot of direction, although Catrin had said nothing. He was a good policeman but he wanted too much validation from others at times. But the two questions he had raised on the call were fair game; he had been right to ask.

He had been in the ACU about a year now. Catrin had returned from a holiday in Hong Kong, a long-planned and once-postponed visit with Jian Li Yeung.

She recalled his nervousness at the beginning and her own adjustment to her promotion that took effect the same day he started. She had come back from getting her warrant card updated to be asked to look after him at lunch time. He had called her 'Sarge'; she did a double-take on whether he was poking fun and saw that he was deadly serious. It had felt strange.

~~

Catrin had changed trains in Truro for the short but picturesque ride to Falmouth. Steadman had told her she would be met at the station there and she assumed it would be a police officer, but no police car was there nor anyone in uniform. As she trundled her case along the platform a man came forward.

"DS Sayer?"

"Yes."

"I am Chris Treneer, a computer specialist with the Devon and Cornwall Police Service. Inspector Hicks said you were on your way so I said I would meet your train. I just got here."

He was about her age, dark haired.

"That's very good of you, Chris, I'm Catrin. I thought DI Hicks would have a uniformed officer meet me but this works out well."

He said, "I will take you to your hotel. My sister lives near there and I stay with her when I have work in the Falmouth area. I am based in Exeter, at headquarters."

It was about a two-hour drive to Exeter, she knew.

As they drove the short distance from the train station to the St. Michael's Hotel Catrin asked, "Are we going to discuss the case this evening?"

A hotel public area was not the place to talk about this sort of thing, Catrin thought, but she wasn't sure what was planned.

Treneer looked a little lost, uncertain.

"I shouldn't do so without DI Hicks or his team, really. I provide technical support."

Catrin nodded. "I see. It was just that in the briefing at Scotland Yard DI Steadman told me that you had made a significant contribution to the progress so far and had been the one to ask for a female officer familiar with art. Can you talk about that, at least?"

He smiled. "Well I can tell you the reason why I asked for someone like you to help, yes. Would you like a drink, or a tea or coffee, at the hotel, perhaps? We are nearly there."

~~

The following morning her mobile rang as she re-packed her bag in the bedroom. She wasn't checking out but it was habit; unless she knew she was staying for a longer period she re-packed. Occasionally she would find herself finishing her work early and collecting the bag rapidly to head back home rather than have to stay away another night.

"DS Sayer, good morning, this is DS Wastle. I am to collect you; DI Hicks just mentioned it to me this morning. A change in his plans, I think. I am in the lobby."

Catrin said, "I will be right down."

As she entered the lobby she saw him; late thirties, a tall man, thin but with a bit of a paunch developing. Conventional, but not a smart dresser, she noticed.

"I'm Oliver. Hello."

Not 'Olly' then, at least, she thought. "Good morning, I am Catrin."

He smiled. "From Wales, I hear. Like myself."

She had heard his accent, recognized it. "I am from Pontypridd, yes. And you?"

"Swansea. I came across the Bristol Channel for work and never went back."

On the short drive to the police station they talked of things Welsh.

Catrin was shown into the office of a middle-aged detective in a nice suit. He was busy talking on the phone. He nodded her into a seat across the desk and then kept on talking, occasionally looking at her but not engaging her in anyway. Then he swivelled the chair round, looking sideways at the wall as he talked. As Catrin overheard the discussion, she got the impression that it was going to drag on a bit. She just sat and waited.

Finally he put the phone down. "So, DS Sayer, you have come down from 'The Smoke' to help us."

His tone was neutral, his eyes boring into hers.

"Yes sir, good morning."

May as well show manners, she thought.

He said, "I am not sure we need it, to be frank. It was the computer guy's suggestion and Sergeant Wastle thought it was a good idea, so I agreed."

One of those, thought Catrin. She had experienced a few regional crime squad people with this attitude over her time in the ACU. The look said, 'my fiefdom, don't enter; even if you are here'.

"If I can, sir," she said brightly, "And if not, I will go back to London."

The exchange of looks spoke more clearly than the words.

He paused then said, "OK, I will have them brief you and then you let Wastle know what you think. If you can help, right?"

He checked his watch.

"First we have the morning briefing. There are two cases, so sit in on that."

"Yes, sir."

He was done. He stood up and led her out to the main area.

He introduced Catrin. "This is DS Catrin Sayer, from London, a specialist from the Art Crime Unit of the 'Met'. Oliver, you and Treneer will brief her on the Mitchell case immediately we are done here. We will start with the robbery."

There were two cases in the West Cornwall area that had members of the Exeter Serious Crime Team working from Falmouth for the duration; the Mitchell case and another, a violent robbery at Tunstall's, a bookmaker's shop. Clearly DI Hicks was leading the Tunstall's investigation himself and it was his top priority. A number of the plain-clothes and uniformed officers assigned to the group were working on both cases. DS

Wastle was leading the Mitchell enquiry.

Catrin wondered if Hicks and Wastle were staying in the same hotel as her but she hadn't seen them last night. She listened to the review of the robbery and then Hicks moved on to the Mitchell case, letting Wastle update the team. From the review, the focus seemed to be on the identification of suspects among other students or members of the faculty at Falmouth University, people who may have a grudge against Mitchell or an obsession with her.

She noticed Chris Treneer sit there silently. He wasn't asked to speak or give an update.

"That's it, people; back to work," said Hicks.

Most of the team assigned to the Mitchell case would continue with the existing interview list.

Catrin went into another smaller office with DS Wastle and Chris Treneer. The two men seemed to get along well.

Wastle kicked off. "Chris suggested we ask for some help, so thank you for coming down. He gave you a background briefing on the computer aspects of the image last night, I gather."

"Yes," said Catrin. He was more comprehensive than that in the discussion but she said nothing.

"I'll take you through it all again, if you don't mind."

Wastle talked through the background information, giving a lot more detail than Chris or Steadman had provided. She made notes of key points as they went along.

"Janis Mitchell attends Falmouth University but she models at a nearby college, the Truro and Penwith College, near Truro itself. She is one of the models for figure drawing or painting for classes held there. The college is new, one of the tertiary education colleges and is about a twenty minute drive from her university hall of residence.

"Life drawing classes are part of the Fine Arts curriculum at both the college and the university, we understand, but she signed up only for modelling at the college."

"She didn't want to be modelling nude in front of people she knew and studied with, I take it," said Catrin.

"That was the reason she gave, yes."

He went on. "Her home is in Exeter. We have no obvious suspect; a dumped boyfriend, a squabble with another student, that sort of thing. And we have asked around, not just Janis herself."

He took her through the timeline of the case; the call, the period the image was on the web site, how Mitchell had reacted during interview.

He looked at Treneer. From the glances she suspected there was more, but they weren't covering it with her now, that was clear. There was no specific mention of family or other people in Janis Mitchell's life, no offer of access to their statements. Usually when she arrived at a regional location of a crime she was given access to the case file on computer and other materials; not here, though.

Wastle said, "Chris, why not take us through your idea?"

Catrin looked at him, wondering what he would do. Would he say, 'She knows already' or would he go through it again. He took the second option.

9 GESTURES

Treneer began, "We would like to try to identify where the photograph of Janis Mitchell was taken, if it was really from a modelling pose, as she told us. Our idea is to use video imagery of the same pose captured on cameras in the studio that was used for the session. Then, if we align that with the orientation of the image placed on her Facebook page, we can identify the line of sight of the camera used. With the position of the podium she posed on, we should get a good idea of the area where the camera was located in the studio."

Wastle added, "And then we can get the forensics people to sweep anything that could have been used along that line. If the person used a fixed position, say a vent or a fitting in the studio, we can check for fingerprints."

Catrin said. "You have the equipment to do this accurately, I take it?"

Treneer nodded, "Yes, I think so. I did a trial run in a room about the same size yesterday and could get the line of sight within a reasonable area. But it will depend to a large extent on the recall of the pose held and its orientation."

Catrin said, "We will have to see. Artists and models generally have a good sense for spatial location, the sort of thing you are after. It's whether Mitchell has a clear memory, given the events."

Wastle said, "And whether she will co-operate with us on this. We are hoping you can help there. She is hiding away, we think. We don't rate our chances of involving her very highly, to be honest."

Catrin thought about it.

"Can we make sure the lecturer or class supervisor who took the class that day is also there? We should involve him or her; they normally pay a lot of attention to the position of the model, as they have to compare it with the sometimes less than brilliant output from the students. That is, unless you have reason to exclude that person, if you have already run a background check."

Wastle nodded, making a note. "We ran checks on everyone at the class and also the technician who looks after the studio. Nothing came up."

Chris Treneer said, "Clearly we want her dressed, but in clothes that will still give accurate limb positions for the analysis. We would like her to run through the same routine while we video her from various angles concurrently."

He stopped, looking at Wastle to talk about next steps.

Catrin said, "So you want me to talk Mitchell into it, talk her through it, I think?"

Wastle smiled. "Yes we thought a woman, particularly someone who was clearly an artist that she could relate to as a model, might break through her withdrawal. At least, stand a better chance than we two could."

Catrin nodded. "I will give it a go."

"Fine," he said, "I will set it up and have a female officer take you over to her; she has already met PC Lloyd, Sharon Lloyd. Then it is a female-only discussion at the outset; that might help too."

~~

Catrin was taken by the older uniformed officer to the university, just a short drive away. Janis Mitchell lived during term in a flat shared with other students at Tuke House, part of the main university residence complex.

When they arrived, there was one other student at home with Janis, a woman called Rosalyn. The other students sharing the flat were out in classes or doing other things. Seeing the officers and knowing the reason for their flat-mate's contact with police, Rosalyn got her coat and backpack and said she would work somewhere else to give them the privacy; Janis could let her know when they were finished.

Then it was just the two officers and Mitchell. The student was looking ill at ease.

"Miss Mitchell, I am Detective Sergeant Catrin Sayer. Can I call you Janis?"

The student nodded.

Catrin took her back to her observation of the image and how they were now trying to work with the news that the photographer may have been in the studio during a life class.

Janis said, "I am trying to put it behind me, but it pops up in my sleep, the image, wakes me up. It would have been one thing to put my nude image on the internet, the one they photographed, but this, the way it has been altered, it is really frightening. I don't know anyone who

65

would do such a thing to me and… yet there is someone is out there who did."

She was starting to get upset. Catrin sat down closer to her, trying to build a bond.

"Janis, putting it behind you without help may be difficult, you know. Dealing with it rather than trying to forget it are two different things. I know that from personal experience. Someone did this to you for a reason and, at present, we don't know that reason or whether he or she will do it again, to you or someone else. We hope you will help us."

Mitchell's head went down, closing the subject.

Catrin had arranged for Sharon Lloyd to stop by a stationer's shop so she could buy a large sketch pad, larger than the small sketchbook she carried routinely with her. She pulled the pad out of the plastic bag and took her Rötring drawing pencil from her purse.

"Can I ask you to go through for me the routine you think you did for the modelling session, the 30 second poses?"

Mitchell said, "For you? Now? You want me to do the poses here in my room?"

She looked up, a little surprised. Then she saw the pad and artist's pencil in Catrin's hand.

"You draw?"

Catrin smiled, "I an artist as well as a policewoman; that's why they brought me all the way from London. So yes, I want to try to capture the gesture poses you ran through."

Catrin moved to the corner of the room, maximizing the distance to view the model, knowing it would also reinforce the message for Janis to do it. She could see on Mitchell's face the fact that she had told her she was an artist resonated with her.

"OK. Why not, it's just us; let's do it. At least I will see if you can really draw," Janis said, with a smile.

It took about ten minutes, PC Lloyd noted. Mitchell would hold a pose and DS Sayer would say, after about half a minute, 'fine' or 'next one'. Then Janis would change position. All the time the London-based officer's arm was in motion, pencil on the paper, hand flipping a new page with each pose.

"Aagh! I am out of practice," said Sayer at one point, clearly making an error or losing concentration. "Too much ceramic decoration, not enough figure drawing. That's what I do now, ceramic decoration."

Mitchell responded as she changed position, "I thought you were a police artist, Sergeant Sayer."

"No." Catrin smiled, looking at the pad and the pose, still sketching, "I work in an Art Crime Unit, mainly on art theft and forgery cases, but I am also a ceramic artist. I can show you our web site later if you want. I work with a potter, a friend of mine."

Lloyd noted that as the conversation about art flowed between the two women, the posing and drawing seemed to get easier. Sayer was leading this very gently but was getting through to her, she thought. She just sat there watching them.

Janis Mitchell asked Catrin, "Where did you study art?"

"At Aberystwyth; I did Fine Arts and Art History."

Janis said, "What degree did you get can I ask? This is my final pose, by the way. I like the short poses a lot better than holding longer ones, like any model."

Catrin said, "An Honours degree, both subjects," not looking up from the sketch page.

"That's impressive," said Janis.

Sharon Lloyd saw that the student was being honest. She too was impressed to hear about the visiting police officer with this strange role at Scotland Yard.

Mitchell said, "Did you choose to be a policewoman, I mean, from college or did you try something in art first?

Catrin smiled, "I always wanted to be a policewoman; that's the problem. Two equal ambitions, art and police work."

"Well," said Janis, sitting down on the settee and picking up a glass of water, "today you get to do both. You should talk to my dad, he had the same decision."

Catrin laughed. "That's one way of looking at it. Why talk to your dad?"

Before she could answer, PC Lloyd said, "Her father is Superintendent Mitchell, with us, in charge of Traffic Division."

Wastle never mentioned that, Catrin thought, nor did Steadman. But she said to Janis, "The choice thing; why talk to him about that?"

Mitchell shrugged her shoulders. "He talks about it the same way as you. He went to university to be a musician and then joined the police. He told me he had two ambitions, too. And he told me to call it the police service, never the 'force'."

Catrin smiled, "That's right; that's what we are. But visiting sergeants don't get to have social conversations with superintendents."

"Nor do local constables," said Sharon, "We get pep talks or the Riot Act, generally." Then, realising what she had said, she added, "Not from your dad though, don't get me wrong."

Janis Mitchell laughed properly for the first time in the interview. "I get both of those from my dad at times, believe me."

With the three women sitting together afterwards, Catrin explained to Sharon what she had been doing.

"Short poses are to catch gestures, the dynamics of the figure and to limber up the artist, familiarize them with the model, the figure and proportions. They are not finished sketches. You can see mine - they look largely like lines, curved and flowing, with some body outline but little else. I tried to add a little more detail than I would normally do in a gesture drawing when I could, to see if that would help Janis remember."

She stopped flipping through quickly for Sharon Lloyd and focused on Mitchell.

"Janis, let's look through these together, one by one. See if you can spot in my sketches anything similar to the pose that made you call DS Wastle."

About half-way through Janis said, "Go back one. It was something like this, not quite, more from the left I think."

Catrin marked it and said, "Let's go through the rest also, just in case..."

Eventually they went back to the original pose identified.

Catrin said, "Can you strike the pose again?"

Janis did as Catrin moved across the room to a different spot and drew again. Janis looked at it.

"Yes, that's much closer to it now."

Catrin would have liked to photograph her doing it again, but didn't dare ask. It could be too touchy. The young woman was clearly still rattled by the whole thing.

Instead she said lightly, "So will you come with us later? Sharon will come and bring you over and take you back afterwards, won't you?"

Lloyd nodded. This was the crunch point, would she get more involved?

Catrin continued without waiting for an answer.

"What we are going to do is go to the same room at the college once DS Wastle has clearance that we can use it with no-one else there. I will strike the pose for the technician instead of you, but it would be helpful if you could watch me, correct me. Will you do that?"

Catrin didn't want to ask her to do it. It was a long time since she had posed as a model herself, for her boyfriend at Aberystwyth. They had posed for each other, in fact. She smiled encouragingly.

Janis Mitchell was clearly debating it internally but said after a moment, "If there is no-one else there. No class or other people watching. I am not sure how I will react, to be honest, going back, that's why. I could make a fool of myself and burst into tears."

"But you will do it, Janis; good. Thank you, it will help a lot," said Catrin.

As the two female officers headed back into town Catrin called Oliver Wastle and said they were good to go; they were heading back.

"That's good news, DS Sayer. We are working with the college and should have the studio a little later today."

Catrin closed her mobile and said, "Sharon; is there any chance of a cup of coffee somewhere nice back into the harbour area rather than at the station? This is my first visit and ..."

The PC smiled, "I know a place. Pretty view, good coffee too. And I can poke your brains about your strange job in London. How did a Valley girl get to work at Scotland Yard?"

Catrin smiled, "Let's get that coffee and I will tell you

all. Well, almost all."

~~

Later, back at the police station, Wastle confirmed they had the studio shortly.

"Treneer is getting the equipment ready and I have an officer arranged to be outside, to keep the place secure so there are no visitors while we are there."

As they went through the plan DI Hicks appeared in the doorway. He said nothing, just listened.

"Ok, I go along with it," he said at the end, as if they had been waiting on his approval. "If I have time in the Tunstall's case, I will come along and watch."

"I would rather you didn't, sir," said Catrin immediately.

"Why not?" said Hicks, his annoyance level visibly rising.

Catrin replied instantly, "Well, the girl is really leery about doing this anyway… and you do come over as a little intimidating."

"Sir," she added, as an appendage, looking at his face.

Oliver Wastle looked as if Catrin had just committed suicide in front of him, she noticed.

DI Hicks said, "Do you find me intimidating then, Sayer?"

"No sir, we have some really intimidating coppers up in London. But Janis Mitchell will, I think, and we don't need that. And I gather that her father is a senior officer here, so it might not be a good idea to mess this up."

Hicks said icily, "The link between the victim and a D&C police officer has nothing to do with the art aspect, does it? That's what Wastle was told to brief you on; just that."

He gave Oliver Wastle a look, then smiled at Catrin and walked off.

Oliver said, "You tread dangerous paths, Catrin."

He was looking at her scar as he spoke.

As she returned from getting some water fifteen minutes later, Sharon Lloyd came up to her and whispered. "Good for you, Catrin. It's going round the station that you stood up to Hicks. About time someone did."

Then at a normal voice level, she said, "I am to head back to Janis Mitchell; DS Wastle is ready to head over to Truro, he said."

10 FIGURE CLASS

It was early afternoon by the time Oliver Wastle drove Catrin to the Truro and Penwith College. Treneer had gone there a little earlier to set up the recording equipment once he had the go-ahead.

As they arrived she saw that it was a new, good-sized college facility set in its own campus, with countryside behind. She could see Janis Mitchell's logic; model for classes with students and staff she wouldn't encounter otherwise at a location not too far from her own college. It struck Catrin as they parked that being new, the art studios would be recently equipped. They probably had track studio lighting and fittings for multi-purpose use.

As Catrin had requested, Wastle had arranged for the lecturer who had taken the life class to be present. He had interviewed the man earlier in the investigation, a Lyman Hearne.

After introductions and entry into the studio, Hearne gave them a general description of the class set-up that he usually used. It was, he said, the one used that day. They worked with him on the placement of the small square podium; the one the model had posed on to increase her visibility for the class. Chris Treneer and Catrin were particularly focused on the accuracy of its orientation; the 'focal point', as Treneer referred to it.

Catrin also asked Hearne to help her, as best as he could, to recall the approximate locations of students during the class. They went around with masking tape, marking spots on the floor, a rough semi-circle around the podium. When Hearne seemed satisfied, Catrin asked him to give them a few minutes alone. His office was not far away, he said, so he would wait there until called. The police officers then had the studio to themselves.

Catrin was reviewing the room and holding in her mind's eye the pose she should adopt based on the gesture lines on her pad. She stood on the podium, looking at the walls and posts, thinking about how a camera could have been positioned. It would have been too visible to conceal on an easel, she thought. There had been a few of those, Hearne had said. Most students had used pads or paper mounted on boards, hand-held or propped up on a desk or chair-back.

"It was a drawing class, not a painting session," Hearne explained during the set-up.

Catrin was eyeing the long wall across one side, the most logical area where the camera had been situated. It had various fixtures, lighting racks and paraphernalia to accommodate everything artistic from art to music to acting. Unless they narrowed it down, it would be a little like fingerprinting a hospital corridor; there would be a lot of prints to eliminate.

Chris Treneer asked, "Can we get Don in now?" He was the studio technician, also waiting outside to be called.

She nodded then watched while the two men re-checked the three cameras on tripods they had positioned earlier. It didn't take long.

Treneer nodded. "We can run through it now, Sergeant Sayer."

Wastle was outside, on his mobile. Whether he was reporting into Hicks, she had no idea.

Catrin took out her mobile and phoned PC Lloyd. "OK, Sharon, bring her over now."

They had about twenty minutes, she knew.

She turned to Chris. "So show me how this works."

He was standing in front of a small table with a laptop connected to a couple of boxes she didn't recognize.

He said, "It's pretty simple really. The software picks up images of the person on the podium from each of the three cameras and integrates them into one 3D image. Once a pose is struck and held, it will capture that image. We will then overlay on it the same pose outline I developed from the hacker photo and match the two as close as possible. This will give a projection line - a probability cone, actually - on to the image of the room."

She followed the logic of it all.

He added, "The digital arts lab at Falmouth University has much higher precision equipment for this sort of work, as they do a degree course in animation there. If needed, we could involve them."

Catrin shook her head. "Let's see how this goes, we need to keep it in-house. We would want DI Hick's to approve the involvement of other parties, if needed."

Treneer smiled. "I thought he was going to insist on being here, back at the station; he does like to be on top of everything."

Catrin said, "Well, I think Sergeant Wastle is keeping him informed quite regularly."

They looked at each other, understanding the working ground they were on.

She changed the subject. "How long do you want me to hold the pose?"

He said, "Not long; it will integrate the small movements to give an average position; let's say five seconds. Within half a minute of each pose I will show you the most probable line for the photo shot."

Catrin said, "The image on the computer from the hacker's photo … is what?" She was thinking of Janis Mitchell looking at it at some point, possibly.

He started answering before she finished. "It is a 3D outline of a generic female, anonymous."

She nodded. "Let's do it."

Catrin took off her jacket and shoes and moved to the podium with a roll of masking tape and her sketch pad.

She placed two metre-length strips on the podium floor parallel with the room walls. Then she put two more at 45 degrees, intersecting them; a make-do 'compass rose' positioned where she was standing; her own reference points.

She struck the pose that she had drawn, holding it for a few seconds then moving it through about fifteen degree segments, re-establishing the pose each time. This way she covered a ninety degree arc and a range of normal variations in the position of her legs, torso and arms. When finished, she put her shoes back on and waited.

Chris Treneer said after a couple of minutes, "Here is the set of best fit 'cones'."

She looked at the screen, at a 3-D image of the studio outline and a coloured band of circles across the rear wall. He touched the screen, rotating and magnifying the image. They overlapped and touched the far wall about eight feet high.

Just then the door opened and Sharon Lloyd came in with Mitchell. The student was looking nervous again, back at the scene that now troubled her so much. Wastle entered behind them, closing his mobile.

"Janis, we have a police officer at the door; no-one will be coming in without checking with us first," he said to her, then to Catrin, "I'll get Hearne back now."

He left again, re-appearing a minute or so later with the lecturer who greeted Mitchell and they began talking.

Catrin left them a moment then went over. She smiled and asked them to join her near the podium. She hadn't said anything to Treneer or Wastle, but she wanted to re-work the pose in stages. Janis's increasing anxiety was evident as she looked at the podium and Catrin wasn't sure how involved the student would become.

She said, "I am going to strike the pose as best as I can. Janis, if you can say if it seems right or not please tell me. Mr. Hearne, I would ask you to do the same thing, but could you go to wherever you were during the class and cast your mind's eye back as I try to simulate one of Janis's poses, please?"

He said, "Well, I was moving around between the students. It is going to be hard to recall where I was located for a single pose, but I will try."

As Catrin moved to the podium and took her shoes off again Janis moved closer. Catrin struck the pose and Hearne said, "The problem is, I can remember the first position and some of the others, but not that one, frankly, nor where I was at the time."

Janis suddenly said, "I will do it; run through the thirty-second set. It's a regular sequence I use."

Mitchell had looked around the room, Catrin noticed, and must have been satisfied with the security arrangement and the people present. She had hoped this would happen.

She smiled at her. "Janis, it would really help, honestly. Thank you. Chris?

He nodded. "Five seconds for each pose will do, Miss Mitchell, thank you."

The student moved on to the podium and said, "I started looking at the post there, for line, and as I recall it went …"

Catrin quietly watched the young woman hold each pose. In the studio setting, it was more evident than in her residence flat that she was a good model and clearly had some ballet or gymnastics training. Catrin let her work through the sequence once. Then she asked her to repeat it while she joined Hearne. This time she mainly watched Janis's face as she moved around the room with Hearne.

At the end, she thought it was time she asked the question that had been on her mind since her first view of the original image. There was nothing to lose now.

Earlier she had asked Chris Treneer about the facial expression on the image placed on the Facebook site. He had said it had not been altered as far as the technicians could tell but they weren't absolutely sure of that. But Janis Mitchell's face during the re-enactments was neutral, almost serene as she settled into it each time, not animated or open-mouthed.

She walked over to the young woman who looked as if

she was finished. Catrin hoped that she wasn't, just yet.

She said, "During the class, when you were posing for this set, were you talking to Mr. Hearne or the students?"

"No," Janis replied, "I don't do that. Most models don't talk during a posing session."

Catrin knew that from experience.

Hearn suddenly spoke up, as if it had jolted a memory. He said, "The only thing I can recall was when a student asked for more a more dynamic action in the pose, remember? She spoke to you, but you didn't say anything. You were a bit put out, I thought, rightly so."

Mitchell nodded, evidently recalling it for the first time.

Hearne said to Catrin, "I intervened. I said, 'Marilyn, these are thirty second sketches; lines please, we can save details until later'. That's what I told her. She was out of order really. It is my job to direct the model, not a student's right to do so, they all knew that. Otherwise they would all want something different and there would be bedlam."

Catrin thought, now we may be getting somewhere. She looked at Wastle. He nodded; he had picked up the significance of the comments, was his message.

Without explanation, Catrin moved to a part of the room where she would be able to see clearly Mitchell's face during the pose sequence.

"Janis, could you do the poses just one more time, please? Mr. Hearne, you have good recall, I think and now have the sequence fresh in your mind. When you see the pose around the time Marilyn asked for more action, could you clap your hands? I will ask Janis for more action in the pose, you repeat again what you said at the time. It's a bit artificial, I know. Janis, can you try to react the way you felt at the time of the exchange? Don't think about in advance, just react, OK? It will be alright, I promise you."

As they went through it again and parodied the request and the model's own response, Chris Treneer moved to the wall behind Catrin. They watched Janis's face change, part mock-surprise, then annoyance and finally amusement as she heard Mr. Hearne give his original response. Then her features returned to a neutral expression as she went on with the pose sequence. Catrin said, "Chris?"

"I saw it, and we can pull it off this camera too, to verify," he said softly. He looked at her, understanding. It was a glimpse. Catrin had seen exactly the facial feature mix that was on the altered image.

Catrin thanked Mitchell and Hearne for their help and looked at Oliver Wastle. It was his case, she had done her part, as requested.

Wastle thanked them also and asked PC Lloyd to take Janis Mitchell home. As they left the room Catrin went out with them to say goodbye.

"Janis, you have been tremendous. We appreciate it, particularly running through the set for us. It has been very useful."

The young woman nodded. Clearly she wanted to get out.

Catrin said, "Think again about talking with someone, it could help."

Mitchell asked her, "Will you tell me - ." She stopped, uncertain, what to say.

"If we find out anything concrete or have any more questions, we will get back to you. And you can always call Sergeant Wastle."

Mitchell smiled. "I think, to be honest, I would rather

talk with you."

Catrin returned the smile. "Thank you." She said no more. She knew she would be long gone before this investigation was anywhere near completion.

She looked at Sharon Lloyd, thinking to say goodbye but knew she shouldn't, given Mitchell's last comment. Lloyd's expression was reflecting the same dilemma. She mouthed, "Goodbye' silently as Janis turned to leave, then she set off with her.

Catrin returned to the studio. Wastle was talking to Hearne but said to him, "One moment please," and came up to Catrin. He said softly, "How would anyone know in advance whether Mitchell was going to be modelling?"

He had realised the significance of the last sequence that Catrin had requested and he too saw it as highly unlikely that the request to have the model change her facial expression was a coincidence. Either the model had been unlucky, the one chosen on that day as the target, or it had been planned in advance.

Catrin nodded and said more loudly, "Mr. Hearne, where was the student Marilyn positioned during the class, do you recall."

From his careful response, she could tell that the lecturer had clued in too. He had been told in advance the purpose of the exercise.

"Actually, she was in the same area as you were standing during the last run-through, approximately, Sergeant Sayer."

"And who is Marilyn, her surname?" said Wastle.

"Marilyn Greaves, she is a mature student; a pretty good one, too; not playing at it. She is doing very well in her course."

Wastle said, "How do students know which model is

being used?"

Hearne looked at him, a little perplexed. "They don't; they don't care, really. They are just drawing or painting the figure. They prefer younger models, most of them; easier lines, you see. Older people tend to have more folds, more wrinkles; it makes for a harder subject to draw."

Catrin smiled. This was exactly her recollection of the chatter during her own life drawing classes.

"I think you have some experience of drawing people as well as modelling, from that smile," said Hearne, looking at Catrin.

Wastle continued, "So who has access to the booking list for the models, to know their schedules?"

Hearne nodded, "You will have to ask Mrs. Hardacre, in Administration. She handles it all, not the teaching staff. I know we draw from a roster of about ten people regularly over the year on a rotating basis and, of course, depending on their availability. Janis Mitchell was an addition to the roster last year."

Wastle nodded. 'Where can I find Mrs. Hardacre?"

Hearne offered to take him along.

Wastle looked at Catrin, "You and Chris keep on with…." He waved his hand at the computer.

She nodded. Wastle started to leave with Hearne then he stopped at the door and said, "Chris, follow me along when you wrap up."

As the door closed Catrin said to Chris, "He is going to ask about a voluntary forensic audit of a computer system, I think."

She also got the distinct impression that she was being excluded from other aspects of the investigation.

Chris Treneer looked at her. "That was clever, the face

thing, the way you teased it out. I had actually wondered about that as she did her first set; her face was so composed throughout."

Catrin said, "Most models keep a neutral or constant expression for a class, so it was puzzling me too, right from seeing the image DI Steadman showed me in Scotland Yard. When he said it was from a figure drawing class, I couldn't understand it."

He said, "Do you want to see the results?"

They went over to the computer and Treneer pulled up a 3-D diagram of the studio. It showed the new band of probability lines similar to the layout set that Catrin had begun with. They overlaid the first set but the area was smaller, better defined, centred on a post that was part of the lighting array.

"Is it your call or Sergeant Wastle's, to bring the SOCOs in?" she asked, a cheeky grin on her face.

"Put it this way, Sergeant Sayer," he said formally, "it is the responsibility of the investigating officer to do so. But don't be surprised when the fingerprint team arrive with impossibly short notice. Someone may have sent them an email… possibly from this very computer."

His phone rang. He listened and said, "I'll be right over, Oliver."

He closed the call. "You should come too, to Mrs. Hardacre's office. He wants me to check the computer system records for access to the roster of models, as you said."

He started to shut down his system.

Catrin said, "I'll stay here. We need the area cordoned off and the SOCOs in. And this room has two extra entrances besides the door to the corridor currently being guarded. You head off; I will talk to the officer outside, get another uniform in here."

"I'll do that," he said. He went into the corridor and spoke to the officer on the door who stepped inside.

Chris Treneer said, "No one will be allowed in before we get back. Let's go, Catrin."

~~

They were delayed a little. The studio technician was a bit put out as they left, telling him the news about no-one being allowed to re-enter. He had been told the police needed the studio for about an hour and there was a class due in. Chris phoned Wastle who in turn made it clear to the vice-principal that it was a crime scene until they said otherwise, that they would be out of there as fast as they could but the college would need to make other arrangements. And they would need access to the computer system.

When Catrin and Chris Treneer arrived at the administration area they found Wastle talking to a female employee. Mrs. Hardacre turned out to be a friendly, chatty person. She signed in with her password and showed Chris the set-up for booking personnel of all sorts, from models to contract technicians and staff covering holiday absences and sickness. Then Chris focused on the system.

She then tried to chat a little with Wastle but he wasn't in the mood, it was clear. He left to deal with the security arrangements until the SOCOs arrived. So Mrs. Hardacre turned her conversational skills on Catrin as Treneer worked away on the computer in front of him.

"Do you have many figure models on the list?" asked Catrin.

"Not many; we only have three courses that involve life class models and each needs two to three per term.

Most are the same people each year, a range of young and older men and women but we move them around a bit; they all want different hours and times and some want more work than others."

"And Janis Mitchell?"

"She joined last year, the year she moved to Falmouth University. No prior professional experience but she told me that she had been encouraged and coached by her mother, I recall, when I met her. It's sad to think …" she stopped, blushed.

"The word is going around that someone photographed her and put it on the internet. Something weird, is that right?'

Catrin nodded, "Yes, Mrs. Hardacre, that is correct. That's what we are looking into."

"We have never had it happen before, not that I know of," she said. "I hope it doesn't link into anything at the college."

Catrin noticed that Treneer had stuck a thumb drive into a port on the machine and had sat back, waiting. He interrupted them. "Mrs. Hardacre, this is the current employee list page; correct?"

"Yes," she said, "How did you get there? I thought it needed a separate login."

He smiled and pressed the keys, "And this is the address listing of all students taking classes here this year?"

She nodded, clearly surprised that this man had found his way around the system so easily.

"Thank you," he said, withdrawing the thumb drive. "Sergeant Sayer, I am finished here, at least for now."

11 PAPER

On her return to Falmouth Police Station Catrin suddenly found herself with nothing to do. She checked in with Aina. Everything was surprisingly quiet back at the office and there was no news on DCI Worsley that Aina could pass on, other than the surgery had gone well, she had heard.

Catrin had a sense that they were now just waiting for Hicks to appear, to inform him about the progress. She would have liked to go out, walk around and be a tourist for a bit but given the exchanges with Hicks today, she didn't want to put a foot wrong.

The SOCOs called Wastle, who in turn brought Catrin and Chris up to speed. "They should be wrapped up in a couple of hours. It is surprising how many fingerprints they lifted in that area, eight feet off the floor from the posts and the wall."

"Not really, Oliver," said Catrin, "if you take into account the number of times people change out lighting equipment, the odd tall student who puts an arm up and

86

leans on the thing for a moment in the middle of a project, that sort of thing."

She added, "I take it you have elimination prints from the technicians?"

He nodded, "Yes; at least the ones working at the college now."

She asked, "I don't suppose you could find a way to add in the fingerprints of the woman who asked for more dynamic action during the class, could you; the mature student, Marilyn Greaves?"

He paused. "Catrin, I don't think we can ask one student for elimination prints without asking all in the class... and I don't think we are ready to do so, unless DI Hicks makes that call. We will check her background again more carefully, though, to see if there are any links."

There was a noise in the corridor. Hicks appeared with another detective sergeant, one she knew had been working on the robbery.

He said, "We have two people brought in for interview on the Tunstall's case but before I do that, what's the update, Oliver?"

He came into the room and leaned against the wall.

Wastle reported that they had made good progress and started to give the update of the day's events.

Hicks interrupted him. "Did DS Sayer sort things out with Janis Mitchell, then?"

"Yes," said Wastle, "We did the run-through and I think it paid off, we -"

Again Hicks interrupted.

"DS Sayer, thank you. I think you can catch the train back to London. The Art Crime Unit has been very helpful and I will let DI Steadman know that."

His face was all smiles but the eyes were clear; time to

go.

"You can be back at work in the morning on your art crimes," he added unnecessarily.

Catrin looked at him.

All she could say was, 'Thank you, sir', as coolly as she could.

He said, "Treneer, can you go with DS Sayer and collect her things, get her to the train station or ask an officer out there to do it, please?"

He looked at Wastle, "Then we can get on."

Clearly he wasn't going to talk about the case with Catrin present. It annoyed her, not being invited to give input.

Chris Treneer said, "It's on my way, I have to head back to Exeter anyway. I will take DS Sayer back to Truro; no need for her to change trains on the way back."

"Thank you, Chris, it's much appreciated." said Hicks very pleasantly, waiting.

Catrin picked up her shoulder bag then shook hands with Wastle, who was looking a little embarrassed. "It's been good working with you today, Catrin. Safe travels."

"Goodbye, Oliver."

She shook hands silently with DI Hicks and walked out, Treneer following her.

They were a few steps along the corridor when DI Hicks's voice came after them.

"Do you think he is sweet on her, Oliver?"

There was no response that they heard from Wastle as they turned the corner.

Catrin stopped suddenly, annoyed by the remark. She felt Treneer's hand gently touch the small of her back. Whether it was to keep her moving or just to stop him colliding with her, she wasn't sure.

"Let's go," he said, walking past her, leading the way.

~~

As they got into his car Catrin said, "Chris, do you have to put up with this all the time?"

He sighed. "It's DI Hicks. There is no problem with other teams, to be honest. Look, the sleeper leaves Truro at 10.30 tonight. Let's collect your bag from the hotel, have dinner and I will see you to the train. Does that work for you?"

She looked at him. He was being quite assertive for a change. Probably his annoyance with Hicks was driving it.

She smiled, "It would be very nice, thank you. Could we go to a seafood place, perhaps? I will catch the train but dinner would be lovely. I just need to call Aina, our Admin person, to sort it out."

She thought a moment.

"But that means you will get back to Exeter later; you could be on your way a lot sooner."

He smiled, "Trust me. In this job I have driven the roads from Falmouth, Truro and other places back to Exeter much later than I will be doing tonight. And killing time in Truro Station for you is less enjoyable than seeing Falmouth."

They collected her suitcase from the hotel and went to eat at pub called the Boathouse on the road leading down to the centre of town; it served seafood. Treneer called ahead, asked them to keep a table by the window; it was high enough on the hill to give Catrin a great view.

Before they ate, Chris gave her a quick tour of Falmouth town centre and harbour while talking about its history. He turned eventually into a small side road, Hull

Street, and suddenly pulled into a reserved parking space in front of a shop with the name 'Treneer Handmade Paper'.

Treneer said, "Come in and meet my sister."

Catrin followed him inside. The ground level was divided into a shop area with a wide array of paper products; writing paper in various hues and flecks, greeting cards, examples of wedding stationery and art paper. The watercolour stock and sketchbooks caught Catrin's eye. Further back, through a door, it looked as if it was a work-space of some sort.

Treneer had called out on entry that it was him and he had a visitor. He introduced Catrin to the two people who came from the back, a woman a little older than her and an older man, looking to be near retirement. Both were wearing aprons with the shop name and logo.

"Catrin, this is my sister, Jenifer, with one 'n'. And Harry, Harold Oates who has worked as a papermaker before either of us was born, he says. This is Detective Sergeant Catrin Sayer, from London. We are going to eat and I will drop her at Truro for the train. But I need the loo... excuse me."

He left them talking as he disappeared into the back of the shop.

As they exchanged pleasantries Jenifer said, "But you are from South Wales, not London."

Catrin smiled, "Yes; from Pontypridd. And the one 'n' in Jenifer is Cornish, I think. I love your paper; you make it here, it seems?"

Jenifer answered, "Yes, we make all our paper on the premises, there is none brought in. It's all handmade paper."

"By time-honoured techniques," said Harry.

Catrin was looking at the samples area. "You make watercolour paper, I see. I am an artist, I don't use much now, but I used to."

She walked over to a display unit. "Can I buy two of these sketchbooks? They look very nice."

Jenifer smiled. "Of course you can."

As she rang up the order, Jenifer said, "I know you are a ceramic decorator, Chris told me. He looked you up on the internet last night and showed me the web page."

Catrin suddenly realized that perhaps she had made an impression on Treneer if he was looking into her online profile.

She smiled. "Well, I go back tonight on the sleeper; it was just a quick trip to help out."

Jenifer nodded.

Catrin changed the subject. "Is it a good business?"

"Parts of it are, but it is very seasonal; we struggle in the winter season. In summer the population around here increases about seven-fold with tourists and summer residents. People will buy handmade notepaper even if they haven't written a letter in ages; they like the look and the feel of it. We do a range of colours, flecks and markings then.

"We are building up stocks for the summer season right now, aren't we, Harry?"

Harry nodded. "Our biggest regular sales each month are archival quality paper for professional artist use. We make the paper that Mason Carrington uses all the time, for example; as do many of his students," he said proudly, just as Chris reappeared from the washroom.

Catrin was impressed. Carrington was one of the most successful watercolour artists in the UK in recent years, with a loose style; flamboyant, many would say. Catrin hadn't seen any originals by him but had seen articles about him and images of his work. She recalled a television documentary about him she had seen about two years ago.

She smiled at Harry. "That must be quite a coup."

Then on the wall behind his head she saw a painting, a Paris scene, realising that it was a Carrington. It looked to be an original, as well, not a print.

"Yes," said the old man, "He goes through a lot and so do his students - and he pays a handsome price for it."

"I see Harry is giving away all the business secrets," said Chris, joining them.

Jenifer smiled, "Mason has been good to us, good business for us, too."

Chris smiled at his sister, "And good for my sister; they are a couple, a strange couple, though."

He pulled a face at her.

Jenifer smiled and said, "More secrets. Catrin, would you like some coffee or tea; we can stop working."

Catrin was about to say 'yes' when her brother said, "No, we have work to discuss and a reservation at the Boathouse. Catrin is on the 10.30 train tonight so… no."

~~

At the pub Chris said, "Can we talk about the case?"

Catrin said, "Sure, but I am off it now, so shouldn't you be talking to Wastle?"

He smiled, "I want to bounce some thoughts off you before I do."

"Fire away, then," Catrin said.

They had ordered their meal and drinks.

"Now…" began Treneer.

Catrin's mobile rang. She looked at it; it was John. "A

moment" she said, then, into the phone, "John?"

"Sarge, Aina says you are heading back. So can you be with me tomorrow afternoon at the Malaysian High Commission? DS Hatcher in A&A said that he could come, but...."

Catrin's mind did a hundred and eighty degree turn to get back to the Coventry case. She knew his reservation; Hatcher knew Asian art but he was no diplomat.

"Yes, I can be there. I am on the overnight train so it will give me time to go home, shower and change into something suitable before I come into the Yard. In fact, I won't come in at all. I will go home, sort myself out, work from there and meet you at the High Commission. Send me the location details."

His response showed his relief.

"Thanks Sarge, will do. I will talk to you tomorrow. Oh, a woman from the Foreign & Commonwealth Office who deals with Malaysia will be there, too."

"OK John, that's good; it keeps everything linked up properly."

She closed the phone.

Chris looked at her.

Catrin said, "Tomorrow's work, at the Malaysian High Commission, sorry... but you were saying."

He said, "Malaysia; it sounds exotic. Well, what I was about to say was thank you for the help and I am really sorry you are heading back; I think we made good progress today."

She smiled. "I do, too."

"I am also planning to say to DI Hicks tomorrow that I think that they are on the wrong track. It won't go down well, and I think you can understand why."

Catrin nodded. She needed to stay out of local politics, she knew. She said, "What are your thoughts? I will give you my feedback but then… I am leaving, Chris, you understand?"

He nodded.

"This hacker 'Adrestia' is top-notch. I assume his or her rates for contract work are way up there. It's a different world, Catrin, hackers. Money flows are secondary to these people normally. It is about the challenge of the hack, the power of intervention or some other driver as well as money. But to the people who contract them, they know a high price is tied to prestige.

"Some hackers work in grotty rooms; others have luxurious apartments. They all have cut-out systems, alerting systems, exits and escapes that would make MI5 nod with understanding, if not approval. They can leave everything behind, sabotaged to wipe out, then walk over to a bank, get out more money, buy a new laptop and pick up wherever they left off. They are really hard to catch."

He looked intense.

"This is no student 'get back at you' thing. I said that at the outset in the first case briefing and DI Hicks told me not to jump the gun. I think someone has targeted Janis Mitchell specifically to get at her or someone else. The person who did it had a careful plan and wanted the symbolism of it, including the vase. If it was another student, it was a wealthy one; and the reason would not be a slight over refusing a date or something like that. It's deep-seated."

He took a breath just as the bartender called their order, saw where they were sitting and headed over carrying the plates.

When they settled to eat she said, "Chris, everything you said makes sense to me. My impression is that Mitchell has no idea why this is happening. People will often say that, but you can see in their face or their body language that they have a suspicion but don't want to share it. In this case I am pretty sure this is a total bewilderment to her. But I am also struck that she never mentioned the vase. Once it was revealed and she knew about it, you think she would wonder why it is a feature in the image. I would, I think."

He nodded.

Catrin said, "So yes, make your point tomorrow at the briefing. Good luck; it can help focus the investigation, if Hicks accepts it."

She thought to herself that Hicks is focused on the person behind this; Steadman is focused on the hacker. They both need to focus on the reason and the message in the image. But Hicks's curt dismissal had brought back DCI Worsley's message that she was not part of this investigation team.

As they were eating he said, "I looked at your web site last night. I like your ceramics."

She smiled. "Jenifer said you had looked and mentioned it to me."

They talked for a while about art and paper-making then Catrin had the thought she shared without thinking it through fully.

"Looking at art, stolen or otherwise, must be a lot easier than some of the stuff you have to deal with?"

"Yes," he said, "Not easy, a lot of it."

"How did you get into this side of computer work?"

He looked at her, deciding what to say.

"I am a pretty quiet guy, really. Honestly. I was doing large system forensic work on business fraud cases, finding incremental errors that pointed in the direction of big payoffs. It's technical but quite interesting."

He smiled, "At least, to me it is."

He hesitated.

"I got into an argument with two other computer technicians. One had made a remark to the other about a woman on a pretty vile image of an assault. I won't say more. We had gone through training together so I knew them both quite well and we got on OK generally. They thought I was being too straight-laced. 'Prissy bastard' one called me, I recall.

"It must have got around. Last year during my performance review my boss said he wanted to include computer support work on vice and sexual assault imagery in my work profile: I would become the lead resource contact for vice team work. He told me it's hard at times but necessary work and he thought I had the right attitude. I agreed to it, went through some training. So here I am."

He smiled.

"I was sent on a course in Plymouth. The hard part is not the flesh and the sex, frankly; it becomes analytical after a while, like a forensic pathologist dealing with bodies. It's the violence and the sense of waste and degradation in a lot of it. That's the erosive bit. I will be rotated off it sometime; they don't leave people doing it continuously."

Memories of some of the policing issues Catrin experienced when she was in uniform came to mind. Young prostitutes, male and female; images found on phones; materials seen during searches that were glanced at then quickly taken as evidence and sent off to... people like Treneer to go through, to document and analyse. She hadn't thought of it much before.

"Then it will be back to frauds?" Catrin smiled.

He laughed. "Not sure. Could be anything these days

the way people use computers; video piracy, fraud, threatening telephone calls, you name it; it's all part of the job."

She checked her watch to see how much time they had before she needed to go to Truro. He saw her action.

"I guess we had better be going. It's a night on the sleeper for you."

Catrin laughed. "I actually sleep quite well on them; it must be the motion, rocking me to sleep."

12 THE HIGH COMMISSION

Marilyn Greaves woke early, around 3.45 a.m. That in itself was not unusual. She had experienced many periods of broken sleep over her life that she blamed on various causes - at least she gave those as reasons to her husband. But only she knew really why they occurred.

Her course at the college was four classes a week, working towards her arts diploma. She had arranged them to mesh well with her part-time job as a civil servant and, between the two and looking after the home, her days were full. When she made 'The Decision' as she thought of it, her life gained an additional complexity. Her sleep had become disturbed yet again.

As she woke her mind was on the news that the police had been into the college. Some of the students were talking about it, coming up with an array of reasons why a police officer had been placed outside a studio and other plain-clothed officers had been seen talking to the Admin office staff and going through the computer system.

But she knew the reason. They had identified the image and its source, the studio. But not her, she thought;

they would have been around to see her, question her.

She had already decided on the next step and had to little more to do than call the number the hacker had given her and explain her needs. She would do that tomorrow once Callum had gone to work.

It disturbed her that nothing had happened. Not in terms of the police making progress; in terms of the package she had seen dropped through the letter box. She needed to up the ante.

~~

Somewhere between Swindon and Reading, Catrin read the emails received overnight while having her first coffee. The one from John was brief; it provided the address of the meeting venue; the Malaysian High Commission in Belgrave Square. He also provided the coordinates of a Madeleine Turner-Jones in the Foreign & Commonwealth Office. She was the liaison assigned to the meeting and would accompany them.

The final sentence was, "We talked; she told me a lot about protocol and Malaysia."

No doubt she did, thought Catrin. The longer email was from Turner-Jones herself.

Dear Sergeant Sayer,

It was unfortunate that you were not available for the briefing discussion on the protocol for the meeting tomorrow, but I understand you are tied up on other matters. I will meet you and Detective Constable Obi at the High Commission of Malaysia entrance foyer at 13.55 sharp.

We are meeting with the Dato' Amhat Budi, the Deputy Commissioner, and a Miss Suriawati, a cultural attaché at the High Commission. Malay honorifics are very complex, with formal titles such as Dato, Tun and Datuk for people of rank, so please just use 'Sir' and 'Miss' and follow my lead.

Also, please dress formally and cover your legs. Thank you.

Sincerely,

Madeleine Turner-Jones (Mrs.)

Executive Officer, Malaysia Liaison

'Cover your legs'. Really? I'd not thought of that, Catrin smiled.

As the train made its way closer to London the issue of her curt dismissal by Hicks came back to mind, nagging at her. She tried to put it to one side, but as she processed it, beyond the personality conflict that defined their interactions yesterday, she knew there was something she had wanted to say about the investigation. In the end she dialled Stephen Hicks' number; he should be in the Falmouth police station by now, she thought.

After he answered she said, "DS Sayer here, sir."

Hicks sounded happy. She could hear voices in the background.

"Yes, Sayer, I was just about to call some order in this room and told people to mute their phones when, guess what, mine rang. How can I help you, DS Sayer?"

His voice had risen in volume during the response. She realised that her call was being made known to others, including DS Wastle, no doubt. They were about to start their morning briefing.

Out with it, she thought.

"It's the Mitchell case, the exercise yesterday at the college. I wanted to emphasize that the intervention by the student Marilyn Greaves asking for more expression in the model is just… strange. Students don't do that with warm-up sketches; it's irrelevant. There is something more to it that needs examination. I wanted to make the point…"

I would have made it yesterday she thought, if I hadn't been tossed out.

There was a short silence.

"Sayer, I thank you for bringing it to my attention."

His voice didn't sound rude, but it was a mechanical response.

Then he asked, "How long have you been a detective, DS Sayer?"

"Three years, sir."

So you were taught that in assault cases, other than random victim attacks, there is generally a correlation between the length of time and the degree of contact between a victim and his or her assailant. It's why family members are always the first suspects, correct?"

"Yes sir, I know that. But I was pointing out an anomaly in …"

His voice rode over hers. "She has one and half years of almost daily exposure to students and staff at Falmouth University during term time and, literally, less than seventeen hours contact with the current batch of students she modelled for at Truro and Penwith College. She has no friends there, no reason to be there other than her contract. I personally checked that with Janis Mitchell, the number of times she had modelled there this year. So which group of people are most likely to be associated with some event, not yet identified, that has caused this oddball assault over the internet, I ask you?"

Catrin didn't respond; they were talking at cross-purposes.

Hicks said, "Thanks for the call, DS Sayer."

The line went dead. Catrin realised she had been steamrollered in front of the team of D&C officers gathered for the morning briefing. She wondered whether Treneer had said his piece yet on his theory and, if not, whether this would send his head back below the parapet.

By the time she arrived at Paddington Station she decided that she was well out of it and glad that Jane Worsley seemed to treat the West Country as her patch; she was welcome to it.

~~

Catrin turned up at the Belgrave Square address on time in a navy blue pant suit. John Obi was waiting outside dressed quite elegantly in a charcoal grey suit, white shirt and light blue tie. It must be his 'Sunday Best', she thought; she hadn't seen him in the suit at the office.

The woman that emerged about the same time from the taxi was tall, middle-aged and… simply big. She was dark-haired, large-framed and was carrying too much weight on that frame. The flowing pale blue dress matched a three-quarter length coat. Designer stuff, Catrin thought, not off the rack.

Catrin's mother had once bought a matching coat and dress for a wedding but it was not something that Catrin or her friends would have done. But this woman has money and a sense of style, despite her size, she thought. As the FCO representative dealt with the taxi and walked over to them Catrin noticed she also had great balance and deportment.

Mrs. Turner-Jones shook hands with Obi and then said, "Detective Sergeant Sayer, nice to meet you. You were in Cornwall, I gather."

The tone was pleasant but somewhat imperious. She was in command, it said.

Catrin smiled inwardly, resisting the urge to curtsey and say, 'Yes, ma'am' as they shook hands. Instead she said, "Good afternoon, and thank you for your email yesterday. Yes, I was on another case, Ms. Turner-Jones."

"Quite." She said, "And it is 'Mrs.', please."

She led the way in as if it was familiar ground, which it turned out to be. She announced their presence and then chatted convivially with the receptionist, a male, in what Catrin took to be Malay. John stayed silent, eyeing the décor and art.

There was no real delay. They were taken up in a small lift and along a corridor into a large office where an older man and a younger woman were waiting.

The cultural attaché did the introductions and after they settled down it was clear that the Deputy High Commissioner wanted to make an opening statement.

"We are very pleased to have this meeting, to thank you for your diligence and for bringing these items to our attention. When we received the photographs on Monday I knew what the kris signified; Detective Obi was quite correct, it is valuable. We are currently checking on its origin, but we need details of the way in which it was… removed… from our country. I assume there is no sales record or related documentation for the kris or the painting?"

Obi took them through the details of the case, carefully keeping names and identification elements out of it. Catrin had already heard more about it on Monday morning, during the briefing.

A senior citizen in Coventry who lived alone, a man called Ted Jackson, had been found by his social worker; he was semi-conscious on the kitchen floor. She had let herself in after getting no response to find him beaten and the house ransacked and robbed.

In enquiries by the police, a neighbour had thought that she recognized a young man leaving by the back gate of Jackson's small garden a day earlier. She told the police who she thought it might be but couldn't recall his name. A 'dinner lady' at a local school, she said she remembered the faces of all the troublemakers over the years.

It didn't take long before they had searched the school records and obtained a name to match the woman's memory of the face, which led to a warrant to search the teenager's home. The painting, a sum of money and the unusual knife were found in his bedroom with other items he had stolen elsewhere.

It was a constable, Ryerson, with the arresting team who had suggested that the knife and painting could be valuable art rather than junk. He had no idea why, really; he just had a growing interest in antiques. But the Detective Inspector leading the case liked the young officer's enthusiasm and had him flag them routinely to the Art & Antiques Unit at Scotland Yard, who in turn forwarded the notice to the ACU. DCI Jane Worsley had assigned it to DC Obi to check out and then had the idea that if Catrin's trip back from Scotland worked out, she could bring him back also.

Jackson had been suffering more from dehydration than any long-term effects of the beating. In hospital the investigating officer had interviewed him the day following the arrest and had also asked about the possessions stolen from his home.

A number of items, including the painting and the

knife, had been passed to Jackson by the widow of an old friend at the Royal British Legion. In clearing her husband's belongings she had asked Ted to see if his old regiment wanted them. That had been four months ago.

He said, "To be honest, I thought they were junk but didn't want to hurt her feelings. And I haven't been out much to do anything about it yet, not that I have a clue what I would do with them."

On his return to Coventry this week, Obi had talked to the widow, which hadn't helped. Then he had visited her husband's Legion branch. One person who knew the deceased and who was willing to say something looked at him with steely eyes.

"You won't get anything here, I think, nothing that would tarnish the reputation of a dead comrade, young man. But you should know that the black market on stuff like this was big in Malaya during the Emergency, as the war was called. I wouldn't look much further than that, I suggest."

Obi had thanked the man and beaten a hasty retreat.

As he finished, Deputy Commissioner Budi said, "Constable Obi, you are to be commended for your work in this matter. We thank you for drawing the discovery to our attention."

The cultural attaché added, "If you could provide us with the regiment or battalion details of the former owner that might help. I appreciate from your summary that we should not get into personal details. Regimental details, postings - that sort of information will assist us in our own search, perhaps."

Amhat Budi continued, "We are also pleased that the British Government has taken the trouble to offer the services of the V&A Museum to assist in the renovation and repair of the items, to address the damages incurred."

Mrs. Turner-Jones just nodded, acknowledging the point. Catrin stayed neutral and silent; she had no idea that the conservation and repair offer had been extended.

Afterwards they said their goodbyes to the FCO staffer as she climbed into a taxi and they headed for the Tube. Both officers were heading home.

"That went quite well, John," said Catrin. "All you have to do now is sanitize some of the info, pass it on through Turner-Jones and it will be finished from our end. We can leave it to FCO after that."

Obi said, "What about the handover of the items?"

Catrin laughed. "In my time in ACU we have had three cases like this. The first one for me was as I arrived at ACU, the Bangor case - the handover of paintings to the Russians. They are always 'gold braid and VIP' events; the troops are not involved."

He sighed, "That's fine."

He sounded relieved.

As they travelled east on the Piccadilly line, Catrin saw that several of her email messages were from Aina, so she called her anyway.

"Did it go well, Catrin? John was nervous after his discussion with Mrs. Turner-Jones."

Catrin laughed, looking across at Obi, "He survived, Aina, didn't put a foot wrong. Is there any news from Jane?"

Aina's voice lightened. "Yes, she called this morning. She plans to be in sometime around the middle of next week. All went well, she said. She will have to take it easy then too, nothing outside the office for a while. You know, like you after the Glasgow thing. No leaping from bridges in hot pursuit."

"That's great news. Thank you for telling me."

"Catrin, my email about Mrs. Mitchell, in Cornwall - have you read it?"

Mrs. Mitchell, not Miss, Catrin noted. "No, I'm just opening it now…"

Catrin was scrolling down her email list and she opened it as Aina said, "She called this morning, wanted to speak to you; she was quite insistent. I passed on the message and her number and I also mentioned it to DI Marshall. He is back and wants to talk with you about it."

"Is Keith there?" she asked, surprised. She thought he would be in France longer.

"He got back just before lunch, Catrin; it was a fast trip. I will put you through."

In a moment Keith Marshall's voice came on the line. He was straight into it.

"Catrin, the Falmouth thing; Steadman called me. Told me you had been sent packing but had done a good day's work, according to DS Wastle there. Steadman said Wastle and everyone else live in fear of DI Hicks."

"I can believe it, Keith. He is like a feudal lord."

"Well, clearly you didn't bow and scrape enough, Catrin," he mocked, then turned serious.

"The thing is this; Janis Mitchell is the daughter of a superintendent there, as you now know, I gather. He runs the coordination of traffic logistics across the basic command units for each region. With the summer population increases and all those festivals, you can imagine the work there.

"His wife talked to her daughter about events this week. She is experienced enough to see that you had a positive effect and she wants you back."

Catrin said, "It's not her call. And I can't discuss the case with her. Even if I was on it, I couldn't do that unless it was an interview. Janis is a legal adult."

"Right," said Marshall, "but I want you to call her anyway. Explain just that."

"You want her avalanche to roll over Hicks, not us."

"Exactly. Charles Steadman is quite annoyed with Hicks; Steadman is after this hacker, remember? DI Hicks is busy chasing computer-savvy students at Falmouth, it seems. His computer tech and Wastle say they should be following a lead you helped to identify, someone in Truro."

Catrin thought, Wastle wants to go after the Greaves woman, the mature student at the Truro College. Good man.

Catrin said, "I'll give her a call once I am off the Tube. It's great news about Jane, back next week."

"Yes, for her and for me. She is largely office-bound so she can deal with all these divisional meetings and the bureaucracy. I will be spending half of tomorrow in a meeting on… it doesn't matter. Look, give Mrs. Mitchell a call, if you would."

"Mrs. Mitchell, this is Detective Sergeant Sayer with the Metropolitan Police, returning your call."

The woman on the end of the line sounded 'public school', not local to Falmouth. It explained why Janis Mitchell sounded somewhere between the two.

"Thank you, DS Sayer. I called because my daughter and I talked. Simply put, I want you back on the case. Now I know you can't talk about it with me. I just want you to be aware that my daughter appreciated your help and I think it would be beneficial for you to continue with the case despite you being a specialist in art crime issues, I gather."

Catrin broke in. "Mrs. Mitchell, you are correct, I can't discuss this with you other than say I was happy to assist the investigation this week. The matter is a local one."

Mitchell said, "I know that, DS Sayer, and... I just ask you to be receptive to coming back to assist further, if requested."

Catrin paused. "My assignments are, of course, a departmental matter."

"That's well understood, DS Sayer. Thank you for calling. Goodbye."

The line closed.

Mitchell wasn't imploring me to do anything and had not requested information, she realised. Catrin gained the distinct impression that the wife of Superintendent Mitchell knew a lot about the Devon & Cornwall Police Service and police procedures in general; and she had correctly surmised that Catrin would be thoroughly unimpressed by Stephen Hicks as well, which was probably the reason for the call.

13 STUTTGART

"Dr. Hintzen!"

The young man hurried towards him. Hintzen had just been about to leave the building, his old leather briefcase in hand. He saw it was Blecher, a teaching assistant, calling him.

Arno Hintzen was an anachronism within the Fraunhofer Institute; a Ph.D., an expert in business ethics rather than engineering. He seemed to spend more time lost in the analysis of past business decisions yet he was a staff member of an Institute firmly focused on the future.

The Stuttgart location was one of a number of applied science and engineering research institutes in Germany within the Fraunhofer structure. This one specialised in organizational technology. Hintzen taught a course there in ethics in business decision-making, a companion course to one he taught in the Freiburg location to software engineers.

"Yes, Hr. Blecher, good afternoon. What can I do for you?"

His voice was controlled but the undertone was clear;

he wanted to leave.

Blecher said quickly, "It's the re-scheduling in lectures and seminars for next week, with the holiday. I sent you an email asking would you exchange seminar rooms on Tuesday morning with my group; it will really help."

Hintzen glanced upwards at the heavens then looked at the man. Help what, he thought and then said politely, "I am sorry. I haven't checked my emails but if I can help at all, I would be glad to do so."

The assistant looked both thankful and a little exasperated.

"I am glad I caught you; I did send it two days ago and wanted to confirm with my group. So it is OK with you?"

"By all means," said Hintzen, pulling out a small, leather-bound notebook and his fountain pen. "Give me the seminar room number and I will send an email to my own class, too."

His tone of voice changed to amused, whimsical. "I have them in a group list; I can send it to them in one press of the return key now, you know."

His frequently humorous sarcasm about modern communication systems was well known. Some enjoyed his quirkiness but most other faculty members were irritated by it. If his insight into ethics and his powerful Socratic teaching style were not so popular with graduate students entering the Institute, he would have been out long ago.

The assistant thanked him and walked away, smiling to himself. Arno certainly lives up to his reputation. He can send a group email. A miracle!

When Hintzen reached his apartment he prepared a snack, poured himself a glass of wine and then locked the apartment door. He fired up his laptop and settled down to work. The second image he was working on intrigued him. Her request was simpler this time technically, but his first attempt at the modifications didn't satisfy him completely, particularly the skin at the edge of the cut; he had re-worked it twice now. The rest of the image was complete.

An hour later he stopped, well pleased with the changes. He went back into the image focusing on the shadow area under her left breast to add the finishing touch. Under the right magnification the police would find his signature; 'Adrestia'.

Finally he took the laptop to the clean area and connected it to the printer there. It was time to send the image to the client and await her call.

When he had finished, he remembered the discussion with Blecher. He started up his desktop computer, sent out the email to the class involved making sure he typed an 'o' instead of '0' in the room number of the new location. Twenty minutes later he sent out a correction. They would smile; Arno is still struggling with a keyboard, someone would say.

He settled back in his living room, listening to music with a second glass of wine. His cat was sitting in one of her favorite places; she rotated through them, he noticed. She was on a side table looking out the window just below the portrait of his mother.

Arno had been born in 1961. That his mother and father had not been married at the time was known to him from a young age. His father, Paul Hintzen, and his mother only moved into an apartment together when Arno was nearly four. And some of the boys at his school obviously heard about it from their parents; it was an occasional, bitter taunt.

It was in his teens he found out that his presumption that they had sex outside marriage and only formalized their partnership later was unfounded. His 'father' was not his biological father. His mother had worked in a retail pharmacy when he was conceived. The only way she could keep her job, it was then revealed, was to have sex regularly with the pharmacist, the business owner.

Paul had been going out with her at the time, was even thinking of marriage. When she became pregnant, she confessed. He ditched her for the deception and her weakness of principle. 'Jobs were hard to find', she had cried; she needed the money, the independence. Her own upbringing had its own horrors from which she needed to escape.

It was several years later that the two former sweethearts got together, a little more pragmatic in their revised relationship. She had in any case been fired from the pharmacy once the pregnancy was evident, discarded from a small business in an era when pregnant women had no rights to continue working nor, to many, to be seen in public in that condition.

Paul Hintzen had always treated Arno as his own child and, to Arno, Paul was his father. Other than the normal cruelties of childhood and taunts generally involving the word 'bastard', Arno had a happy and fulfilling life, it seemed. He was bright, studied hard and was a loving and enjoyable child, his parents thought. If they had a complaint it was that he grew up too fast, he always seemed to be older than his years.

Out of that formative experience came two particular elements of Arno's life. His focus in graduate school on ethics in business was visible; his capacity for clandestine revenge was not.

In his late teens he had visited the pharmacy owned by his biological father on several occasions; making small purchases, checking out the man working in the dispensary, looking at the women serving at the counter wondering if they too had to provide their own sexual services for employment. His sperm donor, as he thought of him, seemed affable and competent with staff and customers, exactly what you would expect. He appeared to be a professional man, a health expert, a man of standing. But all Arno could see was the man forcing his mother to stay behind on some pretext or other after closing.

It was the era of early desktop computerisation. Arno had noted carefully the details of the premises and on two occasions, weeks apart, he took the risk of breaking in. On the first entry he downloaded copies of the business files from the Apple II computer the shop now used. He had brought floppy disks with him for that purpose. Thinking about it many years later, he mused that the software file he stole then was one of the smallest he had ever used. Small it may have been, but the transfer time from the disk drive whispering away in the darkened shop seemed to drag on interminably.

The business accounts were kept on a fancy-named computer program tailored to the pharmaceutical retail sector. It was, however, largely window-dressing; the system was based on a widely-used database program, Dbase II. It took him several weeks to learn his way around the program and come up with the solution. The system and data file modifications took relatively little time after that.

Afterwards he went back into the shop, uploaded the changes and left. Then he waited four months before writing two anonymous letters on another computer he had access to at school. It was only after sending them that he realised that the letters could be examined for fingerprints if anyone was suspicious. It was an unfounded worry, but it caused him such anxiety that his obsession with avoiding detection began then, leading to his 'clean room' approach.

Six months later he went to the pharmacy to make a purchase again. The pharmacist had changed; it was now a younger man. The professional diploma on the wall made it clear he was not a locum. Arno had worked out in advance a pretext to ask for the other man, the older pharmacist who had helped him previously, he said. He was no longer there, they told him. 'Retired' said the sales assistant.

His biological father was then fifty-one.

He said no more at the time, just left. He couldn't do much more, he felt, to find out what happened.

Two years later the man died of a heart attack, his mother told him, feeling he needed to know. She had heard from a friend who still worked at the same shop. That gave Arno another sleepless night; whether one of the counter assistants who served him was this woman and whether she would later recognize him, say he had visited.

He asked her; is heart failure a family trait?

No, his mother told him, at least not on my side. And she knew that the man had a hard couple of years at the end, very stressful. She had long ago forgiven him, Arno knew. He hadn't. She thought the news about the death might upset Arno, she told Paul later, but he just seemed numb about it.

Years later, with the growth of the internet and his increased computer competence, he checked the professional databases of registered pharmacists to find his plan had worked like a charm. In his inventory adjustments to the Dbase data files he had sensibly kept away from the Schedule 1 drugs; the inventories were too tightly controlled. But selling other prescription drugs 'below the counter' without a linking physician authorisation and declaring the discrepancies as obsolete inventory was not appreciated by the pharmaceutical licensing body. Later, when Arno had developed his hacking skills still further, he did some more investigation of files. His father had been struck off; lost the right to practice. The file showed he was still protesting his innocence in letters to the agency at the time of his death, quite unable to account for the stock records that the auditors had found.

Arno's own marriage had lasted only three years. His wife, in leaving him, told him that he was a closed book, watertight. His flare and eloquence in their courtship had disappeared and she didn't know the man she had married.

He disagreed. "Everyone has some small secrets, private things, it's natural."

Her answer was that he was like the brass-bound military travelling chest that they had bought in Aachen in the first year of their marriage. It had fifteen small drawers. In Arno's case, she felt, she had access to just one; the rest were locked off and she knew now that the situation would never change. It wasn't enough to sustain a healthy marriage, she told him. She left with a settlement, disappointed but resolute.

He kept the cat, the previous occupant of the space by the window.

His first client came from a chance meeting at a

conference on ethics and education in Heidelberg, a two-night liaison with a woman, another academic, during which she unburdened her frustrations in more ways than one. He suggested a possible solution. She was bitter enough to agree and wealthy enough to pay for the effort.

"How much will it cost?" she said.

"Five thousand euros," he answered, the number coming off the top of his head. She paid. He never changed his rate nor looked back. These projects now were such a meaningful part of his life.

14 LIZ'S PLACE

"Throwing or working clay into some of the shapes that Catrin and I collaborate on is quite challenging for me at times; it certainly takes me beyond my comfort zone and my regular work at our pottery. And sometimes we get three-quarters of the way through a new work and a crack or a collapse occurs. Then it is fortunate, I think, that both Catrin and I swear in Welsh."

There was laughter in the group assembled. It was the following Tuesday evening. Catrin had been in the office during the day but there had been no sign of Worsley yet.

About thirty patrons and friends were gathered for the early evening reception in the gallery 'Liz's Place'. Each of these evening events featured two of the artists who sold works through the gallery. This was the third time that Catrin and Jean had been involved, this time with the artist Sarah Chambers. It was the first time, though, that Catrin had insisted that Jean should speak for them, not her.

Jean had said, "It's your decoration that they want to hear about."

"It's our work, Jean and I have spoken about it twice now," Catrin responded.

Her friend knew when Catrin reached decisions; she recognized the look.

Catrin had been watching Melanie. Catrin could see how pleased she was both with Jean being at centre stage and her partner's easy style of talking about the work, despite her original fears and protestations.

Jean said, "In closing, I just want to thank again Liz for taking our art under her wing; my partner Melanie, who puts up with all the hours we take out on one piece while she is left dealing with the regular product line and, of course, my friend Catrin. Both her and her talent are a blessing and inspiration in my life."

In the applause Liz Marshall moved forward.

"Thank you everyone, for coming tonight. Mingle, talk, ask the artists some questions and if you have a funny feeling come over you, give in to your impulses and buy!"

It was about 8.30 p.m. when Catrin was ready to wrap up. She had just finished explaining the idea for a design on a vase to two guests when a young couple came over, interrupting their discussion.

"Geoff says you are a police officer," said the young woman.

"Con, we should be going." Her partner, Geoff, Catrin assumed, smiled at them and said, "My apologies, you were talking."

From his body language and tone he was trying to persuade her to leave. His partner sounded as if she had entertained herself a little too much.

"Yes, I am," said Catrin, "My day job."

"You hit that Scot in the balls with a big torch," she said. Her companion, who was clearly her informant, took her arm. Catrin could see he was embarrassed.

She said, "I think you -."

Then Catrin heard a familiar voice behind her.

"Not true, I am afraid," said Neville Coltrane, "She kicked the man there after he attacked her. He was a gang member who disregarded the instruction of a police officer during an arrest; he was too big and dangerous for her to let him get the upper hand."

"Ah, Sir Neville," the young woman smiled, joking with him, clearly inferring he was rushing to Catrin's defense. Catrin saw the woman who had arrived alongside Coltrane wince. Catrin looked at her and the younger woman; they were related, that was easy to see.

Geoff pulled her arm a little more forcefully, moving her back, "My sincere apologies again," he said to the small group, then to Neville's companion, "We will wait by the car."

The couple Catrin had been talking to before the theatrics began smiled at Catrin. The wife said, "It sounds as if you are a brave woman, Catrin; I couldn't have done it, I am sure. Neil, we should leave also, I think. It was really nice to meet you and Jean and find out more about your art. It has been a very enjoyable evening."

Catrin said goodbye to them and looked at Neville Coltrane. She wasn't sure she liked his heavy intervention. She could have dealt with it without the confrontation, she felt, recommending exactly what the young woman's partner had been pulling her towards; fresh air.

"DCI Coltrane, good evening, I saw you earlier but…."

It had been quite busy; a number of other patrons and artists present had recognized Coltrane and engaged him in conversation. There was a still a cluster of people around Jean, who was pointing to a curve on a piece and speaking animatedly about the work.

"Catrin, this is my partner, Sylvia McNair. Sylvia, this is the artist Catrin Sayer."

The woman was subtlety but expensively dressed, Catrin saw, and she had a genuine smile.

"Catrin, it is nice to meet you. I am very glad we came. Neville had suggested it and my sincere apologies; that was my daughter. Not a good introduction to us, is it? A little too much...."

She let it hang.

"I do like your work, it is original. Ceramic decoration is often too stereotyped, I think, so people who make it look fresh and stimulating are welcome."

Catrin said, "It's nice to meet you, too. And thank you for your comments."

The woman looked at her. "It's actually more than that. I am thinking of commissioning pieces for a large dining room. I am looking for three table centrepieces; platters with different but related shapes and designs that could be used for the centre of a long table or used separately, perhaps on smaller tables. Would you be interested?"

Catrin said, "I would, but we would need to meet with my potter, Jean. We work together."

McNair said, "I have your card from the stack over there. Here is mine."

She passed over her own card.

"It has my direct line. Let's talk. Please give me a call when it is convenient. Knowing Neville's life, I am well aware that police work has a habit of taking priority over everything else, so... when it works for you and Jean, we can set up a day and a time."

She turned to Coltrane.

"Neville, we had better be going to catch up with Geoff and Constance. Hopefully the fresh air has done some good."

They shook hands and Neville said, "See you at the Yard, Catrin." He then leaned in a little, "I saw Jane today; she will be in tomorrow, raring to go by the sound of it."

She nodded. "Thank you, sir. And for the 'heads up' too, on the commission."

As they left, Catrin saw that Coltrane and McNair made a distinguished couple; it was strange to think of DCI Coltrane that way, she realised.

~~

Later, Catrin was sitting down having tea with Liz's husband, William Esquith, and Melanie and Jean. They were in Sandi's, the small coffee shop and bistro across the alley from the gallery. The caterers were now busy in the gallery clearing away after the event, with Liz supervising everything; she wanted the place ready for the following morning.

William had been talking about the sales made and the promises to follow up. Catrin had then mentioned the discussion with McNair. It led to her circulating the woman's card and William looking at it intently.

"The Honorable Sylvia McNair; she is Eleanor Sandler's daughter," he said. "It should be an interesting commission; the woman has a good eye for art."

Jean said, "A table that would hold three centrepieces; it must be quite a table."

Melanie was working at her iPhone. "She is the daughter of Baroness Cleary, also known as Eleanor

Sandler, a peer of the realm."

She smiled at the group. "Debrett's peerage guide is on-line. You seem to know a lot, William."

She tapped away a little longer. Catrin thought she was tracking down more on Sylvia McNair on the database of the aristocracy. But she said, "I see you here also, the Honorable William Lionel Esquith."

William looked at her. "I hate young people with their iPhones," he smiled. "All data and no knowledge."

Melanie pouted at him. "How many centrepieces on your long table then?"

Jean said, "So your aristocratic secret is out. You will become a knight or a baron, William, or what?"

William groaned. "No, thank God, my older brother now has that joy. There is a lot of work involved.

"I like art and Liz and our life in London together; I don't want to give that up. Besides, I did my bit in the City for long enough and some of the spare cash went back at times to help the family estate. I retired to start enjoying life. Even selling your clay monstrosities is more enjoyable."

"To think," said Jean, "just how we treat you like anyone else, William, as if you were a real person."

Catrin was watching, amused by her friends but thinking about Neville Coltrane. The trip in the Bentley last week and the discussion at the reception was the first insight she had into his personal life.

Her business mobile buzzed again. It had buzzed several times during the evening but she wasn't on call tonight, so she ignored it. If Marshall or Aina needed her, they would have called on her iPhone if they hadn't received a response from the Blackberry.

In the end she took a peek. Two of the calls were from

DI Hicks and he had left voicemails, so she listened to the messages. "DS Sayer, I need you to call me back as soon as possible", then, "DI Hicks. I left a message earlier, please call me back."

The 'please' sounded 'displeased'.

She ignored them.

She said, "William, I will still love you, even if you do bleed blue…."

Thirty minutes later Liz Marshall had just joined them when Catrin's iPhone rang. It was Keith Marshall. Keith had been the link to 'Liz's Place', introducing Catrin's work to his sister Elizabeth several years ago.

"Catrin, where are you?"

"At Sandi's, with your sister and William; we just finished the reception."

"Right, I had forgotten about that, sorry. There is another image in the Falmouth case. And it involves us more logically now, given the subject; it has a distinctive art element in it now, for some reason.

"Hicks just told me that Mitchell, the daughter, insists on speaking to you. She saw the image, stood up too suddenly, felt light-headed and then tripped over. She gave her head a knock as she fell and is in Falmouth Hospital being checked, but it doesn't appear too serious. DI Hicks was trying to reach you, I gather, but he only has your business number; you must be switched off, obviously with the… how did the reception go?"

"It went well Keith, thank you. But what should I do now regarding the Mitchell file? I am off it, I thought."

"You are back on it. Apparently one of Steadman's people and the assigned computer tech in Exeter are working on the image right now and will be on it for a good while into the night, I expect. I can't see how it can be a different source from the first one but they need to validate that and see if they can find anything else to help."

"Do I need to go down then, and, if so, when?"

"Yes. There is a train in the morning around 7.00 a.m., so you will be in around noon. Take a bag for a week. I talked briefly with Jane at home; she had been told already by Taylor that Matheson wanted you on it if it flared up again. It's politics.

"You can also join the briefing by conference call; Steadman and I are talking with the Devon & Cornwall people at 8.30 a.m. tomorrow."

Chief Superintendent Robert Matheson was in charge of areas of Specialist Crime Command that included both Steadman's and Coltrane's groups. Taylor and Worsley were doing this for Matheson as a favor, she thought; DI Steadman is desperate to get this investigation back on track, to focus on the hacker.

"Yes sir, I will do that."

She closed the call. Her friends were waiting, watching. Liz said, "First Keith, then 'sir'. He is making you work, right?"

Catrin nodded. "Yes, I have to go back to Cornwall tomorrow morning. Not sure when I will be back. Sorry, Jean."

She and Jean had been planning a new piece and were waiting to get the reception over with before starting it next weekend.

Her friend smiled and nodded. "We can have an easy weekend, Melanie. The slave driver is going west."

'The slave driver is my brother, not Catrin," said Liz.

Catrin was feeling guilty. For some reason a lecture

early on in her cadet training came back into mind.

"You are training to become a member of a police service," said the instructor, "and as a police officer it will come back to haunt you at times. You will get a call and your first thought will be 'I am off shift' or 'my partner and I are just going out for her birthday dinner; it's the second time we have re-scheduled this'. If you complete this training and do this job, remember that. You will be a serving police officer and if you are called, you are expected to serve."

It had only been a half-hour delay between the time she had seen Hick's messages and Marshall's call but she knew she had let her dislike of the Cornish detective get in the way.

"I take it you are on an early train?" William said.

Catrin nodded.

"Then I will pull out the Rolls and take you and these two troublemakers home," he said.

Catrin protested. "We'll get the Tube and... you don't have a Rolls Royce, William. You drive a Volvo."

But William was adamant. "Noblesse oblige," he murmured.

15 HIRST

Catrin sat on the dressing table chair in Janis's bedroom in the family home in Exeter. On entering the room she had turned the chair around and brought it closer to the bed where Janis was now sitting up, looking at her. Apparently she had phoned her parents from Falmouth hospital and they had brought her home once she had been checked over and released. With the shock of the new image, the young woman had been awake most of the night, her mother said, and then fallen asleep near dawn. She was still sleeping when DI Hicks and Catrin arrived at their home.

Her mother said pointedly, "I am glad you are back on the case, sergeant. I will wake Janis and you can talk to her; by yourself I think is best, in her room. Please give me a moment."

She left the reception room. Her distaste for DI Hicks was being controlled, but not completely. It was evident to both visiting officers and to her husband.

Hicks said as she walked out, "That would be much appreciated, Mrs. Mitchell. Thank you."

Catrin looked across at Hicks; it was his operation. He nodded. Clearly he had no objection or, if he did, he was hiding it well. Catrin was hoping she was doing a better job than Mrs. Mitchell in that department.

~~

Catrin had been told to get off at Exeter, not Truro or Falmouth this time. Hicks had met her himself at the station, eyes stopping at ground level, taking in the larger case she had brought. She thought he would raise the issue of his calls not being returned, but he didn't. He was all business.

On the conference call that morning while she was on the train she had mainly listened in. It was a crowded compartment for First Class and she had two passengers sitting across from her. DI Steadman was leading the briefing regarding the second image.

"It was placed in two locations; the website of the Tate Gallery and Janis's Facebook page again. It is another pose from her modelling session, this time nude, seated on the podium. Her knees are together, her legs are folded to one side and one arm is behind her for support; a classic modelling position other than two changes.

"Where it gets weird is that her feet and ankles are gold, metallic gold, and a 'P', about two inches in length, has been carved into the hollow of her shoulder, with the bottom of the letter moving into the rise of her left breast. Her expression is calm, distant this time. The hand and part of the forearm of the man in the previous image is to one side holding the same knife, this time with a fleck of blood at the tip, as if it had carved out the letter. The vase is quite clear now, close to the other hand, the one not supporting her."

"It has the same pixel signature, 'Adrestia' and the same attention to detail. Gary and I think it is definitely the same work and origin," said Chris Treneer.

Catrin thought 'Gary' must be one of Steadman's people; Marshall had said that Treneer and one of Steadman's team were analyzing it into the night.

"Any ideas about the gold feet?" said DI Steadman, questioning the people on the call.

"Damien Hirst." Catrin and Keith said the name separately, almost in unison.

Keith continued talking. Catrin saw the man opposite her on the train look her way enquiringly. He had seen her listening on her mobile then heard her say just a single name.

Marshall said, "A British modern artist, he's very controversial. People generally focus on his dead animal exhibits, one of which is a calf with gold horns and hooves."

"I think I have heard of him, now you mention it," said Hicks. "From London, that's why it was put on the Tate, perhaps. But I don't see any link to Mitchell there."

"He was born in Bristol," said Keith. "His 'Golden Calf' was sold at auction, but it is not in the Tate."

"Is it a real cow?" asked Steadman. "I'm not being facetious, but given the dead animal symbolism and the simulation of the knife cut, is this threat escalating towards physical violence?"

Catrin said, "Keith, could we get someone like Herrington? I'm on the train so will leave you to explain."

Marshall said, "Good idea, Catrin. First, yes, it is a real cow, embalmed like forensic specimens. Catrin is suggesting we run all this by a forensic psychologist or more appropriately, a forensic psychiatrist, I think; this is a weird mind at play. Do you have someone?"

DI Hicks said, "Dr. Janet Ryder, in Bristol, ironically; we use her. I will line it up."

"Now we have a detailed image of the vase, I will run it by Art & Antiques," said Steadman. "Catrin, when you see it, check if it strikes a chord with you."

Towards the end of the call Hicks said, "I will meet you at Exeter station, DS Sayer. We are heading to Superintendent Mitchell's home. Janis Mitchell is there now."

"Thank you sir," she said.

As she closed the call the woman across gave a forced sigh.

You should have opted for the quiet carriage; I wasn't noisy, thought Catrin.

The woman's travelling companion said to her, "Do you like Damien Hirst? I saw his butterflies at the Tate. It was very interesting."

The Hirst exhibit of butterflies in a studio setting, Catrin recalled. They had to replenish daily the dead ones and sweep the floor.

"I don't really like that sort of installation art very much, to be honest," said Catrin, "but did you see the Turner watercolour paintings at the Tate?"

"The old stuff, no, I didn't," the man said.

"You should do, if you go again. It was very radical at the time." she said.

He looked at her, unsure if she was pulling his leg. His partner gave her a dirty look.

~~

Catrin had waited after entering the bedroom, saying

nothing other than "Hello, Janis," as she sat down.

After a pause, Janis said, "I am glad you are back. I told my mother about you."

Catrin said, "She called me, but that was before the new image came in."

Janis nodded, "Yes. It's awful, even more bizarre."

She looked away. Catrin felt that the student wanted to talk but didn't know where to begin. So she said, "Janis, did you notice my scar?"

Her head came back to face her.

"Yes, I did. But I try not to stare, it's impolite."

"I get used to it. The reason I mentioned it is that the incident in which it happened, a robbery, was quite traumatic for me. You can relate to that, I think. I came back to London and in my job I had no choice but to see a psychologist. It is police procedure."

She paused.

"When I went to see him the first time I just wanted a sign-off, so I could get back to work. What I got was a series of sessions which brought out a lot emotions and gave me some healing. When I was briefed on your case and then saw you the first time, I thought you were in denial about the need for help."

Janis looked away, not responding.

"But now I think that is not the only reason. Now I think you are in fear. You are scared of talking to a psychologist or to us in case you tell us something you don't want to speak about. Some of us suspect this issue is not about you, you are the victim right enough, but it is about someone else.

"That's what I think and so does the computer technician analyzing the images. I haven't discussed this with DI Hicks or DS Wastle yet. But the team will be consulting a forensic psychiatrist on this case. She will try to analyse the mindset of the perpetrator of these attacks and I will share my thinking with her, including that you are hiding something. And then who knows…."

Mitchell had turned to face Catrin again and tears were forming.

"Why do you say that?"

There was a tone in her voice that gave Catrin a sense she was on the right track.

"I am a Welsh witch," said Catrin.

Janis looked at her, then saw the smile and smiled herself in response.

Catrin said, "No, it's more factual. First, the person who made this happen must have money, quite a lot. He or she is spending it on a hacker who made these images and put them on the websites, we believe. That doesn't sound to me like an angry student getting back at you for some reason.

"Secondly, the symbolism in the two images is deliberate, but it confuses you; it doesn't clarify things for you, I think. But something in the images had struck a chord and you internalize it, for some reason. That's why you don't want to talk about it.

"You never mentioned the vase, for example. I would have been asking myself, 'Why that? What's it doing there? Why was it present but hidden at first and now has been made visible in the second image. When we talked last time it didn't even come up. And you didn't mention it now."

She paused.

"Am I right?"

Janis looked at her and nodded then spoke, a little choked up. "The vase. I have seen the vase before, as a young child, I am sure… but I have no idea where. When the first image was enhanced I wondered. I convinced myself I was wishing it, in the end; that was before I saw you. That's why I didn't say anything about it then.

"This new image, it jolted me. The vase I mean, well, the whole bloody thing. But I have seen that vase. But I have no idea where.'

She wiped her eyes with the tissue Catrin passed over; she was holding the box close to Janis.

"I think you should talk to my parents. This has something to do with them or my family, not my friends or other students."

Catrin nodded. "Thank you, Janis, we will. Does anything else come to mind?"

Janis paused, thinking; clearly she was trying now. "Nothing."

Catrin stood up.

"We can talk more, I promise you. I advise you to tell all this to a psychologist, as well. Given your experiences, ask to see one and you will be there in a heartbeat. It will help."

She smiled and saw for the first time a natural smile appear on Janis Mitchell's face.

"Thank you, Sergeant Sayer."

"Catrin," said Catrin.

When Catrin emerged and went downstairs she saw DI Hicks talking to the Mitchell couple quietly.

Catrin said, "Mr. and Mrs. Mitchell, I mean, Superintendent Mitchell, could you give DI Hicks and me a moment please, then we can talk. It's procedure."

The father nodded, understanding completely.

Catrin walked outside with Hicks and briefly summarized the discussion.

He paused for a moment, looking into the distance. Then he said, "We need to interview them but...

carefully. He is a superintendent."

Catrin smiled. "Then he should understand."

Hicks said, "Why don't you take Mrs. Mitchell and I will talk to him."

Catrin nodded. They went back inside.

Hicks said firmly, "Mrs. Mitchell, I wonder if you could spend some time with DS Sayer. She is not from around here, needs the background on the family and more, of course, on your daughter. Sir, if we could talk, there are a few other matters which we can cover also."

Superintendent Mitchell started to say something then paused, looking at Catrin. He understands full well that they are being separated for interviews, she thought. He is Traffic, DI Hicks is Serious Crime; they probably don't talk a lot at work.

All he said was, "Of course, Inspector; glad to help."

Catrin said, "Mrs. Mitchell, shall we go and have a coffee somewhere? It has been a long ride down and a good cup of coffee would…"

"I could make some," she said.

"I would rather go out, if you don't mind. Just us," she added pointedly.

"Of course," Caroline Mitchell said, catching on, "I know just the place."

Catrin said, "I don't have a car with me and I am new here. Could you drive?"

Hicks said, "Call me; we can meet up after I finish with Superintendent Mitchell."

Caroline Mitchell drove expertly, Catrin thought. She had been trained beyond the norm, it was evident. With her husband in Traffic Division work she could have received 'advanced driver' training easily enough. Catrin realised her mind was wandering, working out how to begin with the woman.

Mitchell said, "Janis really seemed to pick up after your brief visit last week, DS Sayer. That's why I called. I am not sure what art has to do with this attack, but the second image is definitely an art issue."

"I haven't seen the second one yet, Mrs. Mitchell, only had it described."

"But you are with an Art Crime Unit, with the Met, I gather."

"Yes, I was called in, though, not to deal with the image aspect but the fact that it was based on a modelling session where we believe a camera was used; improperly, of course. What do you think of Janis being a model?"

Mitchell said, "What do you think, DS Sayer?"

Catrin thought that inside the coffee shop when the woman wasn't driving, they would turn this into an interview, not a 'who speaks first' contest.

"I am an artist, trained in Fine Arts and Art History, so I am used to models, clothed and nude. I modelled nude myself as a student, for my boyfriend at the time, also an art student."

The older woman nodded. She said, "So you know that it's a closed circle really; artists and models. They are happy talking and working with each other, but not so much to outsiders. There is sometimes a hint of disapproval from others, it seems, not in general of models but that someone they know may be a model. A sort of prudishness about nudity is how I think of it.

"I am proud Janis is a figure model. It's not easy to do; I was one myself once. She is a good one, I hear."

That's news, thought Catrin; her mother was a model, too. Why are we finding this out only now?

"Here we are," said Mitchell, pulling into the car park.

"And can I call you Catrin? And I'm Caroline, so let's drop the formality stuff. I'm not a suspect or anything."

Everyone is a suspect until they are ruled out, thought Catrin. And she knows that well enough, I am sure.

Inside, once seated, Catrin went straight into it.

"Let's begin with the family background; grandparents, brothers, sisters, where you have lived, etc. I know your husband is a career officer, senior rank, but I want to forget about that, frankly. I want to know about the Mitchell family on both your side and your husband's and also what you know of Janis's friends.

"That's a lot of background," said Mitchell.

I'm all ears, Caroline," said Catrin. "You would be surprised how this sort of stuff can help."

16 DARTINGTON

Caroline Mitchell began, "I grew up in Totnes, Devon. My father was a Senior Fellow at Dartington College of Arts, so I went to school near there and then went to the college for my degree in Dramatic Arts. It was quite a liberal, radical teaching approach at Dartington and, knowing it so well, I wanted to study there long before I left school.

"It caused a lot of heat and debate when the government moved the college to Falmouth in 2010 in a merger with the university. You may have read about it?"

"Yes," said Catrin. "I actually followed the issue quite closely at the time."

"Where did you study, by the way?" asked Mitchell.

"Aberystwyth University."

Mitchell nodded and continued. "Of course, we were long gone by the merger; we were here with James in his current role.

"My dad had retired well before then, too; he still lives locally in Totnes, though. I had met James at the college. He was a music student; a good wind player, but he saw early on that he wasn't going to make the top grade and so he became a policeman after he graduated. Some found it funny, but you wouldn't think so, I expect?"

Catrin said, "No, not at all; I wanted to be an artist and a police officer. I try to do both now, but it is challenging."

"You and James would get along, then," she said. "Janis grew up with secondhand memories of how much we enjoyed the life at Dartington. I think that is why she chose Falmouth University."

Catrin asked, "Are there any siblings?"

The older woman replied, "A younger brother, Geoffrey, born after we moved to Exeter. He is at school now but he will be home later. They get along well, so I don't think there are any problems there."

"So Janis was born in Totnes?"

Caroline said, "Yes, we lived there until 1995. She would have been nearly three at the time we moved. No real memory of the place, I think, just our stories. She came with me pretty much everywhere, of course; to my parent's or to the college. I would have lunch with people there and see friends, drop in on dad, that sort of thing. But she was too young to remember much."

Catrin thought it was time to move to the modelling issue. It had been bothering her that no one had mentioned that both mother and daughter had worked as figure models.

"You were a figure model there, at Dartington, were you?"

Caroline smiled. "Yes, I studied dance and drama and I knew someone who did modelling. He said the big thing was the ability to hold poses, understand form and know gestures. I could do all of that and, frankly, I envied people who were good at art - painting and so on. I wasn't myself, my skills were in the performing arts, but being a model was a way to be part of that crowd. And the money was good, it helped my sense of independence at the time, not being dependent on my parents for everything, you know."

She paused.

"Strangely enough, I think we were more liberal then than we are now; and I don't mean about sex or drugs, that sort of thing. When Janis said she was going to model but at Truro College not at Falmouth University I was pleased but also a little relieved, really. It seems that there are more and more attacks on women, physical and on the internet these days. I was relieved it wasn't her own campus where she would appear nude, to be honest.

"But back in Dartington then it was all about art. No one blinked an eye that I modelled... and I think, to be honest, I was also more naïve back then.

"And now this with Janis. My worst nightmare for her taking up modelling has become a reality, someone targeting her, all this perverted imagery. She is in such anguish about it."

She stopped, lost in thought.

Catrin said, "Any friends, people you think might have had a problem with Janis?"

"No," Caroline Mitchell said, pursing her lips. "She has male and female friends. No special boyfriend that I know of... and we have a good relationship. If there was a man in her life she would tell me, I think, particularly if a relationship went enough array that it would cause this sort of animosity."

Catrin kept her face impassive. Mothers always said that.

Now for the next step, she thought.

She said, "Can I go back to your modelling. Anything you recall there. Anyone that you had a problem with?"

Caroline Mitchell looked at Catrin, the eyes showing her understanding of the question, "You are wondering if someone is doing this to Janis in retribution against me for something … or James, perhaps. Interesting. I had not thought of that. DI Hicks had indicated the focus was her peers and the university."

She paused and gave the question some thought.

"The answer, though, is no. It was a very relaxed study environment at Dartington, however the modelling arrangements were handled very professionally. Interviews, contracts, records kept; that sort of thing. Nothing comes to mind of problems with any class I modelled for that I can recall… and I stopped modelling well before Janis was born.

"The only thing I didn't do was model for a class which involved my father. Decorum really. As I said, he taught fine arts there; composition and art theory, mainly. He had also become well-established as an artist, too. He painted quite a bit then, mainly abstracts, but some for which he hired figure models as the basis; not me, obviously."

Catrin asked, "What was your maiden name, then?"

"Staley," said Caroline. "My father is Philip Staley. Have you heard of him?"

Catrin looked at her and nodded. "Yes, I have. Some of his abstract art is well known."

An artist, she thought, and two family members who modelled.

"Where did the other figure models come from?" she asked.

Mitchell concentrated, looking serious.

"I don't recall. A couple of them were local from

Totnes, I know. But not many, despite the hourly rate being good. Several were other students. Some came in from Torquay and Dartmouth. I don't recall any names; God, it's been twenty years and it's hard to dredge this up."

She sipped her coffee then smiled.

"I really enjoyed some of the drawings and paintings of me and there were others… seeing them I wondered why I'd bothered standing or sitting there; they could have used a carrot for a nose stuck on a broomstick head. But I don't recall any problems with students over it."

Catrin smiled, recalling her own experiences of dialogues with figure models. "I know exactly what you mean. In a break in one of my figure drawing classes the model put on her gown and walked around looking at the works in progress and then said to a student, 'Tiffany, I have breasts; breast-shaped breasts, not recovery capsules from the space program'. Generally the models don't say much, but it was true what she said. And the class wasn't being asked to draw just anything; accurate reproduction of the model was the task that day."

Caroline laughed, "Exactly. But it isn't something that leads to enemies."

Catrin brought it back into focus.

"The vase in the images - the one the technician pulled out of the first image and was quite visible in the second. Does it mean anything to you?"

She shook her head. "That's part of my problem with visual arts. That sort of stuff never sticks with me. I can remember lines from plays I read or prepared twenty years ago but the colour of the costume or the 'props' used, no.

She added, "It's not a family possession anyway; I

know that, on my side or with James's family. But you have me thinking now with these questions. Do you think it is someone with a grudge against my husband for something he did, an arrest or something? If so, it's awful that they would take it out on Janis. I really hope you can help catch him, whoever he is."

Catrin thought that no doubt Hicks was going over exactly that ground with Superintendent Mitchell. Every copper has their ghosts. She thought of Colin Cheney.

"We are doing our best, Caroline."

Catrin took Caroline Staley through her recollections of Janis's friendships in Exeter over the years, and her schooling. Nothing came out that flagged a concern. She was still bothered by the modelling link.

Her phone beeped a text. She checked it; Hicks had finished, it told her.

She said, "I think we should head back now. And personally speaking, I would encourage you to support the idea of a psychologist or similar counselling for Janis."

The mother looked a Catrin's scar. "I think you probably know something about that. She told me you had recommended that she seek help."

~~

They re-grouped late afternoon at the Falmouth Police Station to go through the Mitchell case again, in detail. Chris Treneer showed Catrin the image and she asked for a printout of enlargements of the hands, feet and the vase.

DI Hicks said, "I would like the letter P blown up also, run by a graphologist - do you have one we can ask?"

Catrin said, "We do, at the Yard."

Catrin looked again. "The knife is much clearer also.

Can you get a check on that?

DS Wastle was making notes.

She said, "We have a knife expert available, too; we will get the image to him also and get back to you."

DI Hicks was leading the meeting well this time, she felt.

As they worked through assignments for Thursday, DS Wastle and Catrin were to see the forensic psychiatrist, Dr Ryder. She was coming into the Devon & Cornwall HQ in Exeter from Bristol for the meeting.

Catrin said, "I would like to call in at Totnes. We can do that on the way back, I think. I want to drop in on Janis's grandfather, Professor Staley. I looked up his address."

Wastle said, "I will call, make an appointment with him."

Catrin shook her head. "No, let's just drop in, I prefer that."

"Why?" said DI Hicks.

Catrin took a breath.

"It's the modelling thing. The three people in the modelling story so far are Janis, her mother Caroline and her own father; he painted models, the other two were or are models. I would like to touch base with him, get a feel for his perspective, but with him unprepared."

"Good job it's on the way; it seems a bit flimsy." said Wastle.

Catrin added, "And the letter 'P'; her grandfather's name is Philip. I know, there are a lot of people whose names begin with 'p', if it is meant to convey a name ..."

Hicks said, "I think Sayer is right to close the loop; we have so little else to go on. And if the psychiatrist sends you in another direction you can give the drop-in a miss."

He paused, musing. "I would still like to get the vase

identified."

Catrin said, "Nothing from Reynolds?"

The pottery expert at Art & Antiques.

Hicks said, "He says much the same as the comments you gave to Steadman earlier, from the first image. It is not commercial, not a known artist, probably local to wherever. But he is convinced it is English, not European in style, for whatever reason."

Catrin said, 'Can we run it by expert potters in this part of the world, people at a teaching college or who have their own business. I am thinking of the ceramic artist I work with, Jean, who went to Cardiff College of Art. She had tutors there who must have seen a lot of local work. Potters around here must see the same."

Hicks said to another team member, "Can you get a list of places, people; it's a good idea."

At the end of the briefing, as they wrapped up and people started drifting off, DI Hicks said gently to Treneer, "Chris, can you hang on a minute?" and then to Catrin, "DS Sayer, can I see you in my office; alone, please."

He walked off.

Catrin looked at Treneer and he raised his eyes. He said, "I have been up half the night and all day. Hang on…"

She smiled, turned and went into the inspector's office. He motioned her to the chair and she sat, steeling herself for whatever it was to come.

He took a deep breath. "Catrin, I want to apologize. I was rude as hell last week. I didn't want Met interference and I was wrong on that and I took it out on you. I am also a control freak and I am trying to deal with that; I have already been denied promotion once for team leadership concerns. People here all know it. I am trying but… I find it hard to change.

"Anyway, I am sorry and if I bite your leg again, I think you are the sort of person to bite back or let me know, OK? Last week was a bad week for various reasons, but I am trying. You are back on the case and we need your help."

Catrin smiled.

"It's not funny," he said.

"No sir, that's not why I am smiling, I thought you were going to … it doesn't matter. Thank you, it is appreciated. Let's try to make it work and I promise not to nip at your ankles… as I must admit, I did on the first visit."

He smiled back. "OK, that's it, other than -"

He passed over a car key, a black plastic rectangle with buttons. "The Mercedes C-class in the lot; a nice car, it's yours this week to get around and right now I want you to take Chris Treneer to his sister's place; that's where he stays. It's not far from your hotel. He looks knackered and I don't want him driving half-asleep."

He smiled. "A tenner that he is sweet on you. If he isn't, he should be."

From a bear with a sore head to a charmer, Catrin thought. She looked amused and said, "That's a personal matter sir, beyond your control, control freak or not. But thank you for the compliment."

He said, "I am in Torquay on other things tomorrow. Do as you and Oliver see fit but don't leave me blind-sided. There is a superintendent making it clear that he is all eyes and ears on this for his daughter and I have my own people to report to. Agreed?"

Catrin said, "Yes, sir."

She stood to leave. He sighed, turning to his

paperwork.

Catrin said to Chris Treneer, "I'm driving a pool car and I am to take you with me; he doesn't want you driving and falling asleep. You can give me directions."

He smiled. "Suits me."

As they left he looked at the suitcase that she collected from behind the station front desk.

"Are you here for a few days, then?" he asked.

"I plan to be, if I have to. Where do you need to go?"

"My sister's place; I am staying there. Can we have dinner this week, do you think?"

She nodded, "I would like that, but not tomorrow, I think. I am in Exeter and Totnes, right? Probably won't be back in time."

He nodded.

"Let's go," she said.

He took the case handle. "Pulling this will keep me awake, at least as far as the car."

17 MASON

Chris gave her directions but Catrin remembered most of the route. He had told her that the house was in the next road inland from the shop; Jenifer walked to and from work.

"Nicer working arrangements than either of us has," Catrin laughed.

As they stopped outside the house Treneer said, "Come on in and say hello."

Catrin said, "You are tired, I will just drop you."

"I will have some tea and a shower, freshen up; otherwise if I crash now I will wake up in the night. Mason is here. Jen said he was dropping by. Come in and meet him."

Catrin said, "Mason Carrington, the watercolourist, your customer?"

Then she remembered that he and Jenifer were in a relationship. She was intrigued at the thought of meeting the artist.

He saw the indecision. "You are only heading back to the hotel, right?"

Catrin hesitated, then said, "OK, just for a minute. Just to say hello."

She got out and locked the car as Chris said, "Mason lives in Falmouth, when he can. He spends most of his time out painting or doing workshops and stuff around the world. He complains about the travel and then I provoke him a bit; in fact he loves it, loves painting with people of different nationalities in other places. Jenifer never leaves here and he hardly stays around. She is young and he is old as Methuselah… I can't figure it out." He smiled.

Catrin laughed. "Mason Carrington is not old, I think!"

They went inside and Chris made the introductions. Jenifer was preparing supper and she and Mason were in the kitchen with a glass of wine each.

"Would you like one, Catrin, if you are off-duty? Chris?" Carrington said.

"Too tired," said Chris, "I will flake out half-way through dinner if I have wine. Tea, I think."

"I don't drink," said Catrin, not explaining why. She had learned she needn't do that many years ago. "But some water, thank you."

Catrin's mother was a recovered alcoholic; Catrin knew she was too much like her and steered clear of alcohol, had done so from her teens.

"How about this?" he said, pulling a bottle from the fridge, "Cornish Natural Spring water - with a slice of lemon?"

"Wonderful," Catrin said.

Chris said, "Catrin is a colleague, from London; she works with the Art Crime Unit at Scotland Yard."

Mason's eyebrows went up. "Really? I thought you were from Wales. So you know about art. Great! Do you do any creative work yourself?

Catrin nodded. "I am a ceramic decorator; my friend is a potter with a shop in the Spitalfields Arts Market, so we work together on original works. They exhibit and sell pretty well at present."

"Art and sleuthing," Carrington said, "And I thought I was busy."

His face became mischievous. "We will have great debates as opposites. You must stay to dinner, mustn't she, Jen?"

"No," said Catrin, as Jenifer and Chris said 'Yes' simultaneously.

Jen smiled, 'Please do; there is more than enough. Besides, Chris will probably not eat much or fall asleep."

Catrin smiled and said 'Thank you'. The idea of a home-cooked meal with company instead of eating alone in the hotel did appeal, as did talking more with Carrington.

She looked at the artist. "Opposites? I am a police officer and you are a - ?"

He laughed, "Many things, but not an art thief, no. I mean, you are quintessentially precise in your medium, I think, and I am the opposite, a watercolourist, slapping paint all over."

Catrin saw the humorous provocation, so reminiscent of Melanie. An afternoon could fly by once they started this sort of repartee as they worked in the Cwmbran Kiln.

She said, "Your watercolour paintings. So pale, soft and precise, like architectural tints, right? You should see some of our pieces - they can be pretty wild. Expressive I think you would call it."

He laughed, "Touché, Catrin. I will show you mine if you will show me yours." He had pulled out his mobile and pressed the 'pictures' tile.

Catrin laughed. "I know your work. There is one of the Paris scenes in the shop; I saw it when I visited last week with Chris. And I have seen your work on the internet and… it's wonderful." She paused. "There, I have shown my hand."

He smiled, "Thank you. I am sure you must have photos of your work with you too. Can I see it?"

Catrin nodded, pulling out her personal iPhone. He seemed sincere in his interest, so…

Chris said, "I am not hungry; well just a bit. But I need to shower and change, so I will join you later. Don't wait to start."

Later, after dinner, Mason and Catrin left at the same time.

"You know your way?" he asked. He was walking back to the shop where his car was parked; they had loaded his boot with more watercolour paper earlier, Catrin had heard. He was away early in the morning, he had said during dinner.

"Yes. Thank you for being so welcoming. It was wonderful to meet you."

"And for me. I love talking with other artists and I know little about ceramics, so it has been very interesting. How you balance the art and being a police officer astonishes me. I have your email and you have mine and… when I next paint in London, let's get together."

"I'd love to," she said.

As he turned she said, "Is Treneer paper really that good, that special?"

He nodded, "It's very good otherwise I wouldn't use it. But it is not a 'head and shoulders difference' sort of thing, it's that I am really familiar with its properties now. For me it is about knowing your paints and your paper intimately, just like you with ceramic materials. But we can talk more about that in London."

He paused.

"And Catrin, Chris is a really good guy, by the way. He likes you, I can tell; you know that."

She smiled.

"I know."

She thought, I like him a little too. He's bit too quiet, though, and I am just passing through; my life is in London.

~~

Dr. Paula Ryder looked a lot older than she was, Catrin thought. She had googled the forensic psychiatrist last night at the hotel and she was up there, one of the main figures in the field in the UK.

Catrin had seen the sailing magazine partially sticking out of her briefcase as they settled in the meeting room in the Headquarters building in Exeter. She sails a lot and doesn't give a fig for beauty tips and avoiding the sun, she thought. That's where the lines and deep tan come from.

DS Wastle led the discussion with the consultant as it was clear that he knew her from previous cases. After summarizing the situation and showing the images to her, Ryder asked a number of questions about the victim; her background, her response to each attack. Then she took some time to study each image in detail.

"Are these as big as you can show me? I would really like to see sections in detail."

Oliver Wastle said, "Dr Ryder, we can do that but the enlargements won't show any 'cut and paste' elements, if that is your interest. The hacker is too good at this."

She nodded.

After a while she said, "What else do we know about this person, the work he has done? Assuming it is a male; it might not be."

Oliver ran through what he had been told by Steadman.

She absorbed it then said, "It would be helpful to have actual examples of his past work; their timings, the victims, anything in the possession of other police services. If we analyse his 'body of work' we can perhaps understand a little better this 'project', as he sees it. At present, we really don't know if 'Adrestia' is the designer of the image or working to a specific instruction of the client."

Oliver looked a little uneasy. "We don't have much of it, to be honest. We could try to get some more through the Dutch or German police but it could take some time. Given the images… they don't get shared easily once they are pulled from the internet."

The psychiatrist nodded. She wasn't being given much, her expression said.

Ryder took a breath, held it. "At first blush I can suggest some things; informed guesses, really, so nothing you can hold as firm guidance.

"The person behind the attack is probably female, is wealthy enough to pay this hacker and has a deep-seated psychosis built from a traumatic event at some time; something that would lead her to plan this in fine detail. It is carefully orchestrated, but the reservation about full nudity in the first image and then only showing the girl's breasts in the second, with her legs pressed together, all suggest a woman or perhaps a prudish male. Otherwise the graphics would be much more pornographic given the array of nude images he or she must have recorded as the model moved positions.

"Secondly, the symbols; the implied rape in the first image, the vase in both images, the objectifying of the body as 'meat' in the second - this is what I suspect the Hirst element was alluding to - all are important elements the perpetrator wishes to communicate. In turn, they probably tie into his or her psychosis, unless some red herrings have been thrown in to mislead us. I haven't talked with the victim but from what you say I suspect it is targeted at someone else; it's too fancy for a young student to have experiences with this sort of symbolism. Who that target may be, though, I have no idea."

She put the images on the desk and looked up.

"But I can't say any more at present. I need more background detail, Sergeant."

Her eyes had been roving between the two officers. She stopped, lips pursed, looking at Catrin.

"So, DS Sayer, it seems you have probably suggested something along these lines, if I read the look on Sergeant Wastle's face correctly."

Catrin said, "The computer technician suggested that it was a contract job with a deeper motive than a petty revenge issue against Janis Mitchell. He also suggested that it was aimed at someone else, yes, and the way the images were obtained, I suspect that it may involve a person a generation older than Janis Mitchell, a woman.

"And Mitchell thinks she has seen the vase in the second image before, but has no recollection when; it sounded as if it was a very early memory."

"Right." said the psychiatrist, nodding.

Catrin continued, "I also feel that the modelling element is important. Mother and daughter were models; the grandfather was an artist and he supervised life drawing classes - there is a tie in, perhaps. Otherwise, why not start with another image of Janis? There are quite a number of them with family and friends on her Facebook page, for example.

Ryder clearly agreed. "That could well be; at least it needs examination. As does the line that it is tied to Superintendent Mitchell. Police officers develop enemies, as you both know. Have you checked back on his career, talked to him?"

Wastle said, "Yes, DI Hicks went through it with him. We are looking at a couple of possible leads. Looking at their records though, I am not convinced. The people involved would be more likely to beat him up or spray paint his car, not this."

He added, "We are seeing the grandparents later, the grandfather is the artist who hired models."

Dr Ryder nodded. "Good; you should, given Sergeant Sayer's observation. I know you will assess them carefully, of course. But also look for 'distancing' from the problem. It is their granddaughter so normally the grandparents should want to be as close to this as possible, engaged, willing to help and if not, it may say something."

She added, "Do you know how close they were to Janis?"

"No," said Catrin, "I should have checked that with her, but didn't."

The psychiatrist nodded, "It would be worth knowing. It may be easier to assess from their responses than posing the question to Janis now and raising issues in the Mitchell household as to why you are asking."

As they stood up Dr Ryder said, "Sergeant Wastle, if you can send me more on this computer hacker's history, it would useful; he or she sounds interesting, at least professionally so for me. And, DS Sayer, I think your 'modelling' link is very much worth pursuing."

18 TOTNES

Not a big place, thought Catrin, as they drove into Totnes. For some strange reason she remembered that the artist Pegaret Keeling came from here. During her undergraduate studies she had written an essay on her work as a caricaturist during World War II. The names of Totnes and Pegaret had become linked in her synapses, she thought.

A street they passed reminded her of Pontypridd; the incline, the row houses. It brought back that she needed to take some time off, go see her parents.

The house in Copland Meadows was two-storey, with a stone and brick frontage. It looked nicely maintained. When they rang the doorbell they heard a noise of someone moving then a shout of annoyance, male, muffled. The woman who answered the door was middle-aged, too young to be Mrs. Staley, Catrin saw. DS Wastle introduced them, showing his warrant card.

She said, "Come in, please, I'm Katharine, Katharine Sully, the housekeeper. Professor and Mrs. Staley aren't expecting you, are they?"

Wastle said, "No, we are on our way back from Exeter to Falmouth. We decided to drop in at short notice, hoping they would be available."

"Well, they are always here these days," she said.

She led them through to the rear of the house, to a large living room, the southerly part having a glass extension forming a conservatory overlooking a nicely-kept garden. It was spacious but the innermost areas had a cluttered look, with a desk and bookshelves; it was more a home office in that part. Books and magazines filled the bookcases and the overflows were stacked on chairs. An artist's easel without a canvas mounted stood in one corner looking polished and unused.

The walls in the room were filled with paintings. During the walk through to the back of the house Catrin had noticed an array of art on other walls, all originals it seemed, but not by the same hand. And they had passed a room fitted out as a bedroom, the door partially closed.

On the other side of the conservatory closer to the plants, the woman's side thought Catrin, Mrs. Staley was in a high wing-back armchair. She had been reading. Next to her was a wheelchair.

At the desk sat an elderly man wearing casual clothes and a cardigan, with silver-grey hair and glasses. He just looked at them and didn't speak at first, appearing irritated at the intrusion.

"These visitors are police officers," Katharine announced.

"Would you like tea or coffee?" she asked them. "I have just made tea for the Professor and Mrs. Staley."

"Tea would be very nice, thank you," Wastle said. He was making it clear they were here for a while, Catrin knew.

"Please have a seat," she offered, pointing to a divan as she went out. Neither officer sat down.

The man said, "I am Philip Staley, this is my wife, Naomi." He gestured at her; she nodded. He made no attempt to get up.

Wastle went through the introductions again.

"This is about Janis, I take it," said Mrs. Staley.

When she spoke her mouth showed the partial paralysis down the left side of her face. Catrin saw that it probably extended to the limbs on that side also, from their positioning.

DS Wastle said, evenly, "Yes, Mrs. Staley, exactly. We have spoken to her parents and thought we would check with you, just in case. For ideas, anything. We have nothing specific to ask, really."

Professor Staley spoke, his voice sharp. "If my son-in-law can't find enough resources in his police force to track down the young idiot who did this, he should be ashamed."

Wastle looked at him. "Why a young idiot, Professor Staley?"

"Well, it is one of her college people or Facebook lot, that sort of thing, isn't it?"

Wastle replied, "We are checking that, of course, but also making other lines of enquiry. The hacking of the websites was not amateurish."

Professor Staley said, "Are either of you trained as computer experts, then? Every young person these days is an expert on these things, it seems."

His tone was dismissive, like a teacher rejecting an erroneous answer from a student.

"No," said Catrin, responding directly to the question and moving more into his line of sight, closer to the desk,

"Not a computer expert. I work in an art crime unit at Scotland Yard. Are any of these paintings yours, Professor? I gather you taught at Dartington."

"Yes, and yes I did," he said. "Most paintings in the house are mine or by colleagues and students that we have known over the years. So are you trained in art then, if you are working in an art crime unit, Sergeant Sayer?"

They were interrupted by the return of Katharine carrying a tray. They stopped talking during the ritual of distribution of cups and saucers, the choice of milk and sugar, the pouring of the tea. When it was done, Catrin noticed that the housekeeper didn't leave; she moved closer to Mrs. Staley, standing by her chair.

Catrin answered, "I was about to say, Professor Staley, I have a degree in Fine Arts and Art History from Aberystwyth. Do you still paint?

"No," he smiled. "I stopped. I didn't like the decline in quality; a lack of new ideas to spur me forward. If I can't find something new to say in my art I didn't want to churn out the same thing repetitively."

Catrin had moved closer to the wall. "This is one of yours, I take it?"

It was an abstract comprising overlapping squares and rectangles in different colours in a complex pattern. It had a number of spheres of different sizes in one corner, overlapping. Through colour choice and a bolder line density in places, a shape was particularly prominent.

Oliver Wastle caught Catrin's gaze and looked more closely; then he too saw it. The shape she was looking at seemed to him to form a close approximation to the outline of the vase in the images they were investigating. Sayer had honed straight in on it.

He looked away, first at Mrs. Staley, then at his teacup. He decided to leave this stage of the questioning to DS Sayer.

Catrin had seen something more in the painting than the vase design; something that disturbed her. It was something deeper and more visceral about her perception of the entire work. At this stage she knew she couldn't mention it but she felt that, at last, the images Janis Mitchell had received started to make some sense.

But the painting brought back other recollections.

19 SERIES EIGHT

It is one of his 'Series Eight' paintings, she thought. Seeing it brought back the lecture in which Professor Seymour at Aberystwyth had discussed galleries, the process of setting up for exhibitions and 'ways of seeing' when visiting them. There were more than eight of these abstracts, she knew; Philip G. Staley had come back to the theme occasionally but the original eight had been exhibited in several major art galleries for some years.

The 'G' was important she remembered; he was one of the artists who would correct you on it. His signature on the painting, she noted, was P.G. Staley.

During the lecture at Aberystwyth, Professor Seymour had flashed an image of an old press photo from the media coverage of the 'Series Eight' exhibition. The notice on the entrance to the room had said, 'View the paintings from the centre of the room in a clockwise or anti-clockwise direction. One will stand out for you. Which one?'

The press had highlighted first the obvious; that it was the position of the circles in each painting that changed most noticeably as different works were viewed. And one painting did seem to stand out, to be out of sequence. Unfortunately, it was different for each viewer, it turned out.

The debate as to why - and the disputes over who was correct - had caused more news coverage. Staley never explained it. It was about two months later that the art critic of the Guardian had written an article explaining that there was no unique answer. It would be based on the starting point, the precise location in the loose description of 'centre of the room' and the individual's own colour preferences. It was an example of installation art thinking, using oil paintings as the elements of the installation. Professor Seymour said that Staley must have thought through a number of the works before putting paint to canvas on the first one, Catrin recalled.

"Do you know my work?" asked Professor Staley. There was a pride, perhaps a taunt, in his voice as he looked at Catrin, lost in the painting.

"No," said Catrin slowly, apparently defeated by the question, "I don't recall it, sorry. Was it a standard element of the curriculum?"

He looked at her coldly. "At Dartington it became so and I thought it had been taken up elsewhere - even in the far reaches of Aberystwyth. But then you became a policewoman, after all."

She smiled at him. "Yes, I did." She waited.

Staley couldn't resist it. "Yes, it is part of a series of paintings from my heyday. But I thought we were talking about Janis?"

Wastle said, "Indeed, Professor. Do you see a lot of her?"

Professor Staley seemed almost uninterested in the

question; lost in something else. He was still looking at Catrin.

Mrs. Staley said, "Not now, she is too busy and too far away. We used to see a lot more of her when she was very small. They lived close by. Later they visited quite a bit but, after my stroke and with their busy lives, not so much now. We don't see much of Janis or her parents, to be honest."

"Caroline wanted us to get a computer, Skype, that sort of thing. But I talk with her twice a week on the phone."

The emphasis on the 'I' was clear.

DS Wastle said, "Can I ask if either of you have seen the images of Janis which have led to this investigation? I know they are not pleasant to see, but I thought I would check."

She said "No," quietly.

He shook his head, silent.

Mrs. Staley added, "We asked not to, frankly. We don't need that. We want only good memories and images of our granddaughter, not what this pervert has done."

Catrin took out her iPhone and pulled up an image. "This vase was in the second image; quite clear. We don't know why it is there or whether it is significant," she said, "But it has been added to both images. We are asking about anything and everything, frankly."

She showed it to the occupants of the house in turn but made sure she showed it to Mrs. Staley first.

Naomi Staley said, "Wasn't there one like this in the college, Philip? I think I remember seeing something like it there, at least, years ago."

He looked, squinting his eyes. 'It could be, but it doesn't look anything special. But there was a lot of art at the college, still there, some of it, I am sure. But it rings no bells with me. It could be from anywhere, I suppose."

In his emphatic response, Catrin felt something; too much denial around the word 'special' as if he, as an artist, was reluctant to dismiss the piece. She decided to push him.

"I am a ceramic decorator as well as a police officer, you see; but I don't recognize the vase. It is not a standard product line, probably a one-off by a professional ceramic artist. It's nicely decorated though, don't you think?"

He deflected the question. "You are a ceramic decorator, a painter. What, floral motifs, that sort of thing?"

His voice wasn't neutral or interested; it hinted at humor, but had more derisive tone, not pleasant at all.

A little more, she thought.

"Yes," she said, putting into her voice a sense of discomfort at his innuendo. "That sort of thing."

His response was more confident now, as if he was talking to students again. "You studied fine arts at Aberystwyth, became a policewoman and paint flowers on vases."

His wife was looking a little apprehensive at the dominant tone he was taking.

Catrin said, "Not often, flowers, I mean. I am constantly experimenting. Sir John Vale said to me once that experimentation was the essence of art; the constant challenge, pushing the limits. That's what it's about. Our works, the ones I decorate, are exhibited in a gallery in London and sell quite well, including internationally."

Sir John Vale was a sculptor of international renown. She was telling him her art and her appreciation of art was not amateur, not trivial, not to be dismissed. She was staring hard at his face, his arrogant expression, making it clear she didn't like the way he was regarding her. His eyes showed he had registered the comment, she saw; that perhaps there was more to this woman than flower designs on a vase.

Catrin looked again at the painting on the wall deliberately and then looked back at him. He looked away.

She glanced over at DS Wastle; their shared expressions showed it was time to go. Wastle made the right noises and turned towards the door of the room.

As the two officers and Katharine reached the door to the room Catrin turned back.

"Professor, which number is it?" She glanced at the painting.

He had never clarified that it was one of the Series Eight paintings so he looked at her and said after a moment, "Two. It's Number Two in my Series Eight. You know that after all, it seems. What degree did you take, may I ask, Sergeant?"

"A double First, Professor."

His face changed. He regretted his comments, she saw. In making them he had revealed more about himself than he had wanted to, he realized.

"Thank you, Professor, Mrs. Staley," Catrin said and left the room.

At the front door Catrin said to Katharine, "Professor and Mrs. Staley are not internet people, then?"

She had not seen a computer in the room.

Katharine laughed at the suggestion. "No, nothing like that. My mobile is three year old and it's the newest piece of electronics here. They don't even use mobiles. Mrs. Staley keeps the portable phone next to her."

Catrin smiled, showing she understood. "Do they get a lot of mail then, if they don't do emails?"

The housekeeper said, "You know, not a lot. But a lot of their friends have died so, it is to be expected. Now it's mainly books and bills. Professor Staley still buys books and art magazines, as you could see inside. He likes opening those packages; I get to open their bills. Division of the spoils."

She smiled at the joke as she opened the door to show the officers out.

~~

They were out of visual range of the house before Wastle spoke. "It's not right; something is off-base in there, Catrin. He was really evasive."

She said, "Yes Oliver, I agree. Notice how he was particularly so about the vase?"

"That's where I saw it, actually."

She added, "He didn't like me focusing on the painting either, trying to browbeat me as I looked at it."

Wastle said, "I saw what you were looking at, too; the shape of the vase in the painting."

Catrin said, "It's an abstract, part of a series of similar paintings and yes, I do know of them. I will draw it for you when we get back. The shape of the space in that section of the painting is precisely the shape of the vase, outlined between the circles and the rectangles.

"An artist who didn't want to talk about his work, about a set of paintings held in high regard academically. That's what started me off and after that it just got worse. He is hiding something; we need to do a lot more investigation into the background of Professor Staley, I think."

She looked at Oliver Wastle; he was clearly on-side.

She added, "That bit at the end, the discussion of my work. I was provoking him, not showing off. He looked at me like I was... beneath him."

"You really do exhibit and sell art then, it wasn't made up?"

She laughed, "Yes I do, it's my not-so-secret other life besides being a copper. But generally I don't talk about it."

He nodded, impressed. Then he said, "We need to head back. Although I am closer to home here than in Falmouth."

"Family?"

"Wife and two kids; they know I am away the week."

A police officer's life, thought Catrin.

~~

As they drove away Philip Staley's eyes moved to the binding of a slim volume he had received a couple of weeks ago. The best place to hide a book, he mused, is in a bookcase.

Its outer hardback cover was abstract art, a high quality journal for people to record their lives or observations. It contained only two items; a neatly scripted frontispiece entitled, 'A Critique of the Art of Philip G. Staley: Volume 1'. On the next page was a photograph glued in firmly and beneath it, in the same script, a simple instruction.

He should get rid of it, he thought. But he couldn't bring himself to do so yet. And there was a second package, an identical padded envelope to the one the first journal arrived in, now sitting in his 'in-tray' box, as yet un-opened. It had arrived that morning.

20 CONFRONTATION

As they set off back to Falmouth Catrin saw that she had received a text earlier from Chris Treneer. 'If you are back in time, do you want to have a drink?'

She thought for a minute and then sent, 'We should be back around five. Hotel at six? I would like to see you'.

The mobile beeped within a couple of minutes. 'I'll be there'.

She was thinking back to Hicks and Carrington's remarks about Treneer liking her. I am going to have to deal with this, she said to herself.

She said to Wastle, "What happened to the idea of looking into that mature student, Marilyn somebody?"

As he drove, he said, "It's still on the list, Catrin. We ran a background check on her again. Nothing came up. She is a civil servant, a registrar of births & deaths and is married to a teacher, a school principal, I recall. No logical connection, we think.

"DI Hicks said that unless we pulled the entire class in for elimination prints we didn't have enough to single her out or a reason to focus on her."

She said, "That's what you said at the time, Oliver."

He responded, "I have worked with Stephen Hicks for some time now. But I haven't forgotten about the studio session we did. Her surname, by the way is Greaves."

Catrin was about to ask something about Greaves when her phone beeped. It was a text from Aina, with an unrelated question. By the time she had dealt with it her mind went back to Chris Treneer, what she needed to say.

~~

Catrin took Chris through to the bar restaurant. It was busy, noisy enough she thought, and they could eat there rather than in the main restaurant. She said, "What do you want to drink? It's my shout; you looked after me last night."

He chose a bitter and she ordered, adding for herself a sparkling water.

When they were settled she said, "Chris, I like you and I know you like me. In fact, everyone in Cornwall is telling me that, as if I can't see it for myself."

"But you are already...." He didn't finish the sentence. She had gone straight to what was on his mind.

"No, it's not that; that's just it. Let me finish. I don't know much about you and you about me but you are here and I am just visiting and… my job takes me everywhere and my free time is busy with my art. I don't know what to do about that but casual relationships with men don't work for me, sorry. I have tried; I get involved, too involved and then I get hurt. It has happened before. I don't have the answer but I don't want to go through the same cycle. Sorry."

He looked at her.

He said, "But you like me a little? Or what?"

"I like you; you are a nice guy. But it would go nowhere because of me, my job; that's the reason. It just wouldn't work out."

She saw he was hiding his disappointment, but not really well.

She smiled. "But you and Jen gave me such an enjoyable time last night with Mason, it would be great to have dinner with you, me buying; but just that, OK?"

He said nothing. She looked at the food menu, with the selections of the day, partly to give him some time to soak up the news. She had tried to be as gentle as possible about it. The script on the menu was quite good, she thought; someone must be an artist. She was about to choose and looked up see what Chris wanted.

He was standing when she looked up, his drink untouched.

"No Catrin, I don't think I will do that. Thank you for the offer of dinner and your honesty. But I had better leave."

She watched him walk towards the door of the bar, a little taken aback. Then she went after him quickly, catching him just outside, in the main lobby.

She said, "Look, let's just ..."

He turned round and she saw the anger and hurt in his face.

"No," he said quietly, "No. It's my fault. You know, from the first time I saw you at the train station I thought you were lovely, a knockout and... the way you were so self-assured with Hicks and others; you just left me in awe.

"Like I can't stop thinking about you. I don't even know you and I am... it's stupid, I can't explain it."

He paused, lost for words for a moment, then said, "And you talk about trivial stuff, London versus Cornwall, geography and work. I'm a workaholic and I am saying it's trivial. What a laugh, eh?"

He had said his piece; he looked away, at the main entrance, eyes blinking as he pulled out his car keys.

Catrin stood there. This man wasn't just attracted to her, she realised. He was bowled over and prepared to show it too. And me... she thought; so analytical, life so organized. I keep telling myself that I hoped one day to meet a guy I like who would be serious, who would understand the issues of police work, some man to cross my path.

I am a fool, she realised.

He started to walk away and she moved fast again, grabbing his hand. As he stopped and turned she moved into him, kissing him on the cheek. "We are going to have our drinks, and eat and... we are going to get to know each other. Sorry. It's me being stupid; I think I am half-dead inside. You have just woken me up."

Then she started crying, sad and happy at the same time but quite unsure why. He smiled, took her arm and led her back inside the bar.

Later they walked down from the hotel to the shore. Their meal was well over and they needed a respite to talking constantly. Each was wondering what this would mean, where it would go. After a while Catrin said, "What's Jen's number?"

He told her.

She put it into her mobile and dialed. "Jen, its Catrin. I am stealing your brother. He has to be back for work in the morning in Headquarters so he isn't leaving tonight as planned, it will be early morning. Just thought I would let you know it isn't a burglar crawling in at 4.00 a.m.

"Yes, he is, I know that. It sort of knocked me out. Nicely, that is."

Treneer watched her face as she listened to his sister. Then she said, "Thanks, Jen, and I will look forward to it."

He stood looking at her, smiling. "Shouldn't you have asked me or something? Like, will you stay over? Do you want to make love, that sort of thing?"

She laughed. "You are a lost cause on that. You said your piece earlier. And between your sister and me, you don't stand a chance. She is packing your bag and will drop it at reception later. Said she doesn't want to disturb us but she seems happy. She is looking forward to seeing me again."

She smiled, "I have no idea where this is going, Chris, but I know where I want to go right now."

She took his hand and led him back towards the hotel.

21 DARTINGTON HALL

"Met someone? Did I hear right?" Jean said.

It was six-thirty the following morning. Chris was already on the road to Exeter. Catrin was showered but not dressed, sitting in her hotel bathrobe sipping coffee made in the room. She had called Jean and Melanie; she was bursting with it and had to tell someone and they were her closest friends.

Jean added, "Catrin, stop the euphemisms. You phone me this early, stay on the line talking for ten minutes non-stop about dinner with him last night and he has fallen for you, and you think you have 'met someone at last'. Catrin, you are smitten. Now get dressed and get to work."

"We will have to see how it goes...." said Catrin.

Jean said, "Melanie is eavesdropping and is ecstatic and no, she is not going to talk to you, I won't let her; we need to be in the Kiln early today and if you two get on the phone everyone will be late. And you need to be at work.

"And Catrin... I love you and am really happy about

the news, too, it's wonderful."

The phone went dead.

Friends, thought Catrin, smiling, when you need them.

When she had woken in the night and got up trying not to disturb Chris, she saw that he was awake already, lying there, thinking.

He said, "I meant to ask, but there was no time. Are you seeing anyone else currently, or shouldn't I go there?"

Catrin said, "Well, I wouldn't be in bed with you if I was seeing someone else, Chris."

He turned towards her. "I was just not sure...."

She cut in, "It's OK. How about you?"

"Not now," he said. "There is something about my job at present that doesn't exactly lend itself to opportunities. It seems a bit weird, you know, computer work on sex assaults, vice and the rest. I meet someone. At some point they ask what I do and... I tell them if they ask. In the past the finance stuff made me too boring and this makes me too weird; it must be something like that. It's too strange a job and, in a sense, being tied to the police doesn't help."

She switched on the bedside light.

"In a way, it's the same for me. Whether it is the scar or the job or whatever. It's why I was not looking, really, at least outside of people in our line of work."

He smiled and took her hand in his. "Well, you found someone, not a police officer, though; just a civilian computer geek. But do you want to tell me about the scar?"

"Later, in daytime. Sometime. But not now."

She moved forward across the bed and kissed him.

~~

At the morning briefing they reviewed the progress made yesterday. Catrin left it to DS Wastle to talk about the visit to the Staley home; it was his patch.

Hicks pursed his lips thinking.

"You two are on the same wavelength on this?" he asked Catrin.

She said, "Yes sir, we think there is something in the grandfather's evasiveness that is linked to the vase image in his painting."

Now was not the time to share her deeper suspicions; the man was the father-in-law of a police superintendent.

Hicks wrinkled his nose, not sure. "Could just be that he is a cranky old man, but it may be worth following up. Next steps to do that?" he asked.

Wastle said, "We talked about it. I will be getting more information about the hacker to Dr. Ryder from Chris; he went back to Exeter yesterday. Then I will go over to Falmouth University with Lloyd. We will check on their records base for anything relevant from Dartington that may have been brought over when the universities merged.

"Catrin will go back to Totnes, to Dartington Hall, to check on the records held there, the older stuff they didn't transfer to Falmouth, we understand. She can ask about any background on Professor Staley that people there now may recall and also ask about the vase; its more in her line of work, really. Naomi Staley thought she saw one like it there, as we said. That's our plan."

"Good," Hicks said, looking at the team gathered. "But for the rest of you, that doesn't stop us completing the follow-up interview work with the short list of students and staff at Falmouth University."

He paused, checking their faces.

"Everyone know what they are doing? I am meeting Superintendents Mitchell and Pender later; it was already scheduled. I am going to be making no reference to this latest news from Sergeant Wastle regarding Staley. This is Superintendent Mitchell's father-in-law we are talking about. So... I don't want anyone to gossip or give a quiet 'heads up' to anyone. Don't drop me in it. We have about twenty-four hours max before this is out in the open or buried and we move on. Got it?"

Superintendent Pender was Hicks' own boss.

As Catrin drove to Totnes her mind went between the work and the 'what now' question about Chris Treneer. She had been here before, meeting someone while on a case, a bank employee in Glasgow. The Kinnington Church incident had finished that; it had overwhelmed him and he had walked away.

Her plan had been to find someone in London in her social circle, another artist or her job, whatever, but time was passing. No-one of interest, availability or just 'fit' with her had really come up. Now she was reviewing her own feelings. Chris had said he just fell for her and somehow that felt great.

What was troubling her was the adjustment to the way she suddenly had fallen for him, too. That was the only way to describe it; better than 'smitten', as Jean had said. He wasn't someone she would have spotted and said, "He looks interesting...."

And now he was far more than that. In Glasgow it had happened over days with Iain Simmons and here it had changed in seconds.

At least Chris was within the police sphere; he knew the life. He just happened to be living closer to Ireland than to London, but still, it felt good. She felt more alive than she had in a while.

~~

Dartington Hall was impressive, dating from the fourteenth century. It had been derelict when the Elmhirst family bought it in 1925. That was the start of its transition to become a centre of 'progressive learning', eventually encompassing the Dartington College of the Arts where Philip Staley had been a member of the faculty.

Catrin had read that it was still active, an international summer school and sustainability 'think tank'. It also housed another institution, Schumacher College.

The administrative records office didn't date from 1925 but it was largely unchanged from the Dartington College days, it seemed to Catrin. Oliver had arranged for PC Lloyd to phone ahead for her, to give the visit the Devon & Cornwall stamp of authority. She showed her warrant card to a Mr. Jameson, a man about her own age. His examination of it was almost cursory.

"How can we help?" he said.

She explained that she needed records for the years of 1988 to 1995 to begin with, the years that Caroline Staley had attended as a student and the period afterwards. She may need more, in due course. She still needed to find out when, after marriage, Caroline Mitchell moved to Exeter, she realised. She was married then, so they could get that from HQ records tied to James Mitchell's career.

Also she wanted to see that part of the building where Professor Philip Staley had worked, if possible.

He looked at her. "I'm not sure we can do that, to be honest. Everything has changed, including most of the people here in terms of the support staff. Which professor occupied which office then, I am not sure we know. In any event, most of the Dartington records went to Falmouth in 2011 but we did retain some archive material here. Given the years you are interested in, I think our records here may be relevant."

Jameson sighed. "What you need is Mr. Townsend."

He smiled to himself as he said it; making it sound is if she needed a new Phillips screwdriver. He didn't explain further as he called an extension and asked someone to come to his office.

Townsend had white hair, was thin as a rake and in a suit which probably was fashionable when the Dartington College of Arts was first established.

"Mr. Townsend, this is Detective Sergeant Sayer on a police investigation. She needs information on Dartington for the years 1988 to 1995. I told her she needed you. Could you?"

Catrin could sense that Jameson was relieved to have found someone to foist her on. Townsend shook hands enthusiastically and led the way out, suddenly speaking to Catrin in Welsh.

"You are Welsh?" asked Catrin, surprised.

"No, from Bodmin, but I have learned to speak Welsh, Cornish and Breton in the past ten years; a past-time, a passion I think, for the old languages.

"Well," said Catrin, "you speak modern Welsh very well."

She hoped he was not going to try her out on medieval English and Old and Middle Welsh dialects. What am I doing, she thought, speaking Welsh in Totnes and falling for a Cornishman in Falmouth? I am going to wake up soon and find it was all a dream.

Catrin explained her needs to Townsend.

He thought about it. "I can show you the record boxes and leave you to it or you can ask me exactly what you want and hopefully I will be able to track it down more precisely."

"Well, that's a bit of a problem; police confidentiality and all that," she said.

He nodded. "Let's go and get the boxes you need. I think there will be quite a few, Sergeant Sayer."

She looked at him.

"Mr. Townsend, can I trust you?" She smiled.

He looked a little concerned. "I am the soul of discretion, Miss Sayer. I have been dealing with records; personnel records, financial records, disciplinary records for students and, may I say it, some for hare-brained faculty for many years... things about which one has to be discreet. So yes, you can."

She said, "Professor Philip Staley, a lecturer here when it was the Dartington College of Arts; do you know him?"

He nodded. "By sight and his record, yes, from years ago. That's all. We never talked, I think."

Catrin said, "He has a daughter, now Caroline Mitchell, she was Staley then, of course. She studied here 1989 to 1992 doing Dramatic Arts. She also modelled for the figure drawing classes at the college. So I want a list of all figure models for the period and their records; to know who hired and paid them; where they worked; the studios they used; the procedures used and any issues 'disciplinary or otherwise' regarding Professor Staley and the treatment of models by him or any other faculty member. And I need any personnel records here of the two people I mentioned for a start. That sort of thing."

She watched the older man's mind putting it together. To his credit he didn't ask any questions.

Finally he said, "I can find some of these, at least the relevant file boxes. Some of the personnel files may be at Falmouth University, though. It makes it a lot easier now that you told me."

"And," she said, pulling out her phone and digging up the photo of the vase, "do you know anything about this?"

He looked. "It actually looks familiar. Yes, I do, vaguely. A vase like that used to be here in the building back then, I recall. I don't know where exactly, but I have seen it or one like it before. With all the changes, I can say I haven't seen it for a while. I will dig up the files with the minor property inventory listings; it may be among the art items. Hopefully it will be mentioned and possibly, if we are really lucky, there will be a photograph. Assuming I can find all that."

He seemed to be a man on a quest; Edmund Hillary about to ascend a mountain of file boxes.

It was late in the afternoon when he popped his head around the door of the room Catrin had been using. She had been poring through the various boxes that Townsend had brought, marking certain items with sticky notes. The old man had worked away with her, helping as much as he could, she realised, always ready for her next request. Apart from a sandwich in the cafeteria, they had both been working constantly.

"Sergeant Sayer, I can tell you that the vase is not here now. Finding the record led me a merry dance, I can tell you. It was sold to a former student. We don't get many requests like that so it stood out as I went through the inventory. Here are the details, including the artist who made it, a Shauna Courtney. I recall the Courtney family; there have been several generations of them at

Dartington as students. I suspect that it may have been a gift to the college, as both Shauna and her husband were artists."

"Wonderful," said Catrin, looking at the information on the sale. Then she said in Welsh, "Mr. Townsend, you have made my day. Thank you."

He smiled.

Townsend had taken over a photocopier and was copying the pages with her sticky notes. She closed the borrowed office door and phoned Wastle but got no response. She left a message and phoned DI Hicks.

"Sayer?"

"We have it, sir, the link. I have also the history of the vase in the picture, the person who bought it from the college recently and I suspect I know why. I can't prove it yet. We need the fingerprints of Marilyn Greaves, the mature student who asked for more action during the modelling session. We should check them against the prints that came back off the rail where we think the camera was mounted."

"Why? Is she the buyer of the vase?"

"Yes. She was one of the other students here at Dartington who modelled for classes and she also was paid for private modelling sessions with Janis Staley's grandfather. She bought the vase here two years ago. I think something happened between her and Philip Staley that has led now to this attack on Janis. Her grandfather is the real target.

"I also suspect he has seen the images; that's the reason for his behavior. I think that Greaves is trying to force him to confess to something or torture him about it through his granddaughter."

"Sayer, from the report yesterday from Oliver, he

sounded grouchy, not tortured."

Catrin said, "I know. He is either in denial or he just… doesn't care. I tried Oliver, and left a message; I need to brief him too."

Hicks said, "OK, call Oliver again and bring him up to speed then get back with the information. I will get the team together this evening. It will be a late finish, I know, but I feel the bomb ticking on this one; the fact that we are talking about the father-in-law of a senior officer here. I am going to talk again with Superintendent Pender; get her on my side first.

"It was like the Sword of Damocles hanging over me in the meeting with Mitchell and Pender earlier."

"Yes sir, I should be back in a couple of hours."

"And Sayer," his voice lightened. "Can you call Chris Treneer and ask him to attend also, please? I want all the team on this. I will call DI Marshall and see if he can join in by conference call."

"Yes sir."

The line went dead.

If he wants Keith Marshall on the line, then I think he wants to keep me involved further, not head back, she concluded.

Then she realised why his voiced changed as he mentioned Chris. He knows about us. How?

22 ROADBLOCK

"The originals must be kept under lock and key and be the direct responsibility of Mr. Townsend until forensic officers collect them. Otherwise I will get a court order right now," improvised Catrin.

Jameson was nodding, concerned, suddenly aware that there was more to this than the sleepy task he had passed to the older records clerk. Catrin had the photocopies that Townsend had prepared and passed to her in a sealed envelope.

She added for good measure, "He has been extremely helpful. Senior officers will be informed of his support and the co-operation given by the Hall."

Townsend was standing there, smiling. He had enjoyed the day working with this young Welsh woman.

He walked her out. "Thank you, DS Sayer."

"No, thank you, Mr. Townsend. You were a real gentleman."

She called Chris as she drove.

He said, "I already heard, I am on my way. Wastle

called me."

"Hicks knows about us, Chris."

He laughed, "Catrin, he is staying at the same hotel. I saw his car there in the morning when I left. He could have seen us in the restaurant or outside the hotel... but it doesn't matter, does it?"

She thought on it then said, "He has been OK with me this trip."

He added, "Saying 'about us', Catrin. That sounds good to me."

She smiled and said into the speakerphone, "And to me. See you back in Falmouth."

~~

When Catrin entered the meeting room at Falmouth Police Station the whiteboard had been cleared of the robbery details, at least temporarily. The information on the Mitchell case had been re-positioned and DI Hick's team was gathering. Superintendent Mitchell was there, sitting next to another Superintendent, a woman Catrin took to be Pender. Hicks walked over to Catrin, looking at her face. He spoke to her softly, alone.

"I know, but it's not my call; Superintendent Pender invited him. He is a twenty-year veteran officer, Catrin. We have to believe he can deal with this appropriately."

Hicks turned, spoke to the room, "DI Marshall, DI Steadman and Chief Superintendent Matheson from Scotland Yard are on the phone."

Catrin looked at Chris who had arrived a few minutes earlier. He smiled; he was fiddling with the speaker phone set up, helping out.

Catrin thought, this is quite a party. Steadman and his boss - and Keith.

Then Marshall's voice came on the line. "DCI Worsley is also on the line at this end."

Her boss was back. A bigger group again from Scotland Yard but for some reason Catrin felt a sense of relief.

Hicks walked to the front and said, "We have had some significant developments in the Janis Mitchell case over the last twenty-four hours. For those who don't know, Superintendent Mitchell is with us; it is his daughter who was targeted so…"

He looked at Mitchell who leaned towards the speaker phone a little.

He said. "No special consideration, please; it's an investigation. I have a deeply-vested interest, of course, but please treat this like any other. It's the only way and if anyone at any point feels I should leave, say so; it will not be a problem. It's a privilege I am here, but I am not a member of this investigation team."

DI Hicks said, "I am going to get DS Oliver Wastle to begin by briefing us on the meeting with the forensic psychiatrist, Dr. Ryder. I will only add, for DI Marshall's benefit, that DS Sayer was on the right track all along on this one, it appears. I am glad that the Met sent her along."

He looked at Catrin and smiled.

Is this the same guy who threw me on a train last time, Catrin thought?

"Then I will have DS Sayer take us through the findings she reported to me from Dartington Hall."

Wastle took them through the meeting with Dr. Ryder, adding at the end the fact that an updated material list on 'Adrestia', the hacker, had been sent to the psychiatrist and that the fingerprint results from the studio showed currently no known matches. The only prints eliminated were those of the college technician. This left three other distinct sets found on the pole in the studio and more in the same region of the wall behind. A location map of their positions had been prepared.

"Thank you, Oliver; DS Sayer?" said Hicks.

Catrin stood up and moved to the front, closer to the speaker phone. She began, "First I would like to say to DCI Worsley, thank you for joining the call."

Jane would know what that meant, she felt.

Her boss's voice came down the line. "Thank you, Catrin. Glad to be here."

She sounded good.

Catrin then looked at Superintendent Mitchell.

"I am going to begin with the bottom line then take you back to how I got there. Comments are welcome but let me get it all out first, right?"

She paused.

"The attack on Janis was, I believe, orchestrated by a Marilyn Greaves, a mature student in an art class at Truro and Penwith College. Janis has posed as a model for that class. Greaves was formerly a student at Dartington College of Arts concurrent with the period of study there of Caroline Staley, as she was before marriage, Superintendent Mitchell's wife. Greaves maiden name was Samuels.

"She is the wife of a Callum Greaves, a school principal. Professionally she is a part-time registrar of births and deaths, a local civil servant. We will need to do a lot more checking, of course."

She took a deep breath. Here goes, she thought.

"Caroline Mitchell and Marilyn Greaves were both figure models, life class models at Dartington; this was part of the reason that Janis took up the same role here at Truro, it seems. She knew from her mother about the challenges of modelling and had some training from her. During the period that both Mrs. Mitchell and Marilyn Greaves were modelling, her father, Professor Philip Staley, was a lecturer in fine arts at the college. He was involved in teaching and occasionally in life drawing classes but he was also - and still is - an artist of note.

"Records show that Marilyn Greaves was paid for class modelling in sessions he took and also for painting sessions with several artists who were members of the Faculty, including Philip Staley.

"There is also a record at Dartington of the vase found in both the images we are investigating. We have its maker, its inventory acquisition number at the college and, only two years ago, a record of its sale to Mrs. Greaves. There is also a note on the file that in late 1993 it went missing for a two week period, recorded as possibly being stolen. There was then an annotation that it was found in Professor Staley's outer office; his secretary said it had been used as a prop in a painting session and had not been returned. She had found it in a cupboard there and just returned it to a table."

Mitchell's face remained impassive but Catrin saw that his eyes showed he was already at the end of this line.

Catrin wrapped up the summary. "We have a woman linked to Professor Staley as a model who now turns up over twenty years later and speaks to his daughter, while she is modelling, to create the pose and facial expression which enabled the first image on the web site to be created. We have a record of the vase being in her possession and you have heard from DS Wastle of Dr Ryder's initial thoughts on the mindset of the person orchestrating this attack; psychotic revenge on another person linked to Janis Mitchell.

"I think that something occurred between Philip Staley and Marilyn Greaves in which the vase became a significant symbol. This, I suspect, has led to a meticulously planned act. In her mind, fact or fiction, the perpetrator of her perceived injustice was Philip Staley.

"DS Wastle and I found Philip Staley to be dissembling and evasive when we visited him yesterday. He claimed he had not seen the images and he is not on the internet. But there is the possibility that they were delivered to him by mail or courier in books or magazines; he still buys a lot of books and always opens that mail himself, we heard."

She focused again on the senior officers, first Pender then Mitchell.

"I suspect, but have no proof at present, that Philip Staley is aware that Marilyn Greaves is trying to get him to do something, I don't know what. He is resisting or denying it; to the extent, I suggest, that he would not even inform anyone of the woman's possible involvement in the assault on his granddaughter.

She paused.

"I am sorry sir, we can go back through the detail underpinning this now but I recognize this is an additional blow for you."

Superintendent Mitchell nodded, saying nothing.

Chief Superintendent Matheson's voice came on the phone, "DS Sayer, I am breaking into your report and I apologize to all, but I can see where this is going, in fact. I want to set a point straight here before you go through the supporting detail and DI Hicks starts to plan next steps. And it is no small point, so forgive me.

"And James, you will need to forgive me more, I

think. It's a while since we have seen each other but… this is going to get harder still. The obvious outcome for this path of the investigation now is clarification, validation and bringing in Marilyn Greaves. I won't allow that at this stage and, yes it is our call, by agreed protocol, given the international dimension."

DI Hicks looked astonished, then angry.

Matheson continued, "I don't like to put a roadblock in front of any legitimate arrest but, if Sergeant Sayer is right, we have identified the client end of the duo that committed this crime. The hacker expert end is no further forward and, frankly, we want this person. The Germans want him and so do the Dutch. Remember, this hacker has done similar work before and we know of one suicide already firmly linked to this person's handiwork.

"From what I hear we have an intact link to the hacker without, at this stage, any knowledge by him or her of our findings. We have to get both parties, Greaves and 'Adrestia'. I won't take the risk that the interview of Greaves will lead us to the hacker; there will be too many cutoffs."

Catrin could see that the people around the table were starting to see the bigger picture again. Steadman must have prepared Matheson for this in advance.

Matheson went on, "DI Steadman and the team here think that we need to wait for or provoke another attack, track the transaction flows on the assumption that each one is organized and paid for at the time. That is going to take some monumental organization and coordination but until we try it, we can't arrest Greaves."

Superintendent Pender looked at DI Hicks and then at her colleague, Mitchell.

She said, "You are suggesting that Devon & Cornwall Police provoke a further attack on the daughter of one of our own. I wouldn't agree to that for any member of the public unless we had their full agreement and were absolutely sure we were not placing them in danger. Nor would any other senior officer here."

She was clearly not happy with the intervention or the fact that Matheson had just dropped this on her.

Superintendent Mitchell said, "Forgive me, it's not my investigation but it is my family. Bob Matheson is right, I am afraid. Bob, thank you, but no apology is needed. What you said needed saying; we have to take both these people into custody. I just don't know how to explain it to my daughter."

DI Hicks looked at him then at Catrin.

"Sir, any action there is a professional issue, not a family matter. Sorry. The best person to do this, to get Janis on board, is the officer who has built the best rapport with her. That is DS Sayer, I believe. I think Mrs. Mitchell would agree with that also, don't you?

Catrin suddenly found everyone in the room looking at her.

Worsley's voice came down the phone.

"I go along with Chief Superintendent Matheson's position. But I want it clear that this decision is a D&C decision. That if DS Sayer does this and stays involved with the case, persuades Janis Mitchell to co-operate whatever the consequences, she is held harmless.

"Let's be clear on that. I want it in writing. We are, in my mind well beyond now the remit I gave her two weeks ago and, while it is good investigative work, it is well off the path of the Art Crime Unit mandate."

Superintendent Pender said, "We will give you that, DCI Worsley, it's understood."

DI Hicks looked around.

"Let's take a five minute break. Then we can go back through the details. We need to make sure all this stands up to scrutiny before we do anything else."

Catrin's Blackberry beeped as the people milled around. The text was from Worsley.

"Good work, but you are in this up to your armpits, Catrin. Call my mobile tomorrow morning before you go in and do anything further. Let's say 7.30. And all went well."

She texted back immediately even though she needed the loo before she was on again, going through the details.

"Thanks ma'am, for the support and good news. Much relieved. Will call tomorrow."

She walked out and Chris was waiting.

"Later," she said, passing him a small hotel envelope. "I had another room key programmed this morning."

She headed for the washrooms. It was going to be a long evening.

23 SOUNDINGS

Superintendent Mitchell had excused himself before they went into the detailed review. He thought it was appropriate to do so, now he had the picture of where this was going.

DI Hicks had laid it out at the end of the long evening's briefing. Catrin would talk to Janis. He and Oliver Wastle would talk formally with Superintendent and Mrs. Mitchell together. They had hummed and hawed on that point. In the end they decided to inform the mother as well. "She is the wife of a police superintendent. She has doubtlessly her share of secrets to maintain," said Pender.

However, there was to be no release of Greaves' name and only a vague reference to her grandfather's possible involvement. Catrin noted the instructions but made no comment. She knew her role; stay out of the local politics.

The following morning the Mitchell family was brought into Falmouth Police Station. Catrin was waiting for Janis. She had slept well next to Chris.

"Let's go out," she said to Janis Mitchell as her parents were taken into Pender's office to meet with Hicks.

She knew Pender and Hicks were going to brief her parents together as if her father's presence last night had been an illusion.

"Where?"

Her eyes were following her parents.

"Where we can talk as women, not just as a police officer to a crime victim."

Catrin drove Mitchell across town along Swanpool Road to the Beach Café and switched off the engine in its car park. All she had said as they left the station was, "I need to talk to you, get your help and I would rather not talk and drive at the same time. We are not going far."

In the car park, looking across at the water, Catrin began. "Janis, I told you about the scar; I had been physically assaulted."

Mitchell nodded, attentive.

"I am going to tell you something else about me. When I was a student at Aberystwyth I modelled for my boyfriend and he did likewise for me. No big deal. But I also did sessions with two other students, both girls, friends from class, we posed nude for each other; different bodies, different drawing challenges. You understand?"

Janis nodded, "Completely."

"Then sometime afterwards one of the girls made a remark to David, my boyfriend at the time, about my breasts. They aren't big. She had more difficulty drawing them accurately, she said, than when she drew the other student; that the accurate portrayal of smaller breasts relies more on careful shading than on contour. Her remark was meant to be light, but it hurt a lot and I couldn't work out why at first, because she wasn't trying to be mean; we were friends, for heaven's sake. Then I realised what it was; I was modelling for her, not offering myself for criticism.

"I tell you this simply to let you know I have a little understanding, a very little understanding of your situation, based on something very trivial compared with what was done to you. And I do that because we are going to ask an awful lot of you. And you can say no and we will find another approach somehow."

She pushed open her door. "Shall we walk?"

They got out of the car, it was a little blustery and damp but the two women crossed the road and walked along the beach path.

Catrin stopped a short distance along the path and faced Janis head on.

"We now know that there are two people involved; an expert hacker who made the images and a client. That was our suspicion. I told you that previously; now it has been confirmed. The hacker isn't even in the UK. Whoever it is has done it before and will do it again - for money and vanity, we think, but we don't know. No-one has tracked this person yet. And at least one person - a victim like you - has committed suicide as a direct result.

"The client, we believe, is a former student of your grandfather with a grudge, for whatever reason, real or imagined. Whatever is driving the person to do it, we don't know yet. Frankly, there may be some basis; there also may not be. That is going to be hard to sort out, deal with. For everyone, including your family."

"But we desperately want to catch the hacker too and the only way to do that is to get the client to make another attack on you. It's the transaction between them, to order and make a third image that we can follow to find him or her. You see, there won't be any other links we can trace; that's the nature of computer hackers, they cover their tracks and good ones are experts at it. So we want you to help us to provoke that attack."

She was watching her carefully.

"We had a big debate about it last night. I pushed for telling you, asking you, so that is why I am doing this. I think you want closure; you have the right to know the identities of both the people who did this. You may want to tell them directly how cruel it was sometime or make a victim impact statement at their trials.

"And the other reason I pushed for it is that I think you have the guts to do it."

She waited.

Janis said, "Is there likely to be a physical assault provoked. Could I be hurt?" She was looking at Catrin's scar.

Catrin said, "We talked about that, too. We don't think so, because you are not the primary target. This is aimed at your grandfather we believe, as I said."

Janis said, "But he hasn't even seen the photos; he doesn't have a computer and he is not on the internet. Mum has been trying to get them on to it but he is stubborn."

Perhaps, thought Catrin.

She said, "You have to remember the distorted perspective of the person doing this. He or she will assume your grandfather will hear about it from family members; they will describe the weird photos in detail. The perpetrator will think that this will trigger something with your grandfather - what, we don't know - and, at this stage we don't want you to talk about it. The only people who will be in the loop are you and your parents; they are being briefed now."

Janis said, "So why aren't we hearing this together?"

She's quick, like her father, thought Catrin. She looked at Janis Mitchell, assessing her.

"Two reasons. First of all we want you to make the decision without anyone else around. It's you on the line here and, frankly, you have been through a lot. We can assign a woman police officer as your bodyguard if you worry about the physical aspects.

"Not you?" Janis asked.

Catrin shook her head, "No, not me. Someone younger who would fit in it at the college better, with firearms certification, trained in protection."

She paused, "You know, I did that once, went on assignment at a university on a case. They put me in then as a post-grad, so I wouldn't really fit as a second-year student now, would I?"

Janis asked, "Do you think I need it?"

Catrin said, "I don't, but I can't read the mind of the person involved. I think the hacker is just that. The person who is using you hasn't shown physical violence, just a disregard for you and your rights, a callousness driven by their own need for... whatever. But if you feel what we ask makes you want the extra security while this is unfolding, we will do it, I guarantee. We will provide the right sort of protection."

She had been briefed on this point by Pender herself.

Janis thought about it, looking into the distance at the bay, at the water, the wind blowing and her hair getting damp. Then she looked at Catrin.

"But you said, 'two reasons'."

Catrin smiled.

"Yes. The second was the vase - remember how you had seen it but couldn't place it? Having told you this new information, I wondered if it triggers anything. The vase was at the college, we discovered. I thought it might be easier to talk about it here, just with you, if anything comes to mind."

Janis looked thoughtful. "No, it doesn't. Other than you now tell me my intuition about keeping it secret was along the right lines after all, even if that was the wrong thing to do."

Then she said, "Will you be able to do this and trap them before the next image is placed... wherever? It has been escalating and, it could be anything, hacked in anywhere."

This was the hard one, Catrin knew.

"We will do our best to close this out before the image is either prepared or released. But we can't guarantee it, unfortunately. There is a risk, I have to be honest, but we will do our best. Think about it."

She could tell that Mitchell was realizing that it could happen yet again. All she could now do was wait on the woman's decision. She turned and started walking again and Janis Mitchell fell in step.

They had not gone far when Janis took a deep breath and stopped. "You know, the first shock was awful. Then it was the feeling that this wasn't another student, it was closer to home. That drove me crazy. I didn't think I could talk to my dad, funnily enough, because he is policeman. Sounds stupid, I know."

She spoke firmly. "I want them both, too, so I'll do it. The person who made those images should not be allowed to do it to another person again. What do I do?"

Catrin said, "Well, the first thing you need to do is agree to discuss this only with the police and your parents; no-one else must get a hint, do you understand? No-one at all. It really is important."

She nodded.

"If you can do that, we are off to a good start. Let's head back and go through this with your parents and the other detectives."

~~

"Miss Mitchell and I waited until the end of the class; she did not want to disturb the mood for the work today." said Lyman Hearne. "You have all seen her in this course, drawn her and, unfortunately, that is part of the problem."

Janis Mitchell had entered the room close to the end of the session. Hearne had beckoned her over and stood by her side in a show of solidarity as she faced the class, holding the iPad. He switched on the wall display screen as she connected wirelessly. They had set this up before the class.

She looked nervous, Catrin thought; she was supposed to. This was a mid-afternoon class, the first of three art classes at the college that would be addressed in this manner over the next couple of days. To the police, it was the only one that really mattered. The other two classes didn't include Marilyn Greaves; they were window dressing simply to re-affirm that they didn't have a suspect identified yet.

DS Wastle, DI Hicks, Chris Treneer and Catrin were in an office in another part of the building watching on the cameras placed in the studio. Chris and a police technician had installed them in the early hours of the morning. No one would see them. One camera was focused on the podium and Janis, another on Marilyn

Greaves and a third provided a pan of the group. They were all in existing light housings, a lot less visible than the camera that Greaves must have installed. No-one had noticed that one in the equipment array.

Janis swallowed nervously then began speaking.

"Thank you for giving me a few moments. Some of you will know, others probably not, that I have been the victim of an assault. Not physical, but certainly sexual, violent and malicious."

She tapped the iPad and both unaltered images showed on the screen behind her, side by side.

Catrin sighed. DI Hicks smiled. 'She is over the hump, Catrin. Well done."

Janis waited a few moments to allow the class to absorb the images. One student said loudly, "That's awful."

Janis said. "The police experts say the images are derived from the sessions I did in this room as a model. Someone had a hidden camera. Someone played around in Photoshop and put this one - she pointed at the first - on my Facebook page and later put the second image on my page and also hacked into the Tate Gallery web site. It was put there also."

"Damien Hirst," said another student, "but no originality."

Janis said, "I am not saying it is any of you. It could be. It could be another person in the college with access here who did it, perhaps someone in the other classes I posed for. I will speak to them also. It could also be someone from anywhere, really, who decided to pick me and gained access to the room.

"But it is really hurtful, for me and my entire family; you don't know how much. And we have no idea why.

But it has to stop; this perverted or sick person needs to stop or be stopped. I doubt the police can do much about it; they have been interviewing people at Falmouth University, where I study, but I feel the investigation is going nowhere. People here can help, though."

Catrin said, "She remembered; 'entire family', she said it."

Janis touched the iPad.

"This is going on my Facebook page when I leave this room. With more or less the words I said to you now. It must stop. You can like it, share it and support me. I can't face modelling any more, you can understand that, I think. But this is me, not those images."

The image she now displayed was a composite. The large picture showed a head and shoulders photo taken of Janis outdoors at Falmouth, tanned, smiling, relaxed. The two smaller images by its side simply said, 'censored'. The text below said, "This is me. Someone I don't know made inappropriate images of me and posted them on-line. Say 'No' to sexual harassment in all forms. You should; everyone should."

"Good for you," said one student. "Stand up to the bastard." He started applauding and others joined in.

Janis said, "Thank you. Thank you, Mr. Hearne."

She walked off the podium and started talking to people. Some clustered round her offering support.

Catrin watched Marilyn Greaves carefully. She had joined in the applause and talked to the person next to her; she was clearly making the right noises. But she did not approach Janis Mitchell. And her face a few seconds earlier showed a flash of anger as the image of Janis smiling came up.

DI Hicks said, "Now we wait and watch. You won't get much sleep, Chris."

He replied, "It's mostly automatic, sir. There is not much else to do until someone kicks a tripwire or, hopefully, the surveillance on Greaves shows something."

Marilyn talked with Graham next to her about Janis Mitchell's speech as others clustered around the model. He was not short of an opinion on the inadequacy of the police in this matter. Obviously they should be talking to all the students who had been in classes that Mitchell had modelled for, but no-one had talked to him.

"Nor me," said Marilyn.

"I'm puzzled, though," he said.

"What by?" Marilyn asked.

"Why the Tate? Why not Saatchi & Saatchi or another site that dealt with Hirst images. They should be looking into that, too."

She nodded, her face showing she obviously was lost for an answer to Graham's rapier insight.

Because he loved the Tate above the rest, she thought. He was ecstatic when his first painting was exhibited there. That's why.

As she left she pondered the situation. Mitchell had sounded genuine, not rehearsed. But then her mother had been a good actor, she recalled, perhaps it runs in the family. Perhaps the police are a lot closer than she would like at this stage. And perhaps, again, her nerves were playing up; if they knew, they would be dragging her in.

In any event she was committed now. She knew what she had to do.

~~

Catrin was glad it was done. She wanted to stay here with Chris but she also wanted to go home to London. But it wasn't her call. Worsley had told her to get the train after the session this morning.

Hicks looked at Catrin. "I'll drop you at the station... unless, Chris, you are heading that way now?"

His face gave nothing away. Not even the eyes, thought Catrin.

"I would be glad to, sir. No problem at all."

At the station he hugged and kissed her.

He said, "I can't leave, obviously, with this case being active."

She nodded. "I will see when I can get back down."

He smiled, "Although you may need to heed your boss's advice - make more pots to pay for train fares."

Catrin had talked to Jane Worsley three mornings ago, the day following the evening briefing. Worsley had begun with an update on her surgery.

"They got it all, they say, and it was benign still. I am feeling OK, a bit sore and have to be careful with what I wear and not hang my purse strap on that side. Otherwise, it is 'wait and see,' and frequent checkups. It's good to be back at work."

Then she turned to the case.

"Catrin, I understand why Keith sent you back down and you have done a good job but we are way out of our mandate here, as I said on the call. Fortunately Matheson is speaking very highly of this which helps, but we need to look at closing out. There is other work here that needs attention."

Catrin said, "I understand, ma'am. Probably after the talk with Mitchell and seeing her through the first stage."

It was her tone of voice which alerted Worsley.

"And Catrin?" she said. "There's something else, I think?"

"I met someone down here," Catrin said.

There's that phrase again, she thought.

There was a pause. Then Worsley said, "Not another banker?"

Worsley was recalling the Connolly case; she knew Catrin had fallen for someone in Glasgow. Catrin laughed.

"No, ma'am, he is in the job, a civilian computer technician here with D&C Police."

'In the job'; the language of police officers.

"Well, Catrin, I am glad to hear it but you do pick your places. You will need to make more art and jack your price up. The train to Cornwall is not cheap and it sounds like you will be going back there more frequently on your own budget."

24 PROXY

Catrin was again on the sleeper back to Paddington. Her mind started to focus on things she needed to do at home. Worsley had said she wanted to see her on arrival.

At the Yard her boss looked well. She was feisty, in a good mood.

After they caught up on the Mitchell case, she said, "I wanted to see you about John, this Malay thing. You went with him to the Malaysian High Commission."

"Yes, ma'am. It seemed close to wrapping up."

"That's what he said."

She paused. "You met Madeleine Turner-Jones there, I gather."

Catrin said, "Briefly, yes. She fixed up for the V&A to look at the knife and painting, take any conservation measures."

Worsley nodded. "I know. Madeleine I know, too, from my Diplomatic Protection days. She can turn buying a train ticket into a major project, that woman."

She looked at Catrin. "Look, it's become a little more complicated and now you are back from Cornwall, you may as well throw yourself into this one. The Malaysians want to recognize the officers involved in the recovery of the items."

Catrin said, "That's nice. I told John that handing over recovered art was normally a senior level thing."

Worsley said, "It normally is; but for some reason the owner of the items wants to see the officers involved."

Catrin saw from Worsley's face that a bombshell was about to drop. She knew her boss well.

Worsley continued, "And not simply at the High Commission. At the National Museum of Malaysia in Kuala Lumpur, where the knife is now going; it's that valuable, they say. And John Obi has a young child and his wife is well along in her pregnancy with their second, as you know. He is really worried about doing it. Catrin, I can't do it, I am not flying there with this…"

She pointed briefly at her breast.

"So I want you to go to Kuala Lumpur for a few days, if you would."

Catrin let the surprise show on her face. "But, I had nothing to do with the case, really. I just gave John advice, as you asked."

Worsley smiled. "I know. But John and Madeleine have it all worked out. And FCO is paying for the trip, business class and a nice hotel."

She paused. "It's not that far from Hong Kong to Kuala Lumpur, or the other way round, you know. And I will give you some leave outside your annual allocation."

Catrin looked at her. The idea of seeing Jian Li Yeung, her friend who lived in Hong Kong, was appealing.

"Two days of work and expenses to cover a couple of days of sight-seeing if you stay in Kuala Lumpur, or you can use them in Hong Kong."

Catrin remember telling Jane Worsley she would help

out, given the news of her surgery. This sounded like help she was asking for; it hadn't been a direct command.

"What do I do, ma'am?"

"I will call Madeleine. You and Mrs. Turner-Jones can go back to the High Commission, talk with them. Thank you. I am glad you are going, really. If John had gone I would have had one of us go along also, probably Keith, given my situation. It is too much to put on John so early. As it is, you don't need a handler or a chaperone."

Catrin laughed, "I thought that was what Mrs. Turner-Jones was."

Worsley nodded "It is certainly how she sees herself, I agree."

She added, "I will take over the two other cases you were working on in the interim, while you sort this out with Madeleine; the Howard thing and the preparation for giving evidence against Sewell at trial. I will let John do the running round on them. He owes you."

He does that, Catrin thought.

Worsley continued, "And after the meeting with the High Commission, why don't you take a couple of days off? You have been on the go a lot of late, in no small measure due to stuff dropped on you. Perhaps you can get together with your man from Cornwall; drag him to London."

Catrin smiled. "He will be tied up, on standby in the Mitchell case, ma'am, but a few days to catch up here would be great. Thank you."

She wanted to see Chris but she also wanted to get back into the Kiln and work on some art there. Part of that was the promise made to DCI Coltrane's partner, Sylvia McNair, to be in touch.

~~

The Deputy High Commissioner said, "Following our meeting, Sergeant Sayer, there has been a lot of discussion of this issue; a lot of interest. You and your colleague are to be commended for your work in this matter."

They were in the same office at the High Commission, with the same people present, other than John Obi, who was now slogging through some evidence preparation from one of Catrin's former cases.

"Thank you, sir," said Catrin, "The Metropolitan Police Service is pleased to have been of assistance. DC Obi has been particularly focused on this case from the first news of the items being located."

Amhat Budi continued, "We are also pleased that the V&A Museum is working diligently on the renovation and repair of the items."

Deputy Commissioner Budi settled himself more comfortably in his chair. His formal statement was clearly over. "Sergeant Sayer, no doubt Madeleine has explained the complex nature of Malaysian society."

It was a serious question, she felt, tinged with some humour. From his use of Turner-Jones' first name and the smile, he obviously knew the woman well.

Catrin looked at him, "Indeed, sir; Mrs. Turner-Jones explained it to me yesterday; in outline, of course.

Budi nodded, obviously about to go over the same ground.

"Malaysia was a set of individual kingdoms at one time, the Malay states we would call them now. These became Malaya under British colonial rule, as we know. This led to independence and the current nation state, Malaysia, with this infrastructure I mentioned. Our various royal families, for example, reign for fixed periods, in a strict order of precedence.

"The Datuk Jerome Allam is the rightful owner of the items. He is now an older man. He travels less these days but is highly influential in that world and greatly respected. Greatly respected," he repeated, in case she missed its significance.

The man has clout is what he means, thought Catrin.

"His delight at the recovery of this painting and the ceremonial kris is also tied to a building on his family estate that was destroyed. This painting is, in fact, the best record of it; a sort of summer house, you would call it, of personal significance to the gentleman. He expressed a strong wish to meet and thank the officers involved.

"I am glad to say the Foreign Office has agreed that this is a wish they want to see fulfilled also. DC Obi has quite selflessly pointed out, Madeleine tells us, you were the person most instrumental in bringing to our attention the recovery of the painting; his focus was on the kris. Given work and economic realities, we understand that it is most appropriate that Mrs. Turner-Jones and your good self should attend this ceremony.

"So once the restoration is complete, we look forward to your visit to the National Museum in Kuala Lumpur. While you are there, Sergeant, I hope you will get to enjoy and see something of our beautiful country."

"Sergeant Sayer and I are looking forward to it," said Mrs. Turner-Jones.

Catrin said, "Thank you sir, I am sure that I will."

She had already talked with Jian Li; her friend was delighted to meet her in Kuala Lumpur.

She had said immediately, "We can play tourist together for a couple of days; see the Twin Towers. And Catrin, I want to know more about this man Chris Treneer."

25 PLATTERS

Chris and Catrin started a process on Skype. One chose a topic about their life; the other decided who would speak about it first. They needed to find out more about each other despite the distance; what they liked and disliked, who their families were, what they read, music tastes… in the middle of the romance, the list went on.

Chris couldn't leave Cornwall to come to London; they were waiting on action that would break open the Mitchell case and he had other work to do also. He gave no details of the Mitchell case developments or others. That was the way it had to be, she knew; a relationship between two people whose work is covered by confidentiality agreements; they could only talk to each other in generalities about their roles.

In any event, Catrin had her own work and her pottery to do. She had a weekend with Jean and Melanie already lined up.

~~

She went with Jean to Mayfair to meet with Sylvia McNair and talk about the centrepiece platters. They discussed McNair's design interests, what type of uses the platters would be put to; how formal, how informal, how she would want them to work with her existing dinner services; whether they should stand out, make a splash or tone in.

Catrin worked on several designs, busy on them for a couple of days. She was in the Kiln a lot, talking with Jean about what would work structurally, about glazing choices and overglaze enamel decoration combinations. She then took the proposals to McNair's office for her to see, expecting to leave them with her. McNair turned out to be a decisive person; she had chosen there and then after only a little thought and few questions.

Now it was time to make the pieces. From experience, Catrin stayed out of Jean's way at this stage and went back to work at the Yard. Only when her friend was pleased herself with the raw work would she get to comment. Within a few days the first firing had been completed and by the following weekend Catrin was busy on the decoration of the three 'bisques' before the final glazing.

At one point she arranged a Skype session at the Cwmbran Kiln to introduce Chris to Jean and Melanie and show him some of their works there. Later in the evening in private Chris and Catrin connected again and he said they seemed very nice, obviously good friends and so easy to talk to. That Melanie had grown up in the Yeovil area had come up.

Catrin said, "Wait until you get to know her better; she has a wicked sense of humor; she would make Mason seem tame."

Chris responded, "Speaking of which, he is painting in

London soon; a set of *plein air* paintings with video sessions for a watercolour training course. He will give you a buzz. He did say you two should meet up sometime, remember? You can paint with him for a change."

She laughed, "I would have to dig out my watercolour box, if I did. But life is a bit too busy for that, to be honest."

He said, "Oh, if you do it, it will be fun. Knowing Mason, it will be that."

Catrin smiled, "I will ask him to put a plug in his video for my art and for The Cwmbran Kiln. Then I will tell the Great Artist that I will drop you if he edits it out."

"Isn't that extortion, blackmail or something like that?"

She answered, "Marketing, cariad, marketing; it's the same thing really."

The Welsh for 'my love' came naturally to her now.

26 COURIER

Marilyn Greaves went to the DHL Courier Point in the Staples store in Truro. She felt self-conscious about the two Elastoplast bandages wrapped around the thumb and first finger of her right hand, but she was following instructions to avoid fingerprints as best as she could. She couldn't exactly wear gloves, the weather was too nice.

She reached into her carrier bag, withdrawing the sealed envelope. The service agent looked at it. "Germany, right. You will need to put that in one of our own courier envelopes - over on that wall - and fill in the details, seal it up and then come back and pay."

Whether it was nerves or not, it threw Marilyn into a freeze. She had worked out her exact sequence for passing over the sealed envelope with the money and instructions. This was outside her plan. She just stood there.

The woman said, "Do they hurt?"

She was looking at the fingers.

"Yes," said Marilyn, "The knife slipped and one is deep but they both hurt."

The server said, "Give it here, then; I shouldn't, the customer is supposed to but... Les!"

She turned her head to the man behind her.

"Can you serve these two people behind my customer; she needs help."

Marilyn watched as the server wrote out the address and the reply address on the DHL envelope.

'So you are not local then? You could have done this in Newquay, you know; the DHL location is much closer."

Marilyn said, "I know, but I was with my sister at the Tesco across the road and thought, 'kill two birds with one stone'. The car is parked already."

She had never looked into the sender address that the hacker had put on the envelope. Probably another obscure business, she thought.

The agent told her the cost. They sympathized with each other about the price of things these days and Marilyn paid with the notes she had sorted so carefully in her purse.

"At least it will be delivered within two days, for this price," said the service agent.

Marilyn responded, "Thank you for being so helpful. Goodbye."

She turned to head out the door, well satisfied with the 'finish' to this stage of her project. This image would take the brakes off now, she thought. It would have to be the last because it would explicitly identify Philip Staley. And it would get the police running all over him and in time, no doubt, lead them to her.

She was ready for that, too.

As she drove away from the car park a white Vauxhall Zafira followed her, leaving behind a woman police officer in plain clothes. The officer entered the courier office and spoke to a service agent, briefly flashed her warrant card and asked to see the manager.

Once the courier details had been established, the authorities moved very carefully indeed. Two days later in Stuttgart, the German Federal police had prepared well for the surveillance at the dental supply company.

The following day Arno Hintzen turned up to collect the envelope.

~~

The officer leading the German end of the joint investigation was Senior Investigator Helmut Lautner, a member of the Federal Criminal Investigation Office, the Bundeskriminalamt; the BKA for short. Chris Treneer knew that he had been assigned to this case, underscoring the level of importance to the investigation assigned by the German authorities. He was normally associated with high-impact cybercrime cases in Germany which had financial or security implications.

Chris had told Catrin about Lautner in the hotel room after the marathon briefing at Falmouth Police Station. It started with the comment that he wasn't surprised to hear that Chief Superintendent Matheson had pulled the plug on a direct arrest of Greaves; if Lautner was involved in Germany there would already have been high level international discussions which would have set the priorities. He thought that the speed of events leading to the identification of Greaves had run just a little too fast for Pender to be briefed properly, so she had been caught unawares. She should have been brought into the loop earlier, he thought.

Catrin lay next to him, hearing that the new man in her

life, her 'cyber-geek', had information and insights in this shared case that were way above her own perspective on the investigation.

She asked, "So what's so special about this Lautner, then? If knowing he was brought into the case was sufficient to make Matheson's bombshell a ho-hum for you?"

"It wasn't ho-hum, Catrin, at all. I was enthralled by the Welsh Sherlock Holmes standing at the front at the time. It just wasn't a surprise."

She slapped him gently at the comment.

He continued. "Lautner is a former Intelligence Officer, a spook, Steadman thinks. In our world it is all a question of layers of access to systems. If we can break into and monitor a hacker system, or a fraud network, or a kiddie-trap ring without being detected, we have the upper hand. But if we are detected, the target is alerted. It's a tricky business, cyber-penetration.

"But not with Lautner; he is different. Once he knows the target he doesn't use computers at all, just people."

Catrin looked at him quizzically.

He looked back. "Don't ask me how; I am a computer guy."

She smiled, "So I mesmerized you, with my briefing, then?"

"I wasn't listening," he lied, "just watching and thinking."

"Men," she sighed playfully, "lost in erotic daydreams."

He moved closer. "It's a fair cop. I confess."

Her arms wrapped around him as she realised that she wasn't quite as tired as she thought.

~~

Lautner's group had learned about trapping cyber-criminals the hard way, through a series of failures and frustrations over the years. This had led to a strategy that was now his hallmark, as Chris said. First, identify and confirm the target. Second, do nothing in the way of surveillance whatsoever. Third, prepare the ground. Finally, isolate and strike.

It was step two that caused the most friction with his superiors, the insistence on no tails, no intercepts, nothing.

The bakery next to the mail drop in Stuttgart had provided a first class location for the identification of everyone entering or leaving the location and for recording the licence plates of people parking close by.

Arno had driven there and parked outside. That action and the subsequent facial imagery analysis were sufficient to give Lautner a name for the man who collected the package. That was all they wanted at the time.

His team knew exactly what to do. No on-line checks outside a small set of databases within a high security environment. No internet searches or visual checks of what he was doing, now he had received the payment from the client. But they had found enough to show his workplace and home address. From those, they found others to talk to; including one person in particular.

Gerda Weig was surprised to find a rather studious-looking civil servant-type turn up at her apartment unannounced.

Herr Feil had introduced himself as a consultant, a representative of her employer, Bremer Voight Engineering. He had mentioned names she knew in

Human Resources and had made the offer for her to check his validity, which she did, calling her boss. He then moved straight to the topic of his visit. Clearly he was busy and not enjoying this job, a contract for the Internal Communications Director.

"I should have called to make an appointment, but my last client was close by and frankly, we are behind on time on this. I just thought I would take the chance. I am glad you are here."

Lautner's people had been watching her movements for a day now.

"Your study release from the company for the Fraunhofer Institute is in its second term, I see."

"Yes," she said, eyeing him suspiciously as he looked at the information on his iPad.

He continued, "We are assessing at random a number of the recipients of the company study scholarships to establish the quality of the education they are receiving."

She paused, "So it's not about me? I mean, my scores this term are not as good as last, I know, but…."

"No, it's not about you."

Lautner knew of Gerda's relationship with a post-doc studying at the institute and that she had been missing classes. She had shared it a little indiscreetly with several of her friends in emails.

"However, we naturally check the basis for the perspective given, and that does mean checking the profile of the employee with their supervisor. Good cooperation is the primary element we rate people on, to be honest, although I shouldn't tell interviewees that. We know this survey is of little interest to the student, that you are busy, but we do need it to gauge the future direction of company educational support. The Board of Directors is expecting a report… and you know what that means; it has to be right."

Not about me; about co-operation, she registered.

"What do you need?" she asked.

He pulled up his list on his iPad.

"I want to know about the classes you go to, the assessment of the professors or lecturers, the tuition weaknesses and, most importantly, anything which suggests a bias against female students. We are not suggesting there is any, but it is of great importance to Frau Schemel on the Board, we know, given the corporate policy in this area.

He was glancing down the list.

"And finally, a forthcoming class that you attend that should be very typical or illustrative of the highpoints of that lecturer's style and material. One that we are sure that he or she will give, not defer to a junior colleague. You know how it is? I or a colleague of mine may arrange to sit in; to validate your own assessment, so to speak. It's a random element that we include in our protocol. And we expect complete confidentiality on this; no alerting lecturers to our assessment. We can spot that sort of thing."

Gerda nodded, "Yes, I see." She didn't, but it didn't matter. "And I can see why you want the lecturer to be there. Frankly we get too much substitution by teaching assistants or junior staff at times. I can give you the details on that. Of course, I wouldn't say a word to any of them."

Helmut had connected his iPad into its portable keyboard.

"So let's work through together. Then we can both be on our way."

When they came to Professor Hintzen, Gerda was able to identify a clear opportunity to see him at his best, she thought; the Stuyvesant lecture next week.

"He always invites Professor Stuyvesant; it's an annual thing, a debate between them on business ethics. We were told by others that it was a 'must'. He rarely misses his lectures anyway, but he can be guaranteed to be at that one."

She paused then said, "I did say he has no bias against women at all, didn't I? He is a nice older lecturer; a bit quaint and old-fashioned, but certainly not the sort of person to give Frau Schemel a concern."

Helmut said, "Yes, I have that noted, thank you. Finally, let's move on to the last on your list, this Norwegian, Tippi Olson."

He now had what he wanted. A plan would be put in place that would not be communicated outside his team until hours before the start of the Stuyvesant lecture. At that point a range of technical experts would be working, agents ready to enter Hintzen's home using very careful and unorthodox means. Most important, Herr Doctor Arndt of BKA, his Excellency the Most High, would be walking unannounced into the suite of the Director of the Fraunhofer Institute in Stuttgart demanding complete co-operation with his department.

27 IMAGE THREE

Arno was pondering the structure of the next image that Marilyn Greaves had ordered. He was concerned. He had not so far withdrawn from a project once undertaken. True, he had rejected several at the first meeting with the client; he had just declined, stood up and walked away. But so far for any project he had started he had provided the agreed product to the customer.

As with all his contracts, he did some careful enquiries about the target and monitored anything in internet traffic that could indicate whether he or his client were about to be identified. Without Greaves saying, and well before the announcement by Janis Mitchell at the college, he was already aware that the police had identified the college studio where the images of the student had been obtained. He doubted that Greaves would have used gloves when placing or retrieving the camera so it is likely that they could identify her in time, if they had found her fingerprints. So far they had not fingerprinted Greaves or her classmates, he was sure. He had others in the same line of work as him able to check.

He wasn't too worried about that aspect; it was the risk she took and accepted, he knew. And they wouldn't reach him through Greaves. He didn't want to reject the third image assignment but he was worried about the project failing. One more image wasn't going to do the trick with the target, he had concluded.

Marilyn had left the creation of the image to him specifying only certain points, as previously. Her request was that Philip Staley should be clearly identified in the photo, that he should be watching unconcerned as his granddaughter was being assaulted by someone else. She had misgivings, she said, about making him the rapist only because they were family. He had misgivings too, because he felt that Staley would ignore this image as well, no matter what it was; he knew the type he was now. He was unconvinced by Marilyn's report of 'extreme family anguish'; he felt it did not extend as far as Philip Staley and never would.

Yet he knew this was the last kick at the can for Greaves financially and perhaps before detection. He wanted her to win.

His solution went down a different track and was only partly developed. He had done some checking and felt there was an opportunity to discredit, albeit unfairly, Staley's professional reputation as an artist. Evidence of plagiarism could be placed, damaging his artistic status in a manner that would take years to dispute and correct; years that the old man didn't have left. It would take more work than a third image but he wasn't bothered about the cost, he was concerned about the delivery. It had to be someone tougher than Greaves, prepared to meet Staley in person and hit him hard with it; a one-shot, no-other-option decision; confess or die with everyone thinking your art is not original. Which legacy do you want to be in tatters?

Strangely enough, he knew someone who would do exactly that. For two thousand euros including travel costs, the man would go from Holland to Cornwall and be quite effective in delivering the message. He would even break the man's legs if he refused, for that sum, if asked, given his sister's experience. He knew what Greaves had been through and Arno had resolved this person's own project very satisfactorily. Hintzen was even prepared to cover it out of the total proceeds from Greaves.

But it was such a different direction than Marilyn Greaves had made in her new request. He would prefer to talk to her in person about it and wondered if she would travel back to Brussels to do so.

In the end he left it open. He had the Stuyvesant lecture tomorrow and would deal with the matter once that was behind him. He was looking forward to the discussion with Aaron Stuyvesant. Then he mused, hopefully he would move on to some discussions with Greaves and a man called Johan Dirickson.

28 STUYVESANT

The following week Catrin had returned to work and was given fresh assignments. She was pleased with the way Sylvia McNair and Neville Coltrane had welcomed and admired the platters on Sunday; she and Jean felt they had accomplished well the commission and that felt good.

At the Monday briefing Catrin received news that the V&A Museum had completed the restoration work on the kris but the painting was taking a little longer. There had been some debate with the Malaysians on what level of restoration was required. But it was progressing.

Worsley muttered something about hoping the Datuk Jerome Allam was in good health; if they take much longer Catrin would have the embarrassing job of formally transferring the items to his heirs.

On Wednesday morning Catrin was at her desk when her phone rang. As she picked it up she heard Worsley's voice say, "I am patching you in, Catrin," then she heard more noise and Worsley say, "I have DS Sayer on the line now."

She heard Hicks' voice first.

"DS Sayer, its DI Hicks here. I have DS Wastle and Mr. Treneer with me. DI Steadman is also on-line. We now have a connection between Greaves and a German national in Stuttgart. We think the link is solid and simultaneous arrests are in preparation. We would like you to assist in the arrests here, if you would."

Catrin looked across the office area towards Worsley's goldfish bowl of a private office. Worsley was looking back and nodding at her, with a grimace; a go ahead to say 'yes', albeit reluctantly, was the message.

"Yes sir, how can I help?"

Her first thought was she would be back in Cornwall, seeing Chris in person.

Catrin had been rushed in a police car to her flat in Spitalfields. It waited for her while she packed a case and then took her to Paddington in time to catch the Exeter train the same afternoon. Chris had met her there and taken her to his flat.

"You will need to check in sometime at the hotel," he said. "DI Hicks is collecting you in the morning."

She thought about it.

"Is it a problem for you if around here we are known to be a couple? We don't work for the same employer and there is no conflict of interest that I see. So it's not a problem for me, according to the Met policy. I checked."

"No," he said. He stopped, "I will get some smiles, but I would love it to be known, to be honest."

She picked up her mobile and called the hotel, cancelling the reservation. Then she sent a text to Hicks saying she was staying with Chris Treneer, not at the hotel; he would bring her into headquarters or she would be available at any time for collection from his address.

His text back was brief. 'See you tomorrow at the office. Welcome back to Cornwall.'

At the briefing the following morning the work assignments were given after the review of the status of the arrest plans. Sergeant Wastle and Catrin were to arrest Marilyn Greaves and execute the search warrant with a SOCO team. The timing was important; Chris was to be on-line and available with Steadman's team, who in turn would be liaising with the German police in the arrest at their end. That was to be executed first.

Later Catrin and DI Hicks would go to Totnes to talk to the Staley couple; a last chance to let them co-operate. Pender had suggested it but not admitted that it may have come from Superintendent Mitchell himself.

Hicks said, "Sayer, your specific role at this stage is to look out for any relevant art-related elements linking to the images or vase, either during the arrests, in the interviews or at the locations. You have a nose for it.

"The arrests are timed for 1.00 p.m. here, 2.00 p.m. in Stuttgart; the hacker will be in a situation where he can't access his computer and... arrangements have been made.

"Greaves is at home. A car did a circuit and they saw her vehicle there just ten minutes ago. Her husband is home too; his car is in there also. If they go out anywhere, we will know."

DS Wastle said, "Also, the report from Dr. Ryder is in. There is nothing substantial to add from the preliminary comments for us other than one thing. She warned us that people with such extreme obsessions on revenge often see this as the finale to their life work, that they can also be suicidal. We need to watch out for that. She had a lot more comments on the psych profile of 'Adrestia', but those will be sent over to the German police after the arrests."

Hicks finished, "We will be shuttling across Cornwall a lot today; let's get moving."

The 'nose' for the art element was why Hicks had wanted Sayer involved, he had told Worsley, before she brought Catrin into the conference call. "Sometimes these intangible aspects can be really important."

"Yes," said Jane, not bothering to conceal the irony in her voice. "That's why I brought her into the ACU team."

Matheson was going to owe her and Jack Taylor big time, she thought, but had left that one alone at present. Once Catrin had departed she called John Obi into her office.

"John, Catrin is going back to Cornwall at short notice so, you are now on the Fallon case. I want…"

~~

Hintzen looked up at the tiered seating of the main lecture theatre at the Fraunhofer Institute. He recognized the students there taking his course this year and other faces he recognized from past years, plus some faculty members; people who were re-visiting this particular lecture. The theatre was by no means full, but it was a good attendance, he felt. The 'Stuyvesant' lecture was still a magnet for people.

Aaron Stuyvesant, his invited guest and co-lecturer for the hour, was a professor of ethics at the Humboldt University, Berlin. Their dialogue and differences, including the occasional biting jab, made for entertainment value as much as course content for many of the students.

In the audiovisual room at the back of the theatre a single plain-clothes police officer stood with the AV technician, waiting. Just as the introductions were made and the two lecturers had seated themselves on the adjacent tall stools he spoke into his phone once.

The side entry doors at each side of the stage opened and a mix of uniformed and plain clothes officers entered, causing Arno to break his introductory comments mid-sentence. In the rear of the auditorium a voice said, "I have lost connection".

The speaker looked up from his tablet screen. He realised that his voice was audible to others as the background noise had suddenly stopped.

Arno glanced at both sides of the room and reached into his inside pocket for his phone. Somehow the look on the small man in a suit on the corridor side of the theatre made it clear. 'Go ahead, press any button you want, we won't stop you.' No-one rushed him. Signals to and from the theatre had been blocked, he realised.

The man said, "Professor Hintzen, if you would be so good as to accompany us? It would be appreciated."

The implication was clear; he would be handcuffed and arrested centre-stage as an alternative.

He rose off the stool, looked at Stuyvesant and saw a look in his eyes. Aaron knew this would happen, he realised. He had been set up by the police to help with this trap.

Hintzen said, "Professor Stuyvesant, if you would care to present a monologue rather than our dialogue this year, please. I think you are prepared for this?"

Stuyvesant just nodded, clearly unhappy with the whole situation.

Half-way back in the audience, Gerda recognized the small man and wondered why Herr Feil was walking into the lecture with police officers. She had wondered if he would attend, given their discussion, but if he did so she thought he would turn up with his iPad and keyboard, taking copious notes again. Then she thought back to the interview and, catching on at last, that it was about setting a trap, she looked at Professor Hintzen's face as he left. He seemed unconcerned.

Arno walked over towards the side door, stopped, turned to his students and said, "If you will excuse me."

As he reached the door the small man in the suit said. "Your phone, please. Before we leave the room."

Arno saw that this man knew that the signal sent from his mobile to his home would set in motion certain actions that would ensure no records of anything were found on his computers.

He passed his phone over and the man immediately removed the battery, placing both items in a small case held by a police officer; presumably additional shielding, Arno thought. He was trying to be optimistic. There were other traps installed anyway; someone would have to be very good not to trip those, he thought. He hoped that they weren't.

As they left the room and the door closed slowly on its dampened hinges he heard Professor Stuyvesant begin his talk, trying to restore the session to its purpose. An officer took Arno's hands behind his back and handcuffed him. Another plain-clothes officer searched him thoroughly and professionally as they stood there, a huddled group in the doorway.

No-one said anything to him there or as they left the Institute by a side door.

29 ARRESTS

The fleet of vehicles with the detectives, the SOCOs and several regular police cars turned into Carlyon Road in Truro. With the cars already parked along the pavement, they effectively blocked the road in front of the Greaves' home. Treneer had just passed on Steadman's comment. "They got Hintzen without problem and his systems are intact so far."

Wastle reminded them of the plan as they walked smartly up the path to the cream stucco-fronted home. He knocked vigorously at the door, "Any delay, we go in anyway - and fast."

But the door was opened promptly by the husband, Callum Greaves, looking first annoyed at the severity of the knock from the caller then astonished as he saw the mix of people, officers in plain-clothes showing warrant cards and others in uniform, all lined up on his front path. Wastle and Sayer pressed in, Catrin being the slimmer of the two brushing quickly past the man.

Oliver Wastle said, "We need to speak to Mrs. Greaves now, please."

Callum Greaves said, "She is in the kitchen. We are finishing lunch, but what...."

Catrin entered the kitchen. Marilyn Greaves was standing up looking somehow both anxious and angry.

Marilyn looked at the police officer who entered, a young female detective, and registered immediately that this woman knew. She cursed her own vacillation. She should have acted immediately she heard the commotion at the door. Her delay was simply a passing thought; perhaps they are doing interviews, perhaps there is still time to hear whether Philip has finally said anything, to see if it was all worthwhile.

But there was still time. She just needed to handle it right.

Then the older detective came in and she saw the others behind. Perhaps she was out of luck.

"Mrs. Greaves, I am Detective Sergeant Wastle, Devon & Cornwall Police," he said, without preamble. "Marilyn Greaves, I am arresting you on the suspicion that you conspired to commit assaults. You do not have to say anything. But it may harm your defense..."

Marilyn Greaves plonked herself down in the kitchen chair as her husband said indignantly, "That is bloody outrageous. What the hell is this about?"

Wastle's voice had a commanding tone. "Be quiet until I finish cautioning Mrs. Greaves, sir."

He continued. As he finished the statement Marilyn said, "I need to go the bathroom, please, I feel sick ... please give me a moment."

She started to move but Catrin had placed herself in the doorway from the kitchen through to the lounge. As Marilyn reached her she took one arm and neatly handcuffed her. She took her other hand and finished the job.

Catrin said, "You will have to use the sink, I am afraid. At least until we check the bathroom."

The two SOCOs were now in the house waiting for the go-ahead. Catrin called, "The downstairs bathroom, check there first. And check for pills, sharp objects, whatever else she could use."

Callum Greaves was livid. "I want a lawyer and you, you...," he said to Catrin, "I want you charged or disciplined. This is unacceptable, barbaric; treating my wife this way. She is going to be sick, let her go to the bathroom, please."

Wastle said, "Take a seat, Mr. Greaves, please. We will wait a moment and see. We have a search warrant." He produced it and passed it to the man. They all looked at Marilyn.

Marilyn Greaves didn't vomit after all. She just stood there and looked at her husband but said nothing.

Several minutes later a white-suited SOCO called for Wastle and he went out, returning with a labelled plastic bag containing a bottle of pills.

Wastle examined them and said, "These aren't a prescription medication, it seems; can either of you tell me who they belong to? What they are for?"

He looked at them closely. "The capsules are coated and marked, so it won't take us long really to find the answer, you know."

Catrin saw the husband was nonplussed. She looked at Marilyn Greaves.

She said, "Mrs. Greaves? We know, so...."

The woman looked at Catrin and said impassively, "You spoilt everything. They are mine and I think you know what they are for."

Sergeant Wastle said to Catrin, "They were inside a box of tampons in the cupboard below the sink, not in the medicine cabinet above it."

Greaves looked at her husband. "Callum, I am sorry, there is a lot I need ..."

He interrupted her harshly. "Marilyn, say nothing. Nothing, not now. Nothing until I get Peter with you, do you hear?"

He turned to Wastle. "Peter Albright is our family solicitor. I want him present, no-one else, not your duty lawyer! Peter; understand?"

His voice had risen, a little desperate. He had just realised that there were substantive charges against his wife.

Sergeant Wastle said, "Please do so, Mr. Greaves; that would help. We will be taking Mrs. Greaves to the Falmouth police station, tell him. We will question her there."

As they stood up to take her out, Marilyn Greaves said to Catrin, "Why?"

The question was implicit. Why stop her from going to the bathroom.

Catrin thought whether to say anything or not. Then she responded, "There is a young woman who doesn't understand this. I hope you will explain why. Let's go."

The two officers led Greaves to the patrol car outside, passing her into the custody of the two uniformed officers. Neighbours were watching; curtains and blinds were twitching. Callum Greaves was on the phone speaking to someone in his lawyer's office.

They went back inside and waited until he had finished. He looked at them, uncertain what to do now, beaten by something he didn't understand and the speed of events. The SOCOs were moving through the house.

"Mr. Greaves," said Oliver, "You will need to come in for questioning also. Please get your coat, you can ride with me."

"No handcuffs?" he said derisively to Catrin.

Wastle looked at him. "Mr. Greaves, Sergeant Sayer may have just saved your wife's life, I think. Get your coat."

The man looked even more astonished.

Catrin went on a brief survey of the house. She said nothing to the forensic people; they knew what they were looking for and she saw nothing visible herself in the walk through. She hadn't expected to. As she turned away she had the thought.

"Check her paint box and art supplies, including the pages in her sketchpad, everything. And take apart any painting that is framed."

She didn't have long to wait. "The lead SOCO came over to her, "It wasn't in her art supplies, DS Sayer. This one was in the back of a family photograph upstairs, once we took off the back plate."

It was the first photo prepared by Hintzen, a good quality print now in a clear plastic evidence bag.

He said, "They are still looking for the other one. It's probably here."

"Thank you," she said. She was concentrating on what Marilyn Greaves could have done with the vase.

She went outside and around the back. Catrin saw DI Hicks with a SOCO in the large garden shed. He had said he would turn up, but he had wanted Wastle to make the arrest. At the briefing he had said, "Oliver, you led the investigation; you bring her in." Clearly he wanted the credit for the case to go on his sergeant's record.

"I think it is going to be here or in the attic," Hicks said.

"The vase, sir?"

He nodded.

He said nothing for a minute, then, "What if she didn't keep it?"

Catrin said, "I doubt she would sell it or give it away... she kept the images. We have found the first, at least, hidden inside a painting."

They looked at each other, realizing the same thing at the same time.

"Look for any broken pottery, anything like that," said Hicks.

Catrin added, "And any dust which could be ceramic residues - and bag and check every hammer or blunt instrument that could be used to break up a vase."

Hicks said, "And check the grounds for any digging. She may have buried it, or buried the pieces."

He led the way out of the shed and stood still.

"You and Chris Treneer have hit it off, then," he said suddenly.

She smiled. "Yes, we have; does that cause any problems?"

"No," he replied, "I wish you both well. Even if he is a geek."

She looked at him and saw the impudent expression on his face. For the first time she smiled at him properly, at ease with the man.

She said, "We are going to break into your bank account and run away with the take to live on the Isle of Man."

He let out a hearty laugh.

"Good luck with that. What's there won't keep you for long, it's an expensive place. You should come to Cornwall. Or he will have to go to London, I suppose."

"We haven't thought that far ahead, sir, to be honest," she said.

But it was a good point. She had been wondering about it herself.

She looked at Stephen Hicks. He had treated her well after the first encounter. She thought that for some reason she was a 'flag in the ground' to him in his efforts to improve his people management skills and behavior; a case in which he was on show not only to Devon & Cornwall senior staff but to the Met. A lot of visibility. What would matter most now was how he behaved with his own team next time, on the next case when it was local, when no-one else involved.

"Time to hit the road, head over to Totnes," he said, "We don't want to keep the professor waiting, do we?"

"No," said Catrin, "He's not waiting for us, but I have been waiting for this. It's time."

~~

At the Staley home the same three people, Professor and Mrs. Staley and Katharine Sully, ended up in the same conservatory. Staley glared at DI Hicks and ignored Catrin.

"I still don't know why you are here now. You say you have arrested a former student of mine, Samuels, for the stupidity against my granddaughter and also some German who helped her. Good. You should be interviewing them, not me."

The expression on the inspector's face showed he was

having none of Staley's bellicose behavior. Hicks said evenly but forcefully, "We are here because we believe that the motive behind the action is tied to her time as a model at Dartington College. She modelled for you, in private. The vase in the images with Janis was in the college in your office, actually found by your secretary in a cupboard. We are giving you the opportunity to tell us anything that could help in the enquiry, to assist the prosecution of this case.

"So, Professor Staley; did you and Marilyn Greaves, Samuels as she was then, have a relationship? Did your interactions in some way form the basis for this bizarre action?"

Staley snapped back, "You will have to ask her that. I don't know what is in this woman's mind."

Catrin was watching Mrs. Staley. Whether she knew her husband had been involved with another woman wasn't clear; but the expression on her face was not shock; it was fear.

Hicks nodded at Catrin. She pulled out a folder and from it she extracted the photograph of the vase. Then she walked over to the abstract painting on the wall and held it adjacent to the painting. The contour and pattern in the vase matched exactly.

She ignored Professor Staley completely, focusing on his wife.

"The images of your granddaughter that were placed on the internet contained this vase; the one Professor Staley included in Series Eight; his heyday, as he said to me. In the first image it was buried, tantalizing its extraction; in the second it was made visible. It is important symbolism for Mrs. Greaves, who we believe committed this act."

The older woman looked at her. Then she looked down, saying nothing for a few seconds. She then let out a sob and said, "I can't help you."

Hicks said to Philip Staley, "Last chance, sir. We came today before we interviewed Marilyn Greaves out of courtesy, to you and your wife. And also from professional courtesy to your son-in-law, in a manner of speaking. This is an opportunity for you to help us voluntarily. It could count for a lot down the road because, believe me, this investigation is going to have repercussions on you, I do not doubt. Do you understand?"

The old man said, "Inspector, I have nothing more to say and, if you speak to me again in that manner I will want my solicitor present."

Hicks stopped talking and stood very still. Catrin knew it was over. He had tried. Superintendent Mitchell would appreciate the effort but he knew his father-in-law; he probably understood that the opening to co-operate would fall on deaf ears. The chance to make this easier for everyone was gone.

Hicks' voice took on a formal, impassive tone.

"When I speak to you again, sir, I would advise you to have your lawyer present. Thank you for your co-operation, at least in that regard. Sayer, call them in."

Catrin was looking at the wife. What is it, she thought, that this woman is so beaten and controlled by her husband? She thought of Chris, thinking, I will never let our relationship get like this.

"I thought you were leaving," snapped Philip Staley.

"We are just starting, sir," said Hicks, hearing Catrin go to the front door and call in the uniforms and SOCOs who were waiting in vehicles outside.

He pulled out a sheet of paper.

"Philip Staley, this is search warrant for this house in connection with our enquiries. We are looking for copies of these two images - he nodded to Catrin - who pulled them from her folder, passing them to him. He slammed them on to the desk.

"And we will take any items relevant to your potential involvement with Marilyn Greaves that would assist our enquiries; including that painting and others like it."

Mrs. Staley automatically turned her head away as Hicks moved back from the desk and the images were more visible. The housekeeper looked at them and let out a gasp, "Oh no. I can't -"

Her voice trailed off. She went over to Mrs. Staley and put her arm around her shoulder.

Staley fumed. "I am calling my son-in-law. You will hear about this."

DI Hicks said, "He is at home. He is voluntarily taking time off today to be totally unconnected while this case is proceeding. He made that call himself, informing the Chief Superintendent yesterday evening. You can reach him there."

Catrin said to the housekeeper, "Mrs. Sully, please accompany Mr. and Mrs. Staley through to the kitchen; this study and the bedrooms will be searched first."

Staley went silently through to the kitchen. He was thinking of what to say to his lawyer. At least the two journals and their images he had received from Samuels, as he thought of her, were long gone. They would find nothing at the house, not even the envelopes they came in. He reminded himself that it was all about proof. That's what James had said in the past about police work. Proof. And they had none.

30 INTERVIEW

They had placed Marilyn Greaves on suicide watch overnight. She was brought into the interview room in Falmouth Police Station at 9.00 a.m. the following morning where, through a camera, the police officers watched her lawyer, Albright, sit talking with her. Though they couldn't hear the conversation, they saw he was trying to reach her, calm her agitation, assessing her body language as much as her silence.

DS Wastle and DS Sayer waited for Stephen Hicks to reach a decision. Finally he said, "Sayer, I think Oliver is right. I wish he wasn't, but you go in and do the first phase alone. Soften her up."

He was itching to do it himself, they both knew.

"Yes, sir," she said.

Catrin went into the interview room carrying a file folder, sat across from Greaves and Albright and switched on the recorder.

"DS Sayer, Metropolitan Police Art Crime Unit entering the room at 09.14. Also present is... please state your names for the record."

The lawyer and Greaves both did so and then the lawyer said, "DS Sayer, if my client is to be interviewed, a member of the Devon & Cornwall Police should conduct it or at least be present, I believe."

Catrin said, "Mr. Albright, we agree. I am not going to ask Mrs. Greaves any questions."

She opened the folder and pulled out the prints of the photographs in the sealed, transparent evidence bags. They were quite clear through the plastic.

"Mrs. Greaves, we found these two photographs hidden on your premises, images that were separately used to assault another woman over the internet. And we found one of your fingerprints at the location in the studio where the camera was positioned; not on a desk or a chair near ground level, I might add. It was on a lighting rack higher up. You will be questioned about these findings."

She waited a moment, watching the woman look at the photographs.

"I am a specialist in Art Crime. So I was interested to see if the search team would also find the vase. This one here."

She pointed it out on each photograph for the lawyer.

"They didn't. And I know you bought the vase."

She placed the copy of the sales record from Dartington Hall in front of them. She waited again, watching, looking for a response.

"We didn't find the vase but we also suggested to the search team that they look at anything in the home that could logically be used to smash one. We found the hammer. We are lucky that your husband has good tools in his garden shed; his hammer is a nice old one, he has looked after it. Like all rough-forged metal, the hammer has crevices and gaps in the head. A forensic team is going to analyze the white powder in those crevices and check all the fingerprints on the hammer."

She looked at the lawyer then back at Marilyn Greaves.

"I suspect they will find porcelain dust. I am a ceramic artist so I know what that looks like, you see. They won't find the vase because there is not even a small shard left, I think. You laboriously reduced every piece of it to powder after you took the photographs. But we now know who made it and when it was made, so the forensic technicians can examine similar vases from the same artist, scrape some powder from the base, do the analyses and, I think, come up with a probable match. But it will only be probable because they will never find the vase in the photograph."

She had almost said, 'Will they?' at the end but caught herself. No questions yet.

Greaves face started to look apprehensive.

Catrin looked at Peter Albright who was clearly engaged in where this was going. He was getting more from the police than from his own client.

"Still no questions, Mr. Albright."

He nodded.

"When the forensic team identifies your fingerprints on the hammer, as I think they will, as well as the residues, you will be questioned about that. What would induce a woman to be involved in an assault in this manner? Place an image of a vase in the picture; as a symbol, so to speak, but then meticulously reduce the same valuable piece of pottery to dust?"

She leaned forward slightly, towards Greaves, increasing the momentum.

"Revenge, at least, a strange sense of revenge. That is what it means to me. Look."

From the folder she withdrew five prints. Each one was of a painting, part of the series of abstract paintings by Philip G. Staley. Several were from the 'Series Eight' collection. Others were in the same style completed at later dates. Through each one Catrin had drawn one or more lines and she had also had outlined the shape of the vase.

She laid them out in sequence; the lawyer looking puzzled as Greaves started to cry, unable to avert her gaze.

Catrin ignored the tears. "I am not sure whether it was simply ironic coincidence or deliberation which led to one of the 30 second poses of Janis Mitchell for the first attack. They are called gesture lines. You can do these, Mr. Albright, with a human model or with any art image, really, as Mrs. Greaves knows."

She pointed to the second painting in the sequence. "This is my speculation, but I think this is you; from the timing of the painting being completed and the gesture line matching the pose in the first photograph placed on Janis Mitchell's web site; they match up pretty well. See the lines; I think I know how he had sex with you, even the position. I wonder what the reason for revenge was; a discarded lover? Assault perhaps? I don't know. You will be asked about that too."

She lined the two images; the print with the painting marked with the gesture lines alongside the first image placed on Janis Mitchell's web site, then pushed them closer to Greaves. The woman's head was bowed now, the tears hitting her blouse. Peter Albright was sizing up the two images, putting it all together.

Catrin sat back and stopped. Her voice had softened in the last statement and in response Greaves raised her head, used the back of her hand to wipe her eyes. Catrin reached into her pocket and passed over an unopened pack of tissues.

"I can see the gesture lines in some of the others. They were all painted at different times and convey the same sort of event to me, albeit different positions."

She had her now; Catrin could see it in her eyes.

"Now, I must admit, I don't know if it was you or a different woman, each time; if each student or whomever held the vase or was involved with it in some way. I suspect not; I think it was just you, possibly one other person earlier on involved directly with the vase, if the painting dates are correct. But it became a motif, a collector's symbol for him, our psychiatric expert suggests. Something he used as a reference point. But I am sure you had physical contact with the vase at the time; otherwise why would you make such an elaborate song and dance about the symbolism?"

"But this is pure speculation, interpretation that would give lawyers a field day in court. Isn't that so, Mr. Albright?"

The lawyer looked at her and nodded, 'That is true, Sergeant, this sort of thing is highly debatable."

His voice was neutral but it conveyed he had received in a matter of several minutes a lot of insight into the reason why his client had received such an unexpected and unusual charge.

Catrin picked up all the photographs slowly. "Eight paintings in his first series; then he produced others in the same vein at different times later in his career after the first gallery exhibition. Not all of them are linked to gesture lines of women, of course, but how many are? How many in total from what Philip G. Staley calls his 'heyday' or later; how many hiding a similar experience, burying it? I don't know."

She closed the folder.

"Yesterday I held the image of the vase from your photograph against the original of Number Two of Series Eight - it was in the Staley study, on his wall directly across from his desk. Your image. He was asked about the link with you and he denied totally any role in this matter while his partially-paralyzed wife appeared to me to be in total fear. We won't learn a thing from him, or from her, I think."

She stood up.

"DI Hicks and DS Wastle will shortly come in to interview you about all of this, Mrs. Greaves."

She reached over and retrieved the opened pack of tissues. No plastic items for a person on suicide watch, including tissue packaging. Those were the rules.

"DS Sayer exiting the room at 09.37."

She moved out quietly, closing the door gently on the sobs behind her.

They waited, watched them talking. Eventually Albright stood up and opened the door. Hicks went into the corridor to meet him.

"Inspector Hicks, Mrs. Greaves will make a statement on record as part of interview. I am going to ask that arrangements be made for her to be given access to psychiatric counselling."

Hicks nodded. "We will ask for Dr Ryder to see her as soon as possible; you know her? She can recommend a colleague separately, if you wish."

Albright replied, "Agreed. Mrs. Greaves also requests Sergeant Sayer to be present during the interview. I know it's your choice, of course, and I gather that was not the plan."

He returned to the interview room.

Hicks sat with his colleagues and looked at Catrin. "You made a strong impact. She thinks you understand."

He sighed.

"Oliver, do you want to lead; it's your case? I think we should use Catrin's rapport, as Albright said. I will sit it out."

Catrin and Oliver Wastle looked at each other. They could tell Hicks was struggling with this.

Wastle shook his head. "Sir, I would rather watch from outside, frankly. It isn't going to be easy. You are the best one to do this, with DS Sayer."

He looked at Catrin. She smiled at him, nodded.

"Ready, Catrin?" said Stephen Hicks. "Let's go in, then."

The two police officers with their file folders went into the interview room.

~~

After they had settled and identified themselves for the record, DI Hicks said, "I believe that you want to begin with a statement, Mrs. Greaves."

She nodded, clearing her throat.

"Yes. I arranged for the images, two images to be made and placed on the web sites, as you know. I also sent them to Philip with notes telling him to own up to what he did to me. But he hasn't. He should."

Catrin thought that was simply the opening sentence of something longer, so as the growing silence and body language made it clear that she was not simply collecting her thoughts, Catrin looked at DI Hicks. He was watching Greaves carefully, perfectly aware that the silence was dragging on. But still he waited.

Peter Albright leaned towards his client and said, "Do you want to say more, Marilyn?"

Clearly, he too was expecting something more substantive in this opening statement.

She looked at him and said evenly, "I said I did it. That's it."

DI Hicks said quietly, "Mrs. Greaves, we are going to ask you a lot of questions about this matter. We can start now or you can speak freely. Let me suggest at this point that you look directly at DS Sayer. You asked for her to be present so you may as well talk to her. Tell her what you mean by the phrase 'what he did to me'. It doesn't have to be fancy, just say what you mean by that."

He looked at Catrin, making it clear that she should take the lead now. The plan the officers had come up with earlier was for DI Hicks first to take Greaves through the chain of events in the attacks on Janis, then for Wastle to go into the reasons why. Now all that was out the window.

Marilyn Greaves looked at Catrin, kept her eyes on her. After a moment she sighed and then spoke softly.

"I was nineteen. I thought the world of Professor Staley. You may or may not know I modelled for the college as well as for him in private and I thought his work was so... it was a privilege to be part of it. He did mainly abstracts. Sometimes the model was clear, sometimes not. It didn't matter to me. I loved his art and his teaching, his humour, his brash self-confidence.

"Secretly, ironically it turned out, I wished he was mine; my husband, my lover. Sometimes when I talked with Caroline, I felt guilty about my daydreams, wanting to interfere in what was a wonderful family, dreaming about being 'another woman' in his life. But it was fantasy; I was young."

She swallowed hard, getting the worst out into the open.

"What I hadn't wanted was for him to be my rapist; to drug me, rape me and then tell me that he would ruin me if I ever told a soul. It was a modelling session on a Saturday afternoon in his office. The faculty area was virtually deserted.

"I don't know what he gave me; he had given me a small glass of wine. He was sipping at one himself when I arrived, talking about its quality; I knew nothing about vintages or that sort of thing. It was the weekend, he said.

"When I came to he was standing up, fastening his pants. I was lying face down across the coffee table as I came to my senses and saw first, of all things, the bloody vase. I then remembered him pounding at me, as if it was a dream. For some stupid reason, half-sensible, I had one hand on the vase; I didn't want it to fall off and break. It was valuable, I thought. He had finished even as I thought about struggling."

Catrin could see she was back in the event; the horror and disdain were on her face; for Staley and for herself, perhaps.

"It must have taken that long for whatever he gave me to wear off. He just sat back in his desk chair; said nothing at first, didn't seem bothered at all. I put my robe on and stood there, wanting to leave but wanting to know why; why like that! So I asked him.

"He told me it was my smile, the 'come-on', the way I wanted it. He had given in to 'his instincts'; that was the phrase he used. It was my fault. Everyone knew I was lusting after him, he said."

She paused.

"My last memory, my last good memory before the rape, was holding my pose, hand stretched out, fingers touching the vase as he had requested, eager to see what he had painted. That was similar to the pose in the second picture. I thought he valued me as a person, a good model; but I was just a body; for painting, for sex."

Catrin saw that Dr. Ryder was right; the Hirst image modifications were about being treated like meat. The 'P' carved into the image of Staley's granddaughter was about this woman's feeling of violation.

"When I eventually saw his painting, it was in a magazine article in the College library. All I could see was me, that line you drew, me, across the coffee table. I didn't even get to the bathroom before I threw up. For everyone else except him, I wasn't there; I wasn't even in it. That was the big joke."

She stopped, done.

"What did you do after the assault?" Catrin asked.

"I went back into the private washroom attached to his office where I had changed into my robe before posing. I splashed my face with cold water to wake up fully. I remember that in the mirror, apart from the tears, I looked no different. But I was. I then dressed and went out through his secretary's office, went back to my room and cried. I told myself to forget it. Completely. Never accept it, but never think about it.

"I didn't model again; I finished my course but never went to a class involving him. I ignored him on campus, just as he seemed oblivious to me. He had strung me on his belt; he was done with me, I think.

"I never told a soul this much about it until I told the man who made the images and posted them. But I am not saying more about him. I will admit my part, that's all."

Hicks said, "Dr. Hintzen is in custody in Stuttgart, with enough evidence on him already. Your information, when we come to it, will simply be dotting the 'i's.'"

He placed a photo of Hintzen on the table. Marilyn Greaves' eyes registered that she recognized the man.

She said, "I didn't even know his name."

Hicks said, "How did you find him?"

Greaves looked at him. "Well, he doesn't advertise. But I was at a woman's retreat during a… difficult time for me. I talked with another woman there; not the details I talked to you about, but I told her that I had been raped years ago as a student and so much wanted to get the man, now years older, to acknowledge it and apologize. But he never would, I was sure.

"She understood, I think, for similar reasons. She worked in computers, I know. Out of the blue the man called me and explained he had heard of my situation and told me he would help me, at a price. I spent ages thinking about it before I called him back.

"I had just started the course and I saw Janis Mitchell; she is just like her mother Caroline at that age, you know? It was a coincidence but once I confirmed who it was, I saw immediately how he could now help me."

"I thought that there might be others and… if he saw the photograph, he wouldn't know who sent it, perhaps. He would just tell the police the reason for it. But he would have known, from what you said earlier; he would know it was me. Number Two of Series Eight. I am glad about that."

She stopped, shrugged.

Hicks took a breath. "Anything else that you want to say before we begin our questions?"

Greaves said nothing for a moment, just looked at her

lawyer. He knew that the detailed interview was about to start.

Then suddenly she said to Catrin, "You understand, don't you?"

She was looking for validation, Catrin thought. She wasn't going to get it.

She answered quietly, "What I understand, Mrs. Greaves, is that you worked with a computer expert to figuratively rape a young woman in retaliation for an alleged actual rape many years ago. What I don't understand is how you came to do that; to think that the only option to address your grievance was to perpetrate the same type of crime, in a sense, rather than seek help. I don't understand that."

Greaves looked at her, sad rather than angry.

She said, "If I had gone to the police with my complaint back in the early nineties with no more evidence than the story I told you now, what do you think would have happened?"

Nothing, Catrin reflected, probably. No witnesses, no evidence; a moonstruck student and a lecturer she was known to adore. It would be his word against hers.

She just looked back, saying nothing.

DI Hicks gave the answer. "Marilyn, I don't know. But you could have given us an opportunity, then or later. There are enough retrospective cases like this in the news these days to suggest that you could expect some reasonable hearing. At least you wouldn't be sitting here now, in the trouble you are in."

Marilyn Greaves said, "Funnily enough, I don't care about that. I don't even feel I am here, in a sense. I haven't been here for a long time now. I am just treading water, waiting to drown."

She suddenly looked at Catrin hostilely. "And you

didn't even let me do that."

Catrin thought, she looks normal; sounds normal, but her family solicitor was probably right when he asked for a psychiatrist. He was on the ball on that.

Hicks started the questions.

31 ABSTRACT ART

In Totnes the following morning a uniformed officer driving a Range Rover parked near the Staley home. Inside the vehicle were four other people; Superintendent Mitchell, his wife Caroline, his daughter Janis and Catrin Sayer. Catrin had driven Janis Mitchell over from Falmouth to meet up with her parents there. The uniformed officer had driven her parents from Exeter; neither one was in good shape for the task after the full ramifications of the attack on their daughter had been shared with them. A sick woman seeking revenge for a long-past affair was one thing; the revelations from the interview with Marilyn Greaves and Catrin Sayer's interpretation of the paintings were something else.

Hicks and Wastle emerged from the house with two uniformed officers. They led Philip Staley slowly over to the police car at the curb, not pressing his pace at all as he trudged forward silently. He had just been cautioned regarding the sexual assault of Marilyn Greaves and would be formally charged in Exeter.

As the various vehicles drove away, Catrin said, "We

should go in now, sir."

She made the call. James Mitchell had insisted that he was simply a member of the family on this; he was giving no instructions.

They entered to find the young female PC the team had left behind with Mrs. Staley and the housekeeper. The two women looked stunned.

Catrin stood back with the officer as the family greeted each other and Mrs. Staley said to her granddaughter, "I'm sorry, I should have realised…"

"Shush, Gran," said the younger woman, hugging her grandmother, "It's OK. Everything is going to be sorted out now, honest. I promise."

She paused.

"I am just one in a long line, I think."

Her grandmother looked at her, absorbing the comment but said nothing for a moment. Then she looked at her daughter and her son-in-law, totally lost. "What do I do now?"

James Mitchell said, 'We talk as a family. But unless you tell me you want Philip back here, he isn't returning to this house. We can make that part of his bail conditions. Janis wants to move in with you. She thinks it would be good for both of you. Caroline and I agree, in principle; but only if you want it, too."

Janis nodded at her grandmother, smiling, speaking gently. "Gran, Dad is buying me a car, he said. His idea was that I can commute; spend part of the week in Falmouth for lectures, part in Exeter, at home, if I wanted.

"But what would be good, I think, is if I could stay here with you for the part of the week I am not in Falmouth. The drive is about the same from Totnes as from Exeter and… we haven't spent time together, really, for a long while now. What do you think? Perhaps we should let Katharine decide?"

The housekeeper was beaming from ear-to-ear at the thought.

Naomi Staley was silent for a few moments then looked at her son-in-law.

"First, can you take down the rest of his bloody paintings, please? And, Katharine, later you can pack his things. Everything."

She looked at her son-in-law. "You are sure; he won't be back?"

Mitchell nodded. He said, "First you need to hear Detective Sergeant Sayer; it's not easy, but it is necessary."

Catrin sat in a chair in front of the woman.

"Mrs. Staley, you know your husband has been arrested under suspicion of rape and assault with drugs of Marilyn Greaves. Samuels was her maiden name. She is the woman who has now made a confession about the assault on your granddaughter and provided the basis for the charge just made against your husband.

"There will be a public announcement and press briefing about both arrests to the media in about an hour by Superintendent Pender. We need to handle proactively the communication before it comes out through court coverage of the arraignment or by other means. It has to be as factual as possible but reduce the misinformation and salacious nature of the issue.

"A police presence outside your home will protect your privacy until media interest dies down."

She paused, took a breath.

"Our primary reason in making the announcement now is that we believe other women may come forward with similar complaints. We have reason to believe it was not an isolated incident. You need to be aware of and prepared for that.

"Later, not today, Detective Inspector Hicks will ask you to make a statement to help our enquiries. He will come here with a technician to record the interview. There may also be specific questions about Professor Staley's whereabouts on particular days, albeit a long time ago. Other than that, we see no reason to involve you further. But talk with your family. It is probably best if you have a solicitor present."

The older woman nodded, but said nothing.

Catrin thought, 'reason to believe it was not an isolated incident' was as delicate as she could put it.

"I am going to leave you now. I appreciate these are difficult circumstances. I am glad your family is with you at this time."

Her job was done.

As she stood up Mrs. Staley said to her, "You saw it in the painting that was over there, the first time you visited, didn't you? When you came with the other police sergeant, the one who just left?"

Catrin looked at her. "Mrs. Staley, I am an artist, too. It's amazing what artists can see in each other's works, particularly in abstract art; after all, that is why it's called 'abstract', to fire the imagination of the observer."

Naomi Staley looked at her then at the area of wall where the 'Series Eight' painting had been located. She said, "But this time what you saw, I think, was also in the mind of the painter."

Catrin said, "Goodbye, Mrs. Staley."

One more move in that direction and Catrin would be into an interview and it had been agreed that Naomi Staley would not be interviewed at this time. When she was questioned it would be by representatives of the Devon & Cornwall Police Service. From Naomi Staley's reaction to the arrest there was probably a lot of ground to cover.

She took a last look at the remaining paintings in the house as she left, a little bemused. Some were worth a great deal yet, when Philip Staley had looked at the ones now in an evidence locker, did he see the art that others valued or did he see his conquests?

As she walked out Superintendent Mitchell followed her to the door.

"Sergeant Sayer, I take it you are heading back to London now? I wanted to thank you for coming back and assisting with the enquiries. Superintendent Pender briefed me on the interview with Greaves and I know your involvement was instrumental in the development of this case. As a family... with this being my father-in-law... it will need a lot of work, but I am glad that Jack Taylor and Bob Matheson agreed to have you assist the team on this case. I will tell each of them that myself."

He looked tired, frazzled; he hadn't been sleeping, that was clear. It was too personal a case even for a seasoned policeman. She wondered what he would do with his father-in-law, once he was given bail.

"Thank you, sir. I am actually heading back tomorrow; I have dinner tonight with some friends and will stay over."

He shook her hand formally. "Well, thank you again."

~~

She spent the afternoon and early evening with Chris after talking with Aina about a train reservation for the following morning. Worsley called her back shortly afterwards, saying her reservation was for overnight Sunday; to come into the Yard on Monday and don't leave Cornwall before then.

"If you are seen in London before then, I will have you arrested," she said. "Chief Superintendent Matheson is very grateful, as is Mitchell. It's rolling around Sandra Hunt's level now, the fine cooperation between the Met and the Devon & Cornwall Police."

The Assistant Commissioner, Catrin thought. Again.

"A little easier for her to deal with than after the Glasgow incident, ma'am?"

"A lot easier. Enjoy the time with your man down there; see some of Cornwall. Take it easy. And Catrin…"

"Yes?"

"Turner-Jones called. The V&A work is complete on both the painting and the knife now and the handover is scheduled for the seventeenth, the Thursday. That's just about two weeks from now. You will fly overnight Wednesday to Kuala Lumpur and be free to play tourist sometime on Friday, so you need to let Jian Li know."

Over the next couple of days Chris Treneer took her sightseeing in Cornwall; some places the tourists go to and others they would never know about, places that were meaningful to him. And along the way they made a visit to meet his mother in Penzance; a nice woman who eyed Catrin at times with a look that said, "I wonder if you are the one, this time?"

The second evening they were back in Falmouth, at Jen's place having dinner. After it, Mason Carrington and Chris were washing the dinner things that did not fit in the dishwasher. Mason looked past Chris across to Catrin sitting at the kitchen table and thought she still looked wiped. It must have been a hell of a week. He was glad he was a watercolour artist.

"Will you be back down, Catrin; for work, I mean? I know you will be back for this ungrateful wretch." he said, looking at Chris.

Catrin smiled. "He is my cariad, as we say in Welsh, so leave him alone, Mason, or I will wallop you with that wooden spoon. But no, I don't expect anything else here for work unless I am assigned to something new that comes up."

The artist laughed at the threat. "Catrin, I am back up in London the week after next recording more painting sessions for my training video. If you get the chance, will you join me for ten minutes? We talked about it; now it needs to happen. This will be the final session of the London series, so I hope you will do it."

He smiled. "We will put in a plug for your work; it could help sales."

Catrin said, "That's the week I am going off to Malaysia, for work. I leave in the middle of the week."

Carrington said, "We could do the Monday or Tuesday session, perhaps?"

Catrin smiled. "If I can, it would be fun but… what do you want of me?"

"Bring your potter and your watercolour paint box."

"You want me to paint in watercolour; on video, with you? No way…."

He cut in. "No, I want you to bring your watercolour paint box, that's all."

He was looking enigmatic. "It could be a conversation piece, talking about paint, paint boxes, who knows. I have to have something to talk about with people on camera while I paint. What I know about ceramic decoration would occupy about ten seconds."

Chris picked up the last pan to dry it as Mason dried his hands.

"That long? I'm surprised," he teased.

Jen said, "Catrin, you should do it," She walked over to the sink, putting her arms around Mason's waist from behind. "This man's training sessions and videos sell very well and go all over the world; so make sure you put in a big plug for your work. I am thinking of charging him even more for his paper."

"You two should just hitch up and save the money," Catrin said.

Jen shook her head. "Oh no, we are separate entities, separate businesses. He wants to travel all over doing his painting and I don't want to leave Falmouth. It's fine just the way it is; I love him the way it is. He can come and visit, but can't move in here; I would end up killing him."

She gave him a kiss on the cheek.

Catrin thought, I hope Chris and I can make more of it than that, I want to.

She looked across the room. He was looking at her, smiling, taking in the dishwashing banter. She had the distinct impression from his expression that he was thinking the same thought.

32 MEMENTOS

Aina came over to Catrin's desk with the final travel package in a folder, looking very pleased.

She said, "Your travel documents and visit itinerary, finally. It's all sorted out with FCO. I have made a list of the people you are seeing, their roles and the meeting timings. You also have the e-ticket printout, flight numbers, seat numbers; the lot. From the time you leave Heathrow until you get back you are organized; except for this mystery slot on Friday afternoon through to Sunday evening, just marked 'Jian Li Yeung'. You have the hotel for that period, but that's all."

Catrin smiled, "That's the part I am looking forward to. Thank you for sorting it out - and dealing with Mrs. Turner-Jones."

Catrin had been busy with new cases since her return from Cornwall.

Aina smiled, "I wish I was going; I would love to see Malaysia, or at least part of it."

Then she raised her voice slightly, took on a dramatic tone, "Of course, your visit is not tourism, it is just unstinted personal sacrifice for John and his family."

Obi looked up from his work at his desk, smiling. "For which Kaila truly appreciates you, I should add."

Aina said, "So how did you break it to her, John? That Catrin pulled rank and said she would go and you couldn't; or did you tell her the truth?"

He looked enigmatic.

"Let's just say Kaila is glad I wasn't required to accompany anyone there."

Aina said playfully, "I knew it, Catrin, he weaseled out of telling her; she would have been at him about it, I know."

Catrin laughed. She knew that Kaila and Aina had become friends since John had joined the unit; their respective families were from the same area of Pakistan.

She said, "Well John, you can have the joy of preparing all my disclosure documents on the Keystone Gallery case while I am away; that means seeing DS Netherton tomorrow."

Netherton was her contact with the Surrey Police on the case.

He groaned.

'Tomorrow? I was planning on…"

Aina cut in. "Mrs. Turner-Jones is coming over tomorrow, the 'final briefing' for the Great Expedition, running through with Jane what she and Catrin will be doing. I will fix it for you to sit in on that and…

Obi said quickly, "Guilford; I will be seeing Netherton at the Surrey Police Headquarters. Looking forward to it."

Worsley came out of her office across to them, seeing the laughter. She waited until she had their attention then said, "Steadman just heard the news that another woman has come forward in the Staley case, Catrin. It looks as if you were right. Not that Hicks and Pender had any doubts, but it is good, in a sense, to have at least this corroboration. I have no doubt that there will be more."

Catrin nodded. She felt relieved. The last she had heard was the Philip Staley had continued to deny everything and they had found no evidence at his home or in materials dragged out of Dartington archives.

Obi said, "He is guilty, no doubt about it."

"Why?" asked Worsley, slightly amused at the certainty of the junior team member.

Obi said, "He hired Jacob Newman as his solicitor directly after his arrest. Directly after, not after consulting others and being referred. Newman has defended two other serial rapists in the last three years.

"So I ask you, when an average guy is arrested, not a villain with past experience, do they have a lawyer lined up who specializes in the criminal area in which they are charged? Most times they and their family are lost about what to do next. He prepared the ground."

Catrin smiled, "And he doesn't even use the internet. He must be well read, keeping up through newspapers and the box. I don't think Superintendent Mitchell would have advised him on that choice."

"Right," Obi retorted, smiling.

"It will all come out over time, I am sure," said Worsley. "Pity the only evidence is his own paintings; other serial offenders, both rapists and killers, keep mementos that, once found, open a lot of doors."

She looked at Catrin. "You had a rough time at the Cheney trial. Being a witness at this one, when it happens, will be another ordeal. Interpretation of abstract art is going to drive the defense lawyers wild."

She paused.

"I am going to talk to Pender and Neville Coltrane,

make sure they know each other and then line up some heavyweight expert to work with Ryder and use them at the trial, not leave it just to you."

Catrin smiled. "I suspect that Devon & Cornwall are already thinking along the same lines, ma'am."

Worsley responded, "I want to make damn sure they are. We should get someone from the Tate, just to stick it to him."

Marilyn Greaves had told Hicks and Sayer in the interview why she had asked for the Tate web site for the second image. She knew it was of special significance to Philip Staley.

Aina looked at her watch. "Shouldn't you be heading out?"

She was looking at Catrin, who nodded.

"Yes, I have to meet up with my reluctant co-star in the video soon, get her over to Smith Square."

Jean had already called expressing her anxieties about the video session this afternoon. The entire team knew that they were doing the recording with Mason Carrington.

"I will come and watch," said John Obi.

Worsley said, as she turned back to her office, "No, you will prepare the Keystone file this afternoon, that's what you will do. Break a leg, Catrin."

When Worsley was back in her goldfish bowl Aina said to Catrin, "Not literally, though."

33 SMITH SQUARE

Mason was looking right at the primary camera.

"Today we are painting in Smith Square, in Westminster, a wonderful location. I love being here, in London. My easel is set up and my paints are ready and it's raining a bit… and these are my friends Catrin and Jean. Sad to say, everyone, they are not watercolourists. They are ceramic artists; Jean makes pottery; Catrin decorates it. You know; very fancy, precise painting."

In fact, he had only met Jean and Melanie before the shoot and they had hit it off well.

Catrin smiled at the camera, as did Jean. Melanie was now in their line of sight standing a little behind the video director, a man who had been introduced by Mason simply as 'Gord'. She was holding up her own umbrella and looking encouragingly at her partner. A second camera was weaving behind Mason and his guests at the sides, picking up the easel shots. A large blank sheet of watercolour paper was waiting, lightly marked in pencil, an exercise in layout drawing by Mason earlier in the afternoon.

He continued, "So here are some images of their art they have shared with us for you to look at while I wet this sheet of paper with plain water a little more. We want it wet, just right; we want mobility of the paint when we get started, don't we? Catrin, Jean where can they see your work?

"The Cwmbran Kiln in Spitalfields Market," they said in unison and then Jean, now warming faster to this style than Catrin, said, "And the gallery 'Liz's Place' off Fulham Road; both are here in London, so please check their websites. We love creating our pieces and working together!"

They had been told that during editing the opening and closing sequences, images of both them and their work would be shown with website information, mixed with shots of Mason.

Then Catrin talked for a few moments about her design interests.

"Right," said Mason. "So Catrin, now show me your watercolour paint box. I know you brought it along." His face was full of mischief.

Clearly video recording for an imaginary audience was as much his comfort zone as working with a live class.

Catrin held up her open Winsor & Newton paint box in full view of the camera, as she had promised Mason. It was well-used but cared for; it had been a present from her parents when she was in high school.

Mason said, "Look folks, good paints these, I can see, with Artist grade colours but how clean it is… how sad. Catrin, you must have used them once or twice I think. Is that dust, really? Nina, can we have a close up of this. We need to rescue this paint box, put water on it and make the colours come alive again."

The videographer had moved behind Catrin and to the side, away from focusing on his easel.

Catrin laughed. "I used them a lot before I took up ceramic work, Mason, I told you that. I like painting in watercolour and it doesn't need rescuing, thank you."

Mason said "Catrin you need a paint box like mine." Nina's camera moved to the paint box Mason was holding in his left hand, his thumb through the ring on its base. His brush was in motion between it, the water container, a nearby towel and the easel. Mason used the 'Rolls Royce' of paint boxes; handmade of enameled tin to the classic Roberson pattern. Catrin knew they were very expensive and the makers had a backlog of orders running well over a year, but people still ordered and waited.

She said, "It is a lovely paint box, Mason, but yours is a real mess."

Jean added, "Aren't you supposed to put one colour in each pan?"

Mason was sweeping out his first bold strokes across the paper, wielding a large Kolinsky sable brush and looking hurt. "I paint dynamically, Jean. My paint box is dynamic, too."

Jean retorted, "There are parts of your paint box that remind me of mud banks in Suffolk estuaries."

The artist let out a peal of laughter, stopped painting for a moment and looked at the camera, the audience.

"You invite people on to the set and all you get is insults. I am trying to paint and they are trying to undermine my work, these ceramic people…"

Catrin and Mason became a little more serious as the painting progressed; they talked for a time about the location they were in and the building in the centre of the circle, St. John's, talking about the building's architecture. They moved on to issues of selection; what to include in the painting and what to leave out, the issues of design balance both on a flat paper and curved ceramic surfaces.

Carrington then asked them about how Catrin and Jean had started working together, which paints Catrin liked, what were the different challenges in ceramic painting.

As they finished the topic he looked deadpan into the camera. "So Jean, when she wrecks one of your pieces right near the end, do you throw it at her?

Jean laughed. "It doesn't happen often. When it does it's generally a crack that appears or there is a glazing problem; it's not often the decoration. No, we console each other in Welsh until we are through it. Then I get back to the wheel or the table and make another and we start again."

All the time they had been talking the camera was catching the paint flow, the washes on the heavy watercolour paper, the precise strokes with the sable brush or the dabs with an edge of towel to clean an area; it looked swashbuckling but it was fast and very precise. Catrin was watching the image emerge.

In a minute he stepped back a pace. "What do you think, really? Is it that bad?"

Catrin moved closer to him. "Really? Mason it is entrancing, watching it appear, I am so glad I am here, it's wonderful. These sweeps of paint, the half-formed shapes all come together so wonderfully. There is no doubt this painting is forming up to be London, a square in London, at dusk on a rainy day. I love it."

"And Jean?" he asked.

She nodded. "I am quite amazed. Despite you being

the one to give us a hard time. Catrin said it, really."

He moved round to be between them, putting an arm around each of them.

"Ladies, thank you for being here today painting in London, for getting wet with me in Smith Square."

Jean said, "Are you still holding that brush, Mason? Have I got paint on my coat now?"

Gord said. "OK, folks; that's it. Cut as we say. That's a great take. Mason, you did that with Greg Andrews too. Put the brush down next time. Jean, we will pay for the cleaning."

Jean laughed. "It's OK, it's no problem."

Melanie came forward. "That was very natural, you both did really well. Gord, don't get the coat cleaned. We will hang it in the Kiln; say it's a Mason Carrington original."

"You can do better than that," Mason said. "Simon?"

His assistant came forward with a bag containing a framed painting. Clearly it was a standard part of guest appearances. Mason said, "Here is an original, of a Falmouth scene, for your pottery or home, as you wish. I hope you like it."

They all spoke at once, looking at the framed landscape as Mason continued, "And Catrin this is for you."

He pulled another item from the bag. She saw it was a Roberson paint box similar to the one he had just been using. It was brand new.

She said, "Mason... how? There is a waiting list a mile long for these and... thank you, I never thought I would own one."

He said, "Some of the people on the waiting list are there because they see mine. The maker knows it and he is a friend. I promised him a plug in this video series and you helped me do that. And one person near the front of the queue was happy to go to the back in the line for one of my signed prints; we did a deal. We will get you doing watercolour painting in Cornwall, wait and see."

He passed it over.

"Take it as my appreciation for your company today and my happiness that you and Chris are together. I love you both."

He gave her a hug as she thanked him again.

"Speaking of which," said Melanie, "When is this man Treneer coming to London to be vetted by us."

"Vetted?" said Catrin, in mock outrage, "Vetted! You vetted the last one I fell for; he only lasted a week."

Jean said, "Well, you did cock it up, getting bashed up and frightening him off."

Catrin smiled at her friends. "I don't think this one can be frightened away. I will see when he wants to come up and face the ordeal."

Mason watched them, smiling.

Catrin said, "How about a glass of wine to revive Jean and an early dinner? Mason, can you join us? Or do you need to be here?"

"No," he said, "I don't need to be with these guys tonight. We spend too much time together when making videos. I would love to have dinner with you three."

Catrin knew this area well; Scotland Yard was not far away after all, at St. James's.

"Let's go to 'Osteria Dell' Angolo', around the corner, not too far," said Catrin, deciding on a restaurant she knew and liked. "And it's on me. But we should call; check if we need a reservation."

'Got it', said Simon, who had overheard, and who was

energetically working on his phone. "I will make a reservation for the four of you, if you want to start heading that way. If there is a problem, Mason, I will call you."

He had a half-finished Mason Carrington painting worth potentially a lot of money to let dry fully and equipment to clean and pack; it was all part of his job of looking after his boss.

As they sorted themselves out to go to dinner Catrin dealt with her mobiles; they had been in silent mode during the filming. She saw the email from Stephen Hicks and a text from Wastle. "I have to call someone first, though," she said to them.

She stepped back into the shelter and privacy of the entrance area of Kings Building.

"Sayer, there are now four complaints filed against Staley," Hicks said, without preamble.

"Four women. Were they all students, then?" Catrin asked. From one to four assaults in a matter of days.

"Two of them were. One was a college employee who was interested in art and fell under his spell. And Greaves, of course."

"I saw the original media coverage on the BBC, sir."

Hicks said, "Look, the reason I am calling is the interpretation of the abstract paintings that you did, the process which increased your suspicions. Is there a name for it? Can we use it further? Your boss has been on to Pender just now saying we need heavyweight support on it and I can't even describe it."

Catrin said, "It is simply an artistic interpretation of action lines and gestures seen in a drawing or painting. You probably need a link between an art expert on Staley's paintings and a psychiatric evaluation of why he painted that way, linking his conquests with the images."

Hicks replied, "Thanks, we have Ryder lined up to see him for that; he and his lawyer are objecting to a psychiatric review at present and are delaying things through the courts, but it will happen."

He added, "We finished interviewing Naomi Staley. Ryder put it best when we talked it through with her; the woman believed her husband had affairs with students but had no idea he was a rapist. The biggest element of her fear, her denial really, was that it could be worse, given Philip Staley's dominating nature. She gave us some names and timings which led to two of the additional women, who then agreed to come forward."

Catrin said, "So there could be more again, sir? I think so."

Hicks responded, "I have no doubts about that, Sayer; none at all. Thanks for all your help."

"Thank you, sir, for the update."

They closed the line and Catrin turned round.

She hadn't realized that the sound would echo back from the entrance hallway on to the pavement, but she saw on their faces that she had been overheard. The videographer standing by the easel, Nina, had been the closest to her, but Catrin realised that they had all caught the conversation, at least her part of it.

Nina said, "Is that the thing on the news, the man in Cornwall, Staley, accused of rape? Mason said you are a police officer."

Catrin saw the young woman was interested; her question came out of her surprise rather than impoliteness or anything else, she thought.

"Nina, I can't talk about it, sorry. Part of my job. But I did meet Mason in Cornwall."

"Yes she did," Mason said. He paused then said softly,

"Still want to go to dinner?"

Jean and Melanie were also watching her, waiting, she saw.

She said, "Yes, I do. On Wednesday I fly to Kuala Lumpur for work. A different world for a few days. To be with friends tonight is a very good thing."

Melanie said, "But you will get to see Jian Li. Enjoy it there when you can, Catrin."

Mason smiled, "That's what I try to do when I visit places for my paintings. Let's go and get even wetter as we walk to this restaurant, we can try to enjoy that."

Melanie smiled, "He's from Cornwall." The Somerset woman was waving a finger in a circle close to her head; the man wasn't quite all there, she was saying.

"Watch it, Farrell," said Catrin. "That's where my fella is from, too."

34 TO THE EAST

On Wednesday morning Catrin was in Heathrow Airport clearing security when her phone rang. She answered it immediately seeing that it was Jane's number, leading the airport security guard monitoring the waiting line of passengers to pounce immediately, waving his finger. The sign behind the line said, "No mobile phone use in this area."

She kept the phone to her ear and pulled out her warrant card, holding it close to him. He stood there silently, initially annoyed; then he relaxed as he saw what it was.

Jane said, "Happy birthday. I just realised; well, Aina did. And from her and Keith also. Keith is back in from the Nottingham thing. Of course, John is not here, he is back in Guilford, lamenting the time being spent with Netherton."

Catrin turned twenty-eight today. Her parent's card and letter were in her briefcase, to be re-read.

She chuckled, "Thank you, but I am just clearing security, ma'am, in the line."

"Right," said Worsley. "Then I'll get straight to the point. Neville has an expert lined up for the Staley case to pass on to Hicks so you won't be alone as a witness on the art element when this thing comes to trial. Safe Journey, Catrin. Stay in touch."

"Thank you, ma'am. Goodbye."

She closed the call. The security officer was still standing there, waiting. The man behind her, half-absorbing she had not complied with the Security Officer but had kept on talking, was muttering his annoyance at the breach of the rules.

The security guard said, "This way, Miss."

He took her to the front of the 'aircrew-only' line ahead of two pilots waiting to put their bags and coats into the scanner bins. When she was on the other side of the scanner he said, "You can phone again from over there."

"Thank you," she said, "I appreciate it."

As she walked through the terminal she wondered how many more women would surface with assault charges; the news coverage had been heavy after the first press conference. Yesterday, one woman, a former student, had given an interview to the press around the time Catrin was videotaping. She said she had tried to commit suicide. 'I failed at that', she said, 'and at life. College was meant to be a happy memory, my start in the world, not a recurrent nightmare'. For her, it was something she wanted to forget, but couldn't.

Catrin had steeled herself for the journey from London to Kuala Lumpur with Turner-Jones. In fact it turned out to be surprisingly pleasant. The world of business class on Malaysia Airlines seemed to relax the FCO staffer, made her more pleasant, less officious and, thankfully, less talkative. The eleven-hour flight went by smoothly with no diatribe on the social structure of Malaysia or its aristocracy and Catrin slept well after the meal service.

The trip had also made her more relaxed and sanguine about life, reflecting on the enjoyable time with Mason and her friends on Monday and how she was looking forward to seeing Jian Li. As she lay back in her seat after lunch deciding whether to watch a movie or not before sleeping, she had a deep, warm feeling; she was really looking forward to the trip home and seeing Chris again, thinking about where their relationship could be heading after this jaunt.

It is human nature to focus on the positive when things are going well and look forward to them getting even better, of course. Rarely do we contemplate idly how they can go wrong. That's a reactive exercise to the news and sometimes the associated shock, not a daydream at forty thousand feet in a Boeing 777.

On arrival at Kala Lumpur International Airport, it was 8.30 a.m. on Thursday; a descent into the sunrise of a warm, humid world on a new day. The two visitors were met at the aircraft gate by a security official and two police officers, a smart young police inspector in uniform and a sergeant, an older man in a suit. The Inspector had an accent not too far from Madeleine's, Catrin thought; English public school.

They were whisked through immigration to a limousine, two seats facing forward, two to the rear, with a separate driver compartment. The talk on the drive into the city was of the meetings ahead. Inspector Akmal Khan did all the talking from their side, Turner-Jones for the visitors. Sergeant Jared Farra and Catrin occasionally looked at each other. They said virtually nothing but their glances said it all; they were both there under orders, not by choice.

They were on their way to the police headquarters in Bukit Aman, an area not far from the Parliament building in the city centre. The order of the day was first a briefing, with a formal welcome by a senior officer. Catrin was to run through her short speech; a summary of the case and the efforts made by the UK police authorities that led to the identification and return of the knife and painting. They would make suggestions, perhaps, but just issues of nuance or local context; not substance, of course, Inspector Khan said. It may help in the preparation for the handover ceremony with Datuk Allam at the meeting at 2.00 p.m. The speech by the Deputy High Commissioner had already gone through such review.

'Nuances' thought Catrin. No wonder Khan and Turner-Jones get along so well; they have the same doublespeak.

Catrin had felt the heavy humidity briefly in the airport and when entering the car, so she was glad of the advice Turner-Jones had provided on what to wear. She was relieved not to be required to be in dress uniform; as a police officer representing the service overseas she hadn't been sure of protocol.

In a lull in the conversation on the drive Sergeant Farra said, "Our headquarters is very close to the Lake Gardens, a complex with an orchid garden and the world's largest enclosed aviary. It is a very pleasant area for walks later in the afternoon. If you have the energy, that is, after the meeting."

Madeleine answered for them. "We will see, thank you.

We need to be a little careful with the jet lag and the climate adjustment."

The two sergeants smiled at each other. It was doubtful that Mrs. Turner-Jones walked far anywhere.

Catrin's review of the case had been prepared carefully by Jane Worsley with all her diplomatic skills coming to the fore, so in fact there were no 'nuances' to correct in the short speech. The superintendent who hosted the meeting and greeted them, a seasoned grey-haired veteran, was called Baksh. He was smart about the politics but clearly he wasn't from the diplomatic school that Mrs. Turner-Jones and Inspector Khan enjoyed; he had come up through the route of experience.

At the side table with coffee and tea during a break Superintendent Baksh asked Catrin quietly, "The scar, was it on duty?"

"Yes sir, an arrest that probably I shouldn't have tried myself."

He nodded.

"Do you find it itches unaccountably from time to time, not for long, a little away from the scar line?"

She smiled. "Yes it does, Do you…"

He nodded, pointing at the left side of his abdomen. "Knife arrest. I can't show you. It would upset Mrs. Turner-Jones. Not exactly protocol to compare our scars, I think."

Catrin bit back a snort of laughter as they turned away from the refreshment table to face the room. Superintendent Baksh was looking the epitome of innocence. Catrin liked the man already.

After the meeting they were given time to check into their hotel, the Hilton Doubletree in Ampang, and freshen up. Local staff met them there from the British High Commission, located nearby,. Catrin watched the world of Kuala Lumpur around her as the British delegation headed to the National Museum for the meeting with the Datuk Jerome Allam. She was looking forward to tomorrow, seeing Jian Li, dropping all this formality and becoming an ordinary tourist.

~~

Catrin's energy level hit a wall and started to plummet. The handover meeting was coming to an end; that was clear. The kris and the painting had been shipped out separately to the British High Commission and delivered directly to the museum several days earlier. The handover was purely ceremonial.

Photographs had been taken and formal speeches had been made; first by the Deputy High Commissioner, followed by Catrin for the UK Metropolitan Police. The Datuk Allam and the Museum Director spoke warm words of appreciation as the recipients. Catrin had been word-perfect, Turner-Jones had whispered, as Catrin sat down afterwards.

She felt the wave of tiredness as she finished her part and sat down. The adrenalin driven by her nervousness had stopped kicking in and she had to concentrate hard to keep engaged with the remaining elements of the meeting.

Madeleine Turner-Jones seemed untiring. It was her milieu, to use one of her words. She had met the Datuk previously and he had either remembered her or been briefed to comment on it. She was clearly very happy with that.

After the formalities, when the group had clustered together for refreshments in a separate room, Datuk Allam said, "Sergeant Sayer, thank you again for coming and talking about the matter with me. As you now know, my grandfather was the artist who painted the work. That the building shown in it was destroyed in a fire sometime later makes it of much greater personal value to our family, of course.

"Please also convey to Officer Obi and the young constable in Coventry our thanks and best wishes. It is unfortunate that other duties prevent them from attending also. Now, I know this had already been cleared and I hope you will open it now." He looked at Mrs. Turner-Jones, smiling, and stood up. An aide passed a beautifully wrapped box to her.

Catrin carefully opened the wrapping. Inside was a bright pewter vase, delicately engraved but not overly-ornate. She was impressed.

Datuk Allam continued, "Tin and pewter are important still in Malaysia, so I thought I would give you a memento that has that link."

She looked at it carefully and thanked him formally, then smiled. "I really do like it, sir, it is beautiful."

He smiled back. "And I really did choose it myself."

He added, "There is also a similar gift of appreciation for Detective Obi and Constable Ryerson which is being sent to our High Commission in London. We hope they can receive them there from the Commissioner in due course."

"I am sure they would be honoured, sir, and I know Constable Obi's wife would be thrilled," said Catrin.

"Of course," Allam added as an afterthought as they sat down again, "you have tin mines in the United Kingdom, in Devon and Cornwall, I believe. Have you ever been there?"

Catrin said evenly, "Yes sir, in fact I was in that part of England quite recently."

On the way to the Hilton Doubletree Hotel she said to Sergeant Farra, "Thank you for the offer to show us the gardens but…"

He said, "You are very tired, I can see. This is not a normal sort of day for either of us."

Then he added. "Can I take you both on a tour tomorrow morning, perhaps? I will arrange a car. We will first stop at the Petronas Twin Towers. You will see them from your hotel tonight but close up they are very much worth visiting, I assure you. Then we could visit the Lake Gardens and tour around a little. I know that Inspector Khan is unavailable, I believe."

The Inspector had been less talkative on the return; Mrs. Turner-Jones was also fading, not talking.

Khan said, "That is correct, unfortunately."

Mrs. Turner-Jones said, "Sergeant, it would be delightful, I am sure. I, of course, have seen everything previously but it always a joy to see KL with others, particularly when it is their first visit. Thank you."

It was settled and Catrin had not said anything. She had wondered if either of them would be required to be in meetings in the British High Commission tomorrow but none were in the schedule. But she was OK with Farra's proposal; she was really looking forward to it being over and meeting up with Jian Li.

35 EYES

Overnight, not that Thursday night but the following night, the Friday, the Royal Malaysian Police Incident Analysts earnestly talked about the events of the Friday morning. They were gathered in front of the whiteboard re-examining the lines drawn across the diagram; the car outlines, the bullet trajectories and the evidence layout from the forensic work at the scene. They were building the picture for the growing investigation team that would be working the case on Saturday.

They had already concluded that the call by Turner-Jones to sit behind the driver on the Friday morning tour had been highly influential in the outcome. Inadvertently, given the alternatives, it had probably saved four lives.

In her statement Turner-Jones had made it clear that the seating arrangements arose because she wanted to talk to Sergeant Farra on the drive. She had therefore asked Sergeant Sayer to take the curbside rear seat so Turner-Jones wasn't talking to the back of Farra's head, but was sitting diagonally across from him as he sat next to the driver, a Constable Ashland. Ashland's report, which was very detailed for a young officer, indicated that it was more a command than a request.

In any event, Catrin being seated behind Sergeant Farra had probably saved all their lives, although Farra's would never be the same again.

~~

As promised, the sergeant was on time outside the Hilton Doubletree Hotel with a white, unmarked police vehicle, a Proton Perdana driven by a uniformed constable, a young woman he introduced as Constable Jamillah Ashland. Before they entered the vehicle he said, "It's better to have a driver so that I can talk with you as we go and we will also not need to worry about parking.

"We will start at the Petronas Twin Towers. They are a minute or two away from the hotel and then we will tour the Lake Gardens area stopping for two brief walks; the first one will be in the Bird Park and then afterwards we will visit the Orchid Garden. It will be nothing too grueling; just to take a photograph or two."

"We will then visit the Royal Selangor pewter factory, the workshop that made your vase, Sergeant Sayer. It is quite interesting to see the operation. Finally we will return here, have an early lunch and say farewell."

As they drove along the main road, Jalan Ampang, Sergeant Farra directed Constable Ashland to pull into a filter lane closer to a mall entrance, one that was predominantly occupied by taxis. He was talking about the adjoining towers, encouraging the visitors to return here at dusk to see their transformation into pillars of light. He stopped mid-sentence, causing Catrin to turn away from the view and glance at Farra. He was now looking through the side window rather than the windshield, his gaze on a car parked at the curb.

She saw two men, Chinese, wearing suits. They were standing by a Mercedes with another Chinese male at the wheel. Chinese and Indian ethnicities made up a substantial proportion of the Malay population, she knew, but these two Chinese were noticeable; it was the stance and the stare. The older man was looking intently at Farra. He then said something to his younger colleague who started to move towards their vehicle.

Catrin's first thought that they were police colleagues of their guide, here by coincidence. Then she saw Sergeant Farra look round and registered the extreme concern on his face. He was taking stock of the fact that their exit ahead was blocked by a taxi dropping someone and a small tourist van had stopped behind them, the guide encouraging his tourists to exit the vehicle. She knew instantly the policeman wanted them out of there, but they were trapped; there was no exit. He threw open the door and rapidly stood up saying loudly, "Stay inside. Jamillah call in NOW."

Then he switched to Malay. To Catrin it sounded among the stream of words as if a name, a Chinese name, was being reported as Constable Ashland repeated Farra's comments into her personal radio.

Catrin heard the first shot and saw the red hole appear in Sergeant Farra's left shoulder, through the scapula; a deep red stain appearing on the back of his suit jacket. She noticed uncomprehendingly both bone fragments and blood spurt from the exit wound, some hitting the vehicle. She threw open her door instinctively and got out herself, crouching down behind both the door and the man. She said later that it was a fear of being trapped in the vehicle as the gunman approached, claiming she had not thought about how she could aid Farra at that moment.

The Malaysian officer spun round, his service weapon in hand as the second bullet hit him somewhere in the back. She heard it hit. Looking at Catrin, he passed over the Sig Sauer automatic, holding it out to her crouched body as if he were offering pennies to a street beggar. He said nothing but his eyes were clearly indicating she needed to use it.

The windshield shattered near the driver and Catrin heard Turner-Jones scream, "Oh my God…"

She didn't think about it or hesitate. Somehow the training at Milton on the firearms course years ago kicked in remotely, the way it was meant to. She stood upright, took one step to the side, arms outstretched and with the left hand supporting the gun hand. As she moved from behind Farra's bodyline into view of the assailant the policeman crumpled; his legs folded beneath him.

Catrin saw the young Chinese man, his gun pointed one-handed and aimed slightly to the left, towards Constable Ashland still at the wheel. He immediately saw Catrin and swung his arm back towards her, but he was too late. She had fired twice rapidly, hitting his body in the stomach and lower chest. His gun arm stayed up and she automatically fired two more rounds, adjusting her aim slightly higher. These shots hit as well, both in the centre upper chest. He went down face forward, his momentum proving greater than any arresting impact of the bullets.

Catrin kept the gun trained on him as he fell. She heard car tires squeal and caught in her peripheral vision a glance of the Mercedes leaving, but her eyes were locked on the man prone on the ground. His left leg moved, shook once; then he was still.

The screams were coming now from bystanders, from different directions. Some people, seeing the police officer's uniform on Constable Ashland as she emerged from the vehicle, were running over to help. Catrin dropped the gun arm to her side and bent over to see Sergeant Farra. As she did so her knees buckled, she went down backwards, landing hard on her backside with her head hitting the edge of the rear passenger door, the one she had moved away from as she fired, slamming it closed. She half-lay, half sat there still holding the gun as Jamillah Ashland reached the two officers on the ground.

The whole incident had taken seconds.

"Are you hit, Sergeant Sayer?" Ashland asked, her voice shaking.

"No. See to Sergeant Farra," Catrin said, "I can't move, sorry. Stupid."

Ashland looked at Catrin, saw the pallor and said, "I had better take that."

Catrin saw her pointing at the Sig Sauer. She nodded, passing over the weapon. The constable bent over and checked Farra's pulse.

"He is still breathing," she said.

A woman appeared by her side, pressing her folded headscarf, the traditional Malaysian Tudung, into a pad. She said, "We need pressure to reduce the bleeding." The woman seemed to know what to do, Catrin thought. Yet she found she couldn't get up to help them. She felt frozen, cold. I am in shock, she thought, but knew intuitively that realization wasn't going to help.

She heard sirens in the distance, coming closer. Then Catrin heard a wail from Mrs. Turner-Jones in the vehicle. "I have wet myself, I can't believe it; I have bloody wet myself." Then the Foreign Office representative was sobbing, in tears, in shock herself.

It could be worse Catrin thought, as she lay there, shaking violently in the heat. You could be dead rather than embarrassed. She said nothing; found she could say nothing, could only look at Ashland and the woman working feverishly on the prone body of Sergeant Farra.

A bystander, recognizing that the blonde European woman was in a state of shock, put his suit jacket around her shoulders. As he did so, Catrin's gaze moved upwards and, before she saw the jacket owner, the man she had killed came into her line of sight.

No-one was touching him but several people stood close by, staring down; a dead young man in the street. His gun was still in his hand, his arm in front of him. His eyes were open, staring at nothing, staring at her. Somehow the gaze of the British visitor connected with the sightless gaze of the dead Malaysian Chinese. A young man, she thought. She could not stop looking at his eyes, even as people started talking to her.

Suddenly there were more uniforms and police cars bringing her back to the reality of the situation. In no time, it seemed, she was being led away, an officer on either side of her, over to an ambulance adjacent to the one now firing up its siren. That one had Mrs. Turner-Jones in it, she had seen; the ambulance with Sergeant Farra was already out of sight.

Catrin lay on the gurney inside with the ER technician talking to her; she had wrapped a blanket around her and told her she was in shock. She was taking Catrin's pulse and blood pressure and reporting her condition on her personal radio.

Sayer wasn't listening, really. She was thinking of Kinnington Church in Glasgow, the last time she had been taken away in an ambulance. Then she thought of Chris, of Worsley and of being far away from home. Suddenly she realised that Jian Li was already on the plane to KL expecting her to be at the Doubletree Hotel on arrival.

She spoke up. "I am meeting a friend, Jian Li Yeung, at my hotel, the Doubletree... she arrives from Hong Kong this morning but I can't recall the flight number. We are... were going to have the weekend together but..."

Catrin then saw a police officer sitting beside her, a woman she didn't know, an older woman who nodded then spoke in Malay on her radio. The sounds of her voice and the ER technician's communication system overlapped, indecipherable to her.

Only then did Catrin think of the others.

"Sergeant Farra and my colleague, Mrs. Turner-Jones, who was in the back of the car, how are they?"

The police officer said, "Sergeant Farra was alive when he left in the ambulance, I know that. Your colleague is unhurt, just a little shocked. She needs a change of clothes, but she was talking to people. She was very concerned; she could get no response when she came round the vehicle to see you. We have told her you are being taken to the General Hospital to be checked out. She is on her way there also now, being looked after."

The ER technician said in Malay, "She is talking, keep her doing so, it will help."

"Have you ever used a firearm before?" the police officer asked Catrin.

"Just in training," Catrin said, "We don't normally carry guns in the UK except in specific roles."

The woman smiled at her. "I know. But you did very well indeed."

Catrin thought, 'Well indeed'? I just killed a man in a foreign country. I have no permit to use a weapon and I am a serving British police officer. She wondered what would happen next. She knew there would be consequences; this time she had just been in the wrong place at the wrong time, she felt. It wasn't her decision to intervene, as it had been in Scotland. She wondered what Worsley would say, what they would all say back at the Met.

Then she wanted desperately to talk to Chris, to explain what happened herself before others explained it. She didn't want it to be like Glasgow; she didn't want him to walk away. She knew instinctively he wouldn't, he wasn't like that and she knew immediately that the fear was unwarranted, but it was irrational and overwhelming. She asked for her mobile; did they have her purse?

The officer said, "Yes, we have it. But let's get to the hospital first; we are nearly there. It will be easier inside."

The Malaysian officer knew that talking for her recovery was one thing; DS Sayer talking to the world at present was not on the books until a senior officer approved it. If she wasn't in shock, this British officer would have realised that too.

EPILOGUE
NEW SCOTLAND YARD

Marilyn Greaves entered the small room at New Scotland Yard with her husband a pace behind her. It wasn't an interview room, was her first thought; no recording equipment. She was very familiar with those rooms now.

Sergeant Sayer was standing with another officer, a superior she gathered, a man introduced as Inspector Marshall. This time she was in uniform; she looked every bit a police officer now; a white uniform shirt, uniform trousers and an equipment belt. Marilyn thought it may have only been a little under a year since she last saw Sayer but the policewoman looked a lot older; as if Marilyn had had a far easier time of it in prison than this woman on the outside.

Introductions over, Marilyn said straight away, "Sergeant Sayer, as I said in my letter, I want to apologize in person... but mainly to thank you. Callum thought you were barbaric at the time, handcuffing me, I recall him saying, but you did save my life. It was my intention to take the tablets and finish things. I was... very unbalanced, warped really."

The policewoman nodded. She said nothing at first, then, "And have you spoken with Janis Mitchell, too?"

Marilyn said, "Yes I have. You are the last on my list of apologies for my actions in Falmouth, just because you were so far away, in London. I have met with Janis twice now, the first time with her mother. At the first meeting she wanted to understand why I did it, why I chose her, and what had happened to me that drove me to be so cruel to her. Not just the rape image, the way I... deteriorated into the mindset that led me to choose her."

"Then she contacted me and came to see me some weeks later by herself. She wanted to know how her grandfather had reacted. I had written to him also."

"To Staley, the man who raped you?" Sayer said, her voice showing surprise.

"I felt I had to, for my own recovery. I shouldn't have concealed it. Letting him go on, I was part of letting it happen again to others. I should have screamed blue murder at the time and filed a complaint. At least it would have been on record if some other woman was brave enough to complain. But I didn't have the courage, only the shame. I was the archetypal victim and I turned into the archetypal...."

She trailed off, lost for the word.

"Monster," her husband said, matter-of-factly. "She was a sick woman who behaved monstrously."

She nodded, "It's true. But I am getting help."

Her husband stayed by her, it seems, thought Catrin.

"And how did he react to your letter, may I ask?" Sergeant Sayer said evenly.

"He never responded to me."

Sayer nodded; it seemed to be the answer she

expected.

"Therapy helped me; it still does," Marilyn said. "It was a requirement of my sentence but I also became desperate for it. I think this is why I got parole as early as I did."

Catrin knew she had not contested the charges. Greaves had pleaded guilty and had been sentenced to a year's imprisonment in Falfield Women's Prison near Bristol. She had been released on parole after only five months, including time served, under the condition that she continued to receive psychiatric care and ongoing assessment. The outcry in the media over Staley's victims had been an influence in the parole decision.

She knew also that Philip Staley was now charged with only three counts of rape. He was still free on bail and the Crown was examining new evidence in other cases, which could delay still further a trial date. Several women from the slate of eight alleged victims had spoken to the press, frustrated that their own complaints had not been included in the original set of charges. Given his age Catrin wondered if he would ever serve time.

In contrast, the hacker Arno Hintzen had been recently convicted and was now starting his twelve-year sentence in Stammhein Prison in Germany. He had been candid with the authorities once his computer defenses had been by-passed; his record-keeping was meticulous, the authorities had found.

Sayer said, "Well, thank you for taking the time to do this. You needn't have really, it was my job. It's a long way to come. I am glad it is sorting itself out for you now and that you are helping Janis to understand."

Clearly, Madeleine thought, Sayer wants to get this

over with; they need to go.

"We are taking a short holiday, as well," said Callum Greaves, as they made moves to leave, "the galleries; the theatre." He smiled, adding, "We are even going to see some of your art at the gallery you use - we looked it up on the internet. Janis mentioned to Marilyn that you are an artist too."

Greaves saw Sergeant Sayer smile for the first time. She said, "Well, don't break anything; someone will arrest you. And you are on parole."

Marilyn laughed. "I will be careful. I may even buy a vase."

As she turned she saw Inspector Marshall drop one of the file folders he had been carrying. They were probably both on their way to something else or had broken out of a meeting for this short event, she realised. Sayer bent down, leaned over as she picked it up for him, pushing the papers that had half-emerged back into the folder, moving them out of the visitor's sight before rising.

Callum was standing behind and to the right of Sayer. His view included her back and the holstered sidearm, made more visible by the angle of her body and the direction she was now facing. "You are armed; I noticed that earlier," he said, "but I didn't think British detectives were, in general."

Sergeant Sayer stood, passing the file folder back to her colleague.

"They aren't, generally. Roles change, as in any organisation. Let me show you the way out," she said.

It was the look between the two officers that gave it away. Marilyn assumed that Sergeant Sayer was still working with the art crime team at Scotland Yard, the one Peter Albright had explained to her later. But now that appeared not to be the case. They had asked to meet with Sayer, of course. Marshall was there because the case was part of the Art Crime Unit activity. What Sayer did now, she had not said, and she wasn't offering any more explanation, that was clear.

As Marilyn saw Sayer's arm point towards the door she noticed the flash of the diamond in the engagement ring on her left hand. Her mind went back to the interview in Falmouth; she had no ring then, she recalled. She had a vivid memory of the woman; her clothes, her hair, her voice. Above all she remembered the police officer's clear explanation of her own dark secret and her facial expression, showing she already knew.

"Thank you for seeing me," she said as she entered the doorway then, dropping her voice, she glanced quickly at the hand, "and congratulations."

Marilyn saw a second smile crossed the police officer's face.

As they left the room, Marshall exited after Callum Greaves and behind the two women. He heard Sayer say softly, "I met him in Cornwall" to the woman beside her.

NOTES

I visited Cornwall only once before writing this novel, as a boy, and have vague but enjoyable memories of the family holiday but little detail after all this time. However, I visited it again recently, winding my way through the centre of Falmouth to places I had only seen on Google maps and images, including Hull Street, visualising where 'Treneer Handmade Paper' would be located.

I visited Malaysia twice in recent years and have very specific enjoyable memories of Kuala Lumpur; the Lake Garden complex, the Petronas Towers, the National Museum of Malaysia and the Royal Sengalor Pewter Factory.

The museum has a comprehensive collection of ceremonial knives of the sort described in this novel and Royal Selangor makes items of astonishing beauty in pewter. They are all places I suggest that anyone visiting Malaysia should consider in their visit itinerary.

My thanks go to my wife Gill and my friend Jack Soule for pre-reading the drafts and making editing suggestions. Any remaining errors are entirely my own, of course.

This book, the third Catrin Sayer full-length novel of art-related mysteries, it is set immediately after a Catrin Sayer short story, *The Norfolk Probationer*, available at no cost in various places, including www.wattpad.com. The fourth novel in the series, *The Carnforth Double*, begins immediately after the events in Kuala Lumpur and is set mainly in London.

ABOUT THE AUTHOR

Allan Jones lives in Ontario, Canada. He was born and grew up in Merseyside, England. By profession an industrial chemist, he worked for many years as a consultant on international chemical regulation. He has lived in or travelled to most of the regions featured in the Catrin Sayer novels.

The Falmouth Model

IF YOU ENJOYED
THE FALMOUTH MODEL...

Please read the sequel, the fourth novel in the series, THE CARNFORTH DOUBLE, an investigation into the theft of two valuable paintings by George Stubbs, the noted equine artist, from a merchant bank in London. It begins sequentially following Catrin Sayer's return to London.

An excerpt follows.

Essendon, Hertfordshire. Two cars, a BMW Tourer and a smaller Audi, drew up at the house on the country road, switching off their lights and engines in unison. Four men dressed in black and wearing balaclava-type masks and gloves exited quietly leaving the driver of the BMW to keep watch. They moved quickly to the front door and entered the home. The watcher stayed on alert; there were no neighbours nearby but there were other homes along this stretch of road.

By the time the family sleeping inside realised there were noises of movement in the house, bedroom lights were being switched on and they were being manhandled forcefully downstairs. Once they were sufficiently awake, it was made clear what was happening; the man would dress in his work uniform and accompany some of the intruders. The woman and daughter would wait here with two of the men.

It was the leader's voice which conveyed the menace, even though he was speaking quietly, precisely. Any problems from the man; his family would pay the price. Any problems from the wife and daughter, he would similarly do so, even if he co-operated with them fully. The family's eyes were on the FNP-9 handgun he had placed on the table, emphasizing his point. They saw that two other intruders were also armed. The wife and daughter had never seen a real weapon like this before; the sight of it was as chilling as the man's voice in their ears.

They understood the price being referred to; their survival as a family, their survival individually.

The leader finished with, "It's now 1.10 a.m. Do as we say and by 5.00 a.m. you will be a family again; if you don't, then some of you will be picking up the pieces. Your lives will never be the same again."

The leader had little understanding how, following their invasion and threats, the family's life would never be quite the same again anyway.

After a drive in the BMW into London, mainly in silence and in darkness for the kidnapped man, the wrap-around opaque glasses were removed from his eyes and he realised where he was. He assumed he would be taken here, to the bank where he worked.

He was led over to insert an access code at a panel beside a door. Once inside he similarly disarmed the entry alarm and several sets of wall sensors. Someone had inside information, he knew. He was one of only three people who carried in his head all the current codes needed by this gang. Others at the bank would need access to a physical log book kept in a safe to get these codes.

He had been told on the journey into London that afterwards he would be taken somewhere, locked in and left alone with his own mobile phone. He had his doubts, his terrors really, about that promise now that these men had what they wanted.

At 4.55 a.m. precisely, they said, he was to text a message to a telephone number now entered into his mobile by one of his captors; a three letter code that needed to be sent. They made him repeat it several times. At 5.00 a.m. exactly he could use his mobile to call his wife on their home phone, not before. No other contact with anyone, no deviation from that plan, would be tolerated.

He had worked here a long time and knew the paintings being stolen by name. Two were near-priceless works by the artist George Stubbs; paintings of horses. 'Mr. Frederic Allenby of Hythe, mounted,' was the larger; 'Senator II', a black thoroughbred, was the second.

The third painting they removed had been acquired only recently by his employers. Mrs. Woodley had told him it was called 'Mrs. Rosalind Heaton of Carnforth', painted by an artist he hadn't heard of, a man called Hamlet Winstanley. Despite his plight, the man wondered why they had chosen this one rather than other, more famous works that were there for the taking.

www.ingramcontent.com/pod-product-compliance
Lightning Source LLC
Chambersburg PA
CBHW020409260626
47156CB00007B/2305